WHITE TRASH SUBLIME

Dickson Lee Turpin

I0674109

Nightmare Press
Shepherdsville, KY

To my wife, Kathy

DICKSON LEE TURPIN

Other works by Dickson Lee Turpin
Ballad of Cassidy

WHITE TRASH SUBLIME

Dickson Lee Turpin

TABLE OF CONTENTS

Figment

The steel door banged shut with a boom. He jumped. He looked at its garish shade of currant red. Studying it, all he could do was wait. Chill air cooled the skin. He shivered as a blast of wintry air shoved at him. The office was warm and quiet, but certainly better than the ice-cold production floor. The cheap yet pungent potpourri stunk up the room. He coughed, and underlying chemicals soured in the throat. Beyond the cloister of offices, machinery howled in begrudged life. They were old and out of date. They were newer things in this place, mused Kayden.

Through the steel door's blinds, he saw her. He reached for the handle. Sheila held up a finger with a smirk that almost passed as a smile. An out-of-towner, she had all the self-important condescension. She turned back to another. Tightness gripped his chest. Rumors abounded in a factory. Some said that foreign industry was crushing them. Others said the Van Lear family wanted to push out the company. Rumors were a way for the workers to have an illusion of control and awareness. The town's aristocracy hated the incursion of the plant. The Old Money despised the push by the New Money. Either way, he cursed, they reduced everyone's hours down from overtime to forty, forty to thirty-two hours a week.

"I'm safe," muttered Kayden. Brian Weber smiled at him as if catching the thought. A gleam was in the other man's gaze, which was intense, almost sickly. He clicked his fingers, listening, but nothing traveled through the door.

The smile beneath that gaze held all the charm of a little boy tearing the wings of flies. Tightness turned to an iron grip around Kayden's heart. His stomach felt full of soured coffee. It rose to his throat. Anger had made counting the cost impossible, though he had been unaware of connections. The good-ole-boys' club always wins in Owl Sticks. Merit was determined by family or familiarity. Once he believed superiors were exceptional, but life had shown him that fools ruled him. Kayden ground his teeth, jaw popping. For all their cruel words and mean-spirited acts, they enjoyed him doing their jobs.

"No," He dismissed the nagging thoughts. Kayden shook his head. "Who will do the work so their buddies can stand around?"

Sheila nodded her head as Brian beckoned Kayden with one long fingernail. The color matched to the door when they repainted it. The expense was obvious. He opened it, seeing the Plant Manager Chris Peck. Kayden smiled, light-headed.

"Mister Stone," Sheila mouthed with a smirk. "How are you this morning? How is your wife?" She tried her best to make her voice sympathetic. Her eyes held a look of boredom.

"Still divorced," he admitted. He forced a smile. Jillian had worked at the company. Kayden had no interest in the whole plant talking about his ex-wife. "She still can't work, you know, after the medical problems," he added, almost ashamed. Brian's smile grew, but Chris sighed and crossed his arms and legs.

"That was so unfortunate," her smirk turned to a smile. "I just hate it. Maybe you can get her into rehab." She composed herself as a saint to a repentant sinner.

Kayden glanced at Brian, who laughed, but Sheila waggled a finger at him. Like a beloved but naughty child, he stowed his open glee. "Well, with our hours being cut," he confessed, digging fingers into his palms, "it is hard—"

Sheila waved off his words. "Anyway, we brought you here today to discuss certain matters." She glanced at the other men and nodded. "Oh yes, first, I need your security card."

"Okay," he muttered. He withdrew it from his wallet and set the card on her desk. The beat of his heart grew louder, and lightness at the back of his head bloomed. Grayness at the edges of his vision spread. Kayden's beech wood eyes, light brown, charred at the edges, locked onto Sheila. Every sensation grew more intense. He could feel the hand of the clock tick. The potpourri was a clawing chemical stench.

The Human Resources Manager took a pencil from the cup. She pulled the card with its eraser, lip curled. "Now," she brushed down the wrinkles of her blouse, "there have been some unfortunate events, and things have been limping along."

"Yes," he nodded, "we lost some contracts." Kayden tried to keep his eyes away from Brian. His supervisor's face reddened. "Those quality issues," he said. Everyone knew the reason for them losing customers.

"Sure," she mouthed, looking down at a list of names. "You know that we've been working reduced hours, which has made things harder." Her eyes ticked up to recall part of this speech.

"Yes," he said, but she looked away. A dark part wanted Sheila to at least look at him. She had developed a reputation around town. Despite what she believed, no one believed outsiders were above them. An ice pick of fire stabbed at the back of Kayden's eyes.

"Anyway," she snapped, looking at the computer. Sheila looked at her computer, referring to her notes. "Yes, unfortunately, we have to lay off some people. Then, others can have forty hours."

Part of him knew this was possible. The words hung in the air. Days when they moved him played at the back of his mind. He had managed to be too valuable to terminate. Everyone knew Brian and his buddies hated him, but Kayden always came to help. He went out of his way, lending a hand when no other would. "I don't understand," he grunted, dazed. Through the gray fog, which was turning red. "I've been here a long time," he scowled, "and there are people who're newer than me."

"Well," she blinked, smirk blessedly gone. Kayden had always been polite. His resistance was striking.

Brian crossed his arms. "We need the best! We can make it through these hard times. I figured, with all those books you read, you would understand. I guess you're not that smart." He had peeked at them when Kayden left them unattended.

Kayden pressed his mouth shut. His eyes locked onto the supervisor. The good-ole-boys' club, he thought bitterly. "Smart, there is a difference between smart and being a sycophantic lecher." Brian looked at Chris and Sheila. "There is a distinction between intelligence, and being a boot-licking pervert. The smart thing," he spat the words. "If I were in power, I would be to separate my personal and professional lives. I've heard women here complaining." His neck and face burned. Some had tearfully confessed things. No one else would listen, certainly not Sheila. "Some have told me they've felt pressure to do THINGS."

"There is no evidence," Sheila snapped, holding up a hand. "Besides, I can't do 'anything' if there is no PROOF." Her smirk returned. She placed a hand to her heart as if it bled for any victims.

The ice picks turned to flaming daggers, and he struck his leg with a fist. "Everyone is afraid to say anything!" Kayden growled. The grayness was gone, but now blackness took its place. "You say anything, and you get punished!"

"We have a no retaliation policy," countered Sheila.

"Sure," he laughed, grinning viciously. Anything being a rule never means it unbroken; he thought.

Brian struck the desk with a fist. "I wondered why you were talking to them!" He reached for Kayden's shirt collar. The plant manager pushed his hand down before it could grab him.

Chris stood. "Mister Stone, we no longer need your services," he mouthed. His lip curled, and he pulled up his pants. Despite his belt, the bulbous gut pushed them down. "I have great faith in my supervisors," he raised his chin.

"Because they back your lies," Kayden returned. "When your boss asks why we lost contracts, they lie." Brian and Sheila blinked. Both wore similar looks of shock. Like a surprise finger in the bum, Kayden mused.

Chris's face turned a dangerous shade of plum, finger raised, mouth agape. He froze, closed his mouth, and his color returned to its milky shade. "Don't expect a call, Mister

Stone," he admitted, smiling, although his eyes cut at Kayden. "During your transition, it would be a time for reflection. You may find another employer who needs someone so smart, they're useless." Before anyone could speak up, Chris held up a hand. "Leave, Mister Stone, or I'll call the police." He puffed up his chest, almost daring Kayden to speak.

Kayden looked at them. Chris scowled. Brian grinned like a cat that got the cream. Sheila's ever-present smirk returned, and a hand went to the phone on her desk. He stepped out of the office before anger could get the law called. Part of him knew they held all the cards. He had no money to fight them, which they took advantage of.

He trudged out of the building into the wintry day. Through his fury, the gust of icy wind cooled his passions. Unaccustomed to unemployment, he grasped at every thought. Kayden cursed. He tried to think of any plan, but his mind raced with retorts and denunciations. His mind constructed and discarded workable plans, despite the fog of emotion. At occasional intervals, he paused, until reminded by the cold to keep walking.

Kayden stopped beside his car, frowning. The scene before him broke through the haze of thoughts, slights, and indignities incurred. The door was open, and the contents of his car lied about the lot. Inside, the thief had cut the seats and gouged the wheel. Kayden's head hung for a moment. He studied the scars on his hands. A snowflake landed on his neck, melted, and stung with another wintry blast. No matter how low one fell, he thought, there was always a way to stomp a man deeper.

He gathered up his belongings before putting them back inside the cab. Kayden inserted the key and turned it, but the car was dead. The thief had left the door open, and the battery had died. He rested his head against the wheel, feeling its coolness. A sob slipped out, but he squeezed his eyes closed. Better do something, a worn-out voice inside offered.

Kayden got out. The local parts store would let him borrow a jumper, but they were closed today. He looked at the plant, and Chris watched him. He stood by the security hut. "Better get out of here," he whispered, the fog of his breath hanging in the air.

He trudged over the gravel. His mind snatched at any way to get himself a job fast. The prospects were rapidly drying up in the county. The asphalt was a little better. He barely noted the change underfoot. It had deep cracks running through it. Kayden paused at the edge of the plant's property. I guess I never noticed; he mused.

This revelation revealed more of the world's shabbiness. Along the road, Kayden saw other plants closed. Shuttered, they warned against trespassing. The Van Lear family owned all the land, so none dared to destroy or squat inside the buildings. Some families blamed them for the county's dissolution, but others believed they were purging the outsider filth. He needed a job, but none of the industrial jobs remained.

Flakes of snow grew fatter, and a dusting of snow clung to the road. Beside him, the chain-link fence held icicles. He trudged on, stopped briefly, seeing only more closed businesses. Eventually, the road ended at the edge of the industrial park. The people who could afford better lived in these homes. More of them were empty, he saw. When did this happen? He wondered. No answer came. One had a wrecked vehicle in the yard, which looked abandoned, though Kayden was unsure. Before Jillian's injury, they had lived nearby. He smiled at all the plans they had made within its walls. Hope once abounded. He found none now. He moved past the houses haunted by dead hopes.

At the top of Lear Mountain was Swannanoa, where the Old Money had ruled at the town's founding. Beneath it, the New Money of Duncannon aspired to the family's decadence above. Below all were Owl Sticks. Beyond where Kayden lived was the forest, though he avoided it. The people there were strange. People started calling the town Meridian.

The smart ones moved away. The desperate or foolish remained. Clusters of trailer parks and decrepit houses comprised the lowest section. Breaks in the pavement ran riot through the road. The cat piss stink of meth labs bled over the desolation of the lowland. Busted engines bled oil and anti-freeze, which mixed with dirt. Dogs on heavy chains glowered at pedestrians, ready to bite. Damp boots made the bones in his feet ache. Skeletal, pockmarked figures watched from porches, yards, or houses. They numbed themselves to escape this truth, this desolation. Kayden glanced at the dirty children, whose strung-out parents ignored them. Peeking at a dirty window, his eyes haunted him. He saw the same desperation in his eyes. It marked all that lived here.

The sharp horn ripped Kayden from the darksome thoughts. Its note was strange and old. He stepped off the road. It glided over the road. A vintage model, its beauty was alien in Owl Sticks. It was in mint condition. People retreated from it, yet he could only stare. Its dark glass obfuscated the driver until they passed Kayden on the street. Dressed as eloquently as his ride, the man's eyes were pale, nearly white, and Kayden could swear he was blind. Their eyes met. He felt a curiosity.

The vintage car glided past him. Its engine had a polite rumble. A pothole in the road was before it, but Kayden sensed the driver focused on him. Wheels struck the broken pavement, the trunk popped open, and a package dropped on the road. The man's pale eyes turned from his. Kayden jerked. He called for him to stop.

He picked up the package. Kayden frowned, and he turned the parcel in his hands. His brow furrowed. Wrapped in paper, secured by a grass string, it was light. Empty, I think, he mused. The fall damaged the string. It snapped in his hands. He sighed. This was something else he had to handle. He would have to return it if it had anything inside.

An old bottle rested inside. Like something from an apothecary, he mused. He smiled, enchanted. The label read "HPL-0717." He shrugged and looked at a tag. "Figment," he muttered. "What is that, a street name?" The label had a list of effects. His brow furrowed. It guaranteed a boost in intelligence, so magnificent, it would let one see the 'Truth' itself. "Okay," he laughed, stowing it in a pocket.

Snow fell faster, and Kayden looked up at the sky. Better get home, he thought. He had to remember to call Rutger the Sheriff. The cold bit into the skin. His socks were wet, and his feet ached. He moved at a slow, though persistent, pace through the snow. He hoped the owner of the Figment would pay him for returning his package. A smile dared to break over his face.

Quick as his grin was born, the view of the trailer before he buried it. After moving here, Kayden learned to keep nothing of value visible. They had struck again. He wondered if it was Brian trying to spook him. Like his car, the thief had found little worth stealing. They had destroyed his few possessions. He moved through the mess. Secured through a hole in the floor, all his valuables were in a safe. Kayden stopped. His hidden cache was on the floor. He sat back, butt landed on the bed.

Tears filled his scarred hands. All his bills were due in a week. The utility companies had no mercy on people like him. The thieves had even stolen his mother's wedding ring. It was of no monetary value, but he could never replace it. Kayden, for the first time, felt all thoughts flee. Only the aches throughout his body filled the emptiness. His knees throbbed, and the cold agitated his shoulder.

"Jillian," he whispered. He had saved up money, which was in the safe. "How will I tell her?" He was so close. He looked at the ruin. "I can get out of this." He thought of his ex-wife. Helping her cook dinner would make him feel better. This day would end with a smile.

After the divorce, his ex-wife moved into another trailer. Jillian had told him to stay away the last time they talked, but she was also high. No one else took care of her. He was the only one that cared about her.

He stood, pushed down the emptiness, and wiped away tears. I can get out of this, thought Kayden. I'll talk to Jillian and tell her that Rehab is still on. A plan is better than no plan.

Every trailer court in Owl Sticks was the same. At the bottom, there was little difference in the lives. No one came to the dredges of Lear Mountain. Snow came down harder in bloated flakes. Winter made the rot lower, like a busted freezer in a junkyard. Kayden closed his mouth. Every breath pulled in the decay. At the turning of the seasons, when temperatures changed in sudden sharpness, he noticed the soured putrescence. No matter the filth and stink, you can learn to bear it, mused Kayden. Life has a way of reminding one of their low lots in life. Busted cars rusted away. Houses leaned. As snow went everywhere, people went nowhere.

Jillian's trailer waited at the back of the trailer court. Time and neglect had worn out the trailer, leaving it ugly and broken. The sign, which displayed its name, was long gone. Flyers for churches hung on posts, most were gone too. A waist-high chain-link fence kept no one out. Junkies jumped its fence instead of using the roads. Chicken wire patched the gaps. Although summer was gone, bug zappers hummed, and electric blue light made all appear frozen. The storm was building into a blizzard. It had already covered the yards. The homes leaned away from each other, disgusted.

It hunched. Streaks in vertical strokes of a sickly hue stained the mustard yellow exterior. The carpenter that built the porch was incapable of right angles, Kayden reckoned. Cheap wood had weathered the years poorly, which were nearly black. There hung another bug zapper, which had gone dark. Broken. It had run till it had quit like the black truck out front. He had given it to Jillian, but it had given up. She never fixed it. He was going to repair it after rehab. Kayden felt the emptiness crawl into his heart, but he focused on the next step. He raised his hand to knock, which shook. Tears burst out. How do I tell her?

The icy wind turned the tears to needles. He wiped at them, cleared his throat, and knocked. The repeated repairs failed to fix the damage. It could never properly close. A sigh slipped out. He shook his head.

"Hello," he said, pushing open the door. "Jillian, are you here?"

She sat on the couch, head tilted slightly back. The heater blew tobacco ash-choked air, which mixed with the scorched coffee. Kayden cursed and turned it off. I should have come by and cleaned the place. He thought and felt his cheeks burn. The floor popped with every step. The storm howled outside.

He stopped in front of Jillian. Kayden looked at a small table. She had scored a lot this time. She often passed out after getting a fix. Sores marred her skin, once perfect. Did you run me off to do this? He wondered. Clothes hung off her, bones too sharp under pale skin. Mascara ran from tears. She had shot up with shame, but the drugs dulled that too.

"I'm sorry," he sobbed, looking away from her. "I should have come by sooner. You promised to take care of yourself better." Kayden sighed and wiped his brow. "I lost my job." Silence greeted this, and he looked anywhere but at Jillian. "I promised to get you help," he swore, "and I know you don't think you need it. I'll find another job!" Killian thought of his old bosses. "I guess you're right. They got away with it." He sat in front of her and took her wrist.

Kayden blinked. They were cold. Jillian runs hotter than this, part of him said stupidly. He felt the wrist, but nothing. Again, he checked. He examined the other arm. He stood and checked her neck, but there was no pulse. "NO," he barked. He opened her eyes. Once they had enchanted him, but their luster was gone. "I promised," he groaned, knees buckling. Tears blurred his eyes.

A wail tore out of him as he buried his face in her lap. He could smell her urine. The emptiness returned to drive away all but the sorrow. Kayden wept. His chest heaved, body shaking. All his plans—all his work for nothing. No thought, no path came to give him purpose. Without purpose, he had no reason to move. He cried until tears dried up.

After no more tears would come, he sat back. His head felt woozy. Light glinted from her finger, and Kayden shook his head. Jillian wore his mother's wedding ring. She had put it back on. It was looser now than when they had got married. He thought of his car, house, and safe. He shook his head to dispel the thought.

"I should have hidden it better," he confessed, stepping back. Gray crept back into his vision, and he leaned against the wall. This was his fault. He knew she had problems. How could he be so careless?

Through the numbness, part of him told him to call the police. It was the next logical step. With the storm, it took longer to get through. The absence of thought had cut him adrift in the chaos of emotion. His myriad emotions fluctuated and flashed so fast that he felt dazed. He picked up the phone, hearing a dial tone. Sweat broke out as he talked, and he forgot words as he spoke. The dispatcher asked questions, often repeating them. The phone went dead at the other end. Kayden stared at it.

Kayden looked at Jillian, eyes open to slits. How could it be true? The room's heater blew, and sweat gathered at the small of his back. The smell of stale tobacco ash was unbearable. He pulled at the collar of his hoodie. The space felt too small. He peeked at her gaze.

"No," he muttered, retreating retreated to the porch. Kayden had no idea what he meant, but it was true.

The half-rotted wood creaked underfoot. It barely held on. He walked off the porch, falling back onto the steps. All through Kayden's life, until today, a constant stream of thought occupied his days, often dreams too. He never was unaware. This silence of the mind comforted yet frightened. No path forward came.

Cold crept into his hands, and Kayden thrust them into his jacket pockets. Icy winds or any cold weather turned his joints to molten lead. Cool glass touched his knuckles. He turned his head, brow furrowed. He withdrew the bottle and shook it. Thoughts began to return. His mind pulled towards Jillian, but he focused on the label. Like some cheap gas station candy, it had a wrapper with reflective foil inside. Eldritch blue caught the light, which was unpleasant. It made his eyes ache to look at it. Like something from a magazine, he mused. He recalled x-ray glasses that would allow one to see through things. This promised a boost in brain power and awareness. He chuckled. It was a raspy snap.

If he was smarter and knew more, this was avoidable. There was a way out, at some point. It was impossible, but his mind insisted.

"Watermelon," he muttered, "just a piece of candy." It must have been a gift for a kid, he mused. He placed it on the tongue. Sweet, it was flavorful, though the shell broke to reveal a whipped cream with jelly at the center. Although the Figment was delicious, the image of biting into a snail in its shell ruined it. He shrugged, "Good candy." It was a start on the calories that would keep him going another day. It wasn't healthy, but real food cost money.

He sat, focused on his body. Other than a slight sugar rush, Figment was just another tasty treat. Kayden felt his mind wander back to the contents of the trailer behind him. Shaking his head, he looked at the antique bottle, brow furrowed. Beech wood-brown eyes roamed over the deepening snow. Laughter bled over the torn, tattered trailer park. It was under a blanket of white. He forced back thoughts of Jillian before they could tear him apart.

Just past the badly patched perimeter fence, a small group had congregated. They chattered about nothing. They gathered around a trash barrel filled with debris and wood. The warmth of the flames drove away from the cold. Kayden stood to peek at them, but looked down instead. Something pulled at the back of his mind. Something about their face, a voice whispered inside. They were off, somehow.

The four stood around the flames. One was a teenager, poor yet vibrant. He smiled at the others. He held his hands up to drive off the cold. Kayden's gaze ripped away to the young man's friends. They were dimmer in aspect, though within the fire's glow. Muted features of their faces felt somehow painted on. Though the imaginary artist was masterful, it fell short of real. It was uncanny in its approximation to reality. Emotions rolled over them; yet, they were an act, an accurate mimicry. They were insincere. Arcs of shadow passed between them, each connected, but they never touched the ordinary young man. Reactions were also a facsimile. Their bodies fell almost into scripted responses, but with a tiny jerk.

"Like," he muttered, but a flood came to drown the chaotic emptiness. They're like characters in a story; he thought, but shook his head. No, they're like those things. A voice inside blubbered. Kayden stared until a flake of snow landed in an eye. He blinked, wiping at his eyes, but they remained a falsehood. With a shake of his head, they remained. "They're like those things in games," he blabbered, blinking rapidly.

He held up the bottle of Figment. He held it up to his eyes to see the fine print. "Oh, my GOD," he groaned, "this is this a hallucinogen!" The group looked at him, and Kayden stuffed it into a pocket.

Again, he listened to his body, but all that waited was old aches. I don't feel high, part of him pleaded. Is this high? Why would anyone want to feel like this?

He stared at the young men. They spoke for a moment longer, but left after a few minutes. The unreality of them remained, despite Kayden's denial. He stepped off the porch, drawn by their strangeness. Thought of Jillian stabbing at him, heart feeling split. The only plan was to wait for the police. Not true yet, he promised, but refused to look back at the trailer. She wasn't dead. He was no doctor, Kayden told himself.

He ventured to the edge of the trailer court. Snow fell harder, cutting down visibility. The mountain was gone. The Van Lear family ruled from atop it. All that remained was the cloister of homes, all beyond veiled in white. Kayden brushed snow off his shoulders. Cold boots forgotten; his old pain seemed now distant. Each step casts up little clots of snow that built up on the tops of his boots.

The chatter of his cacophony of thoughts slowed. He focused his mind amid the constant babble inside. Most had placid fake faces that moved by absent string, though some were ordinary. None seemed to notice him. Was his face like theirs? He watched them pass back and forth. They moved over the street. Some glanced at him, but he managed a smile and waved. Some waved back. He shook, wiping the sweat away.

"Useless," he judged, "this stuff is a waste of time." He shook his head with a shrug. I just don't get it, thought Kayden.

A shadow drifted in the snow. Back and forth, it staggered. Kayden ignored them. It was a familiar sight. The only way to live in Meridian was to numb yourself. He thought of the strange people. Their faces were a sham.

Jillian's face swam into his thoughts, too. How did this happen? The question was a constant across life. A voice replied that this was the culmination of her decisions. This was the natural conclusion to her actions.

A stranger came closer as he frowned over the mildly offered idea. Before the strange, new voice could elaborate, the sudden stagger of the other pulled him away. Years of use had worn the biker. Stains darkened the stranger's jeans. Their rips zig-zagged across the knees. You get that from working in the dirt on a car, a voice offered in case he needed clarification. Kayden's beech wood eyes climbed up the man, for something waved atop his shoulders. Like a car lot with a sale, those things that swayed and jerked, that voice added in the pleasant tone of a helpful observer. From the stranger's neck, a tube of cancerous meat waved in the air, though along the sides, legs like fangs scrabbled at the falling snow. The force of this movement made each step a tenuous affair.

"Oh," Kayden breathed. His mind clamored. His stomach flipped as the world turned gray at the edges.

Among the tumult of the thoughts, the unfamiliar voice mulled over the situation, detachment of the intellectual or insane. He has that off-brand of cigarettes; it instructed. You know that one with the name like motor oil. What did you call them? Oh yes, you called them Black Tar Nails.

Where the man's head should have been, the meat centipede finally stilled. Oh, it sees me! The thought blared across his mind, and the Intellectual concurred. It waved. The violence of the undulation almost toppled the mechanic. Kayden fell backward, landing in the snow. He kicked at the earth to back up. A hand reached towards him, but he scrambled back onto his feet.

It shambled after him, meat centipede mewled. Kayden jumped over a fence. He threw himself forward. Behind him, the mechanic jerked towards him. Black tar nails peeked from a chest pocket. Kayden nearly crashed into a doghouse. The lower part of it rotted away. The only remaining evidence of its former occupant was a name above the entrance. He fled to the back as he moved, chest heaving, but the uneven tread of the mechanic grew louder. *I have to get to Jillian*, he thought.

Kayden forced himself to slow, hoping the mechanic would lose him. The man, controlled by the centipede of meat, fell over the fence. Some alien means of perception failed to register it. Kayden watched them flail.

Snow blinded, and the wind howled. The blizzard reduced the world to mere yards. Within the blizzard, the sound of Owl Sticks became deadened. The busted freezer taste pried itself inside the mouth. His cold boots slipped on Jillian's steps, and he fell on one knee. He leaped up and through the door.

Inside, he secured the door. Kayden peeked out the window. The mechanic shambled and jerked about in the snow. It wandered about, pulled by alien thoughts. "Doesn't see me," he breathed, resting his head against the cold wood.

A crinkle rose. It was furtive, like an earthworm dragged over an empty chip bag. Kayden froze. Are her eyes still open? He turned his head. It stopped before he could find the source of the noise. Of course, the Intellectual remarked. The real question is if she is looking at you. Chaos erupted in his mind, though the unfamiliar voice was still cool and detached. Invisible hands gently, though firmly, turned his gaze. A groan drooled out of his slack mouth.

Jillian sat with her head tilted back. Lovely eyes were open to slits. She may be sleeping, he prayed. A ragged sigh slipped out of him, and Kayden's face burned. Tears burst out, face reddened, weight lifted, but his chest heaved. His knees felt ready to buckle. Shivers gripped him. The taste of candy was too sweet in his mouth. The room felt too full. Ghost of the chills bit into his hands and feet.

"I have to think," he announced. "There is a way out, just a bad trip!"

No, the Intellectual corrected, this is the Truth. There was a smugness in this inner voice. It was pleased to perceive something he couldn't.

"What?" asked Kayden, eyes drifting away. He could smell the factory on him. Its aroma clawed at his sinuses.

Jillian, your ex-wife, is dead from a drug overdose, the voice elaborated. A culmination of variables and choices—yours and hers—that ended in her death. You already knew the answer. The voice spoke with a condescending glee.

Kayden frowned at the thought. A question rose, but a sudden shift at the edge of his vision pulled into his eyes. Jillian's hand twitched. One finger pointed, absently, at the remnants of an envelope. From its tip, a fat thread crawled over the paper. It moved, rose to look about, but froze at his gasp. It quivered. The shiver of its body ran down the hand. A thin red line traced down her arm like the voracious roots of a tree. These razor-thin cuts spread over the emaciated body. A dark part of him thought of a broken vase. Skin peeled back. It pulled from muscles. It sounded like ripping paper, though wet. Kayden fell backward, shoulders struck by the wood. He pawed the air to turn an invisible knob. More skin pulled away to lift her like a doll. Like an angel of ruin, her wings spread out, made of veiny flesh. Her lower jaw split. Her tongue lulled down to a too-skinny chest, and an empty eye melted into a luminous blue. Two tentacles extended from the sockets like skinned snakes. Out from the tattered clothes and ruined meat, a pungent mushroom stink choked the tobacco ash reek.

"Oh, GOD," he pleaded. His mind emptied. Even the Intellectual had no thought to share. It watched from within him.

"Just move on," the twin snakes hissed low in hateful sorrow. It was the last thing Jillian had said to him. It was a fervent plea. Jillian had cried when she said it.

That was the last words of your ex-wife before she overdosed, the Intellectual voice insisted. It revealed the thought as if it was the winning answer in a game show.

Kayden screamed. Wings of skin lifted Jillian towards him, and he bucked backward. Badly repaired door barely held together. It fragmented under his weight. The few nails and screws holding it closed gave up. He tumbled back onto the porch. She moved towards him, silent. Another scream tore out of him, and he moved back and then kicked it closed. It banged shut, but the slightest push would open it.

Jillian bumped against the door, but he kept it shut. His wail of anguish broke. Kayden covered his face. Knowing more never changes the past, the Intellectual whispered. It shouldn't take long for her to escape.

"NO," he turned over, jumping to his feet. He rushed off the porch.

You cannot flee your mind, the unfamiliar voice observed. I am wherever you are, it added, almost amused.

The meat centipede head had wandered out of the trailer park. His gaze was wild. He searched for the mechanic.

Kayden stumbled through the blizzard. The other trailers were only pale visages. He loped, carried upon terror, out into the road.

Shadows passed at the edges. People appeared and then disappeared. They pushed through the blizzard. Streets turned, twisted, and bent. No cars dared the road. Snow reduced parked vehicles to white hulks. Every flake of snow had weight, tossed upon howls of wind. The entire world felt sewn into nerves. Even the slightest mote plucked the nerve and strummed the heart. The placid island of his mind drifted into the pandemonium of the infinite. His eyes saw too much. Tastes assailed and sensations assaulted. I can feel every particle, Kayden's mind moaned. Battered by endless sensation, he staggered forward in the blinding white. His eye counted every particle of ice. All senses rose higher and higher until everything was within him, and he reduced to nothing.

Beyond mere yards, an uneasy light devoured the world. It was an eldritch blue, and a bruised hue of purple. It painted all beyond the fleck of the ground beneath Kayden. Sensuous and wicked wares offered in secret. The alien stars, already dead, swept across a strange sky. The blizzard raged, but it was a speck in the boundless sea of the infinite. All of it pressed upon his mind. A man was finite. To see—to feel the fathomless—filled every atom till even the senses of gods fell short, stupid, and insufficient. Better to close your eyes than blinded by revelation, the Intellectual observed. It was better to die than numbed by the sensation this voice knew. Deafened by the chaos left one hollowed out; his mind obliterated. Every facet of taste became one until indivisible, but nothing in the lack of definition. Overwhelmed, the specific was nothing in the endless. Kayden wailed under the assault, hearing the echoes of the hungry void raise its voice in his.

The unabashed truth crashed down upon Kayden, all of it. It hollowed him out. Inside it filled, spilled, and drowned anything else. Naked revelation was before him. It coursed through him, awful as the acknowledgment. The truth was relentless. Layers upon layers wove together. Stupid senses failed to capture it. Together, a bizarre gulf and nothing surrounded each, and the absurd reality of incongruities defied logic. Laws of existence broke, yet held in a paradox unfathomable. Sane and insane bound this reality as the rules of attraction and repulsion. In every universe, galaxy, and each cell this pulled and pushed, warred. Kayden covered his eyes, praying this would stop.

Like the crash of a tsunami, it eventually pulled back into the sea. Truth receded. Although it left him, it had left its mark. Kayden sat, body drawing up. He sobbed, reduced to a child. Beech wood-brown eyes felt heavier, older. He retreated from any thought or sense. Better to be empty than filled to bursting destruction.

You can stay here and mourn your wife, the Intellectual voice observed. It was ponderous. Unmoved by these revelations, it considered him. Or you could talk to Chris, Sheila, and Brian. They're responsible for Jillian's fate. The voice let the idea settle in the air, unhurried.

An invisible hand lifted Kayden's chin. A new day came. He had walked back to his former job in the blizzard. The morning sun blazed across the fields of white. The Plant

Manager stood out in front of the building beside Kayden's old supervisor and HR Manager.

"A new plan," Kayden whispered, smiling at all his knowledge. "It is time to tell them some of what I know." He stood as the razor-thin cuts sealed over his body. The Intellectual agreed.

After a short walk, Kayden stood before Chris. His unrestrained smile was too wide. The Plant Manager asked him to come inside, for things had changed. Kayden sensed something was different. Their body language was open. Brian and Sheila had already waited in her office. They had called his house, since laying off others on the list. His light-hearted smile greeted them, and disquiet built into their hearts. Possibilities burst across his mind. Logic eliminated them, leaving fewer and fewer.

The Human Resources Manager's fingers tapped rapidly on the desk. Her eyes flew from the other two men. She cleared her throat, tears welled. "Mister Stone, Kayden, yes," she stammered, smiling. Her mascara ran. "We've been trying to contact you!" She covered her mouth and coughed, "I mean, we have been trying to speak to you." She wore the same outfit as the other day. Her breath smelled like coffee. She had sweated so much, stains spread beneath her arms.

"The names on the list included all the women Brian had tormented," Kayden ventured, though his voice was pensive and detached. It was the most logical move for his ex-supervisor to make. "You laid off those women." His eyes locked onto hers, and she swore she saw a strange light inside his eyes. A bruised purple light glimmered within. "Now, you have no power over them, and it is reasonable to deduce that they are very mad." He laughed. It was loud and vicious. The Plant Manager, supervisor, and Human Resources Manager blinked in unison, faces paled. They reddened. "To further guess, they've had gotten together to exchange stories," he added, watching them fidget and shift.

"We have a no sexual harassment policy!" Sheila blubbered, and the other two nodded like bobbleheads. Her eyes roamed over Kayden. She wanted to leap across the desk. They were all a bunch of psycho hillbillies.

Kayden's expression remained placid. "Anyway, you are all shaking because they talked to someone." His words flowed like an intellectual at a presentation. "It isn't the home office, because you could all just cover the other, buffalo them like good-ole-boys. No... I think it is most likely the Van Lear Family." All three of them recoiled from the evocation of the family atop Swannanoa. He smiled. "They are Lear County. They are this community's aristocracy." A mechanical laugh boiled out of him, "The Queen of Lear Mountain will come down, because she won't have your nonsense in her kingdom, especially from a New Money project." He looked at Brian, "I hear Miss Van Lear is very swift to bring low any who treat their people with a lack of proprieties." Kayden looked into his ex-supervisor's eyes, knowing he thought of the Blackberry Bog. Often, missing people ended up sinking into its mud.

"They have no proof," Sheila moaned, and the other two nodded in idiot agreement. She glanced at the door. The men had explained the Van Lear Family to her, the rumors.

Kayden looked at her until Sheila's gaze moved away. "The Queen won't care about your bureaucracy," he stated.

Razor-thin lines formed in his skin. They spread. "Now, you have brought me here to silence me," he whispered, suddenly far away. He felt the fragility of reality.

"We want to bring you back," she blabbered in a rush, "but first, you sign this." She pushed a Non-Disclosure Agreement towards him. She hoped it would frighten him and keep his mouth shut.

He ignored it. He had something more important to tell them. Thin tendrils slithered across the floor and then gripped the steel doors. It barred the door. Kayden turned his eyes on them. They filled with bruised purple light. The plant manager, supervisor, and HR manager stared into his alien gaze. Some drilled into their eyes, infecting them. The strange light centered in their mind. Every sensation grew within their skulls. Unpleasant truth, a dark knowledge, leeched into their minds. It let them know exactly what was to happen to them. They felt small, like they had made others feel.

"I think it is time to talk about what I know," he breathed. Lines spread up his face, and his body unzipped to reveal the truth.

Crossroads and Blues

A semi raced past, blaring its horn. Its slipstream nearly jerked him off his feet. He glanced at it, thinking of playing his guitar. His boots beat a unique rhythm on gravel. Heels caught the small stones, casting them forward. The sun was pleasant on his skin. His steps were constant, and their timing kept at a swift pace. Iggy's gait kept in sync with the music, which never ended in his head. He could still taste the mustard from his last sandwich. Soles kept pace with his heart. These notes played even in his dreams. They were born within, and he had to write them down. It was the only way to silence them so more could take their place. Sometimes, he would trudge, strut, or scamper. He would catch the smell of busted engines and leaking oil. Most days, the young man moved in a smooth stride. The chords' melody, major or minor, carried him along. People avoided him as he moved to his eternal beats.

The transition to pavement was as abrupt as a wide-of-the-mark pluck. So smooth was his step that Iggy moved to accommodate the change. The rasp of boots was a whisper sung low. Cut-off mufflers were the bass of a lifetime smoker. Newer cars sang tenor, more electronic and lighter than metal and heavy, he knew. Everything added to his music sheet, though more vehicles contributed. He moved, turned back with a thumb up, but still moved on. None stopped. They passed him by as if a man with a guitar was accursed or trafficked with the unsavory.

He came to the crossroads, still to the rhythm, still on foot. Iggy paused. Superstition ran deep in Appalachia. He considered walking around it. Once, over a decade ago, he had come to such a place, but it was dirt. Desperate to be better on his guitar, Paganini, he'd begged anything that would listen, God or the devil. He had gotten no better for months. The only thing that came was the smell of hand-rolled cigarettes, and the downbeat of steel spurs. Tears had also come, as one consigned to a miserable lot. If no one above or below would help, he had sworn then and now, Iggy would play as his heart moved him. Fame sounded sweet, recognition even better; yet, he strummed his guitar out of love for the eternal music inside. Before that desperate act, they noticed his skill, although it earned him only scorn.

He crossed over the road when it was clear enough to go. His boots slapped the pavement. A black truck passed him, windows tinted dark, and Iggy looked away. Memories swam up and then dived to leave troubled waters. The music turned down in his heart, as he felt eyes upon him.

No motorist gave him a ride or slowed, except to stare. Music turned up to match the dervish of his heart. Closer to home, he kept his thumb down and looked away from all the passing drivers. One old man in a truck rumbled past slowly, but his eyes found the guitar on Iggy's back. The young man sighed and murmured a thank you as the vehicle drove on. He was close to Meridian. Winter Rose County was next to Lear County, and a decade was a long time to some, but nothing to rural folk. Others would pass, but very few slowed.

He had hitchhiked to the Winter Rose Mall as a teenager. It was still open. He felt a weight lift. Once, when he lived just beyond Lear Mountain, he had come to the music store for records or strings. People picked up hitchhikers then, especially a kid. Every spot occupied back then, especially on a Friday night. When a blockbuster movie opened in the theater, every space in the parking lot filled. The last time Iggy saw a movie was that Halloween, he recalled. He pushed away the thought with other memories. He preferred to forget them.

Now, most of the stores closed long ago. Previous occupants had left their mark before they had folded or moved on. Dreams of stepping back into the record store faltered. It was one of his few hopes. People dressed differently. The fashions were alien. Cars had changed too. They were sleeker. Iggy wore the same clothes when he had left, though he was taller and thinner. It was his favorite shirt. Some people noticed him. He was just strange enough to attract attention. They stared at him, the guitar. Their curiosity was quick to pass.

He walked to the record store, considering the money he saved. Iggy stopped. The steel shutters secured. Nothing of Razor Hawk Records remained. Another store's advertisements remained in the window. Some had fallen onto the floor. One of very few dreams. He allowed himself to hit a sour note. He heaved a deep sigh, unsurprised. The music inside him skipped like a damaged vinyl.

He strode over to the bench. There was too much music inside. Playing would clear his mind. He withdrew Paganini and set it down. Iggy rubbed the scar, which ran from above his right eye up into his black hair. Quiet for years, it held a low ache. "What to do?" he asked, too low for others to hear.

He picked up Paganini. The music skipped inside, and he frowned at the repetition. He drew in a breath, held it, and then released it. Fingers picked chords in a smooth motion, and music again played. When his hands pulled notes out, the world felt far away. Nothing except the song remained. They came easy as breathing. The progression was sweet, ensnared by all that heard. Iggy saw nothing, only the rapture of creation. It filled him. Heavy eyes focused on nothing, intense in ecstasy. People gathered. Women held hands to their hearts as their faces reddened like intruders in a secret garden. They swayed. Men frowned, though their heads bobbed. Their faces paled. Creation was the province of the Divine, and the result of mind, heart, and soul in tune. Their mouths worked, and a few trembled; some even closed their eyes to hear better, eliminating distractions. None dared to make any noise. All fell under the music's spell.

"You're that boy," a man barked, face moved from pale to a violent reed. His eyes widened, fists clenching. He jerked forward as if to charge, but halted. The color drained from his face.

Iggy jerked. His eyes found the man, whose calloused hands turned into fists. The man recognized him, somehow. "I... I don't know what you mean," Iggy groaned, looking at the small crowd. They blinked, frowned, and turned to the middle-aged man. They murmured as eyes moved between the two. He snapped back to the world. He could taste the mustard he had eaten. The smell of his sweat was too much.

"DNA, BULL-SPIT," he bellowed, thick brow drawing down, "you need to get going. You should have never come back." He glared at Iggy. His wife, who had a bag with a new blouse, rushed over. She whispered to him, pulled him, gentle yet insistent. "NO, honey, once we would have hung men like him!" he growled. "He should have ended in

Blackberry Bog!" She jerked him away, though the man's baleful eyes returned to Iggy.

Others stared at the young man but moved on, speaking low. They whispered about murders. They asked about the guitarist. Iggy looked down, hoping they'd leave, but a dark figure remained. He blinked, thinking it was a shadow. He peeked at the man's face; yet, he had to look again to make sure it was a man. His skin pebbled at his strangeness.

"Men have sold their souls to play so sweet," remarked the man, who brushed down a tie as dark as the three-piece suit. "I'm Valto, Valto Miettinen, and you are?" he asked, lip twitched, thinned. His eyes locked onto the young man.

"I'm just," Iggy muttered. He saw the angry man talking to another, "passing through. I've got business. I mean to see done." He had nightmares about returning. They seemed prophetic now.

"Yes, I've come to pick up a few things myself," he confessed. Valto's lips screwed up into a smile. His skin held a sheen. Like a bird freshly hatched, Iggy thought. He looked away from him, shivering. No one else looked at him, only the Guitarist. "I'm headed back to Lear Mountain, one county over if you need a ride," he offered casually.

"Thank you," he sighed. The men looked his way. "But I think it is best that I go alone." The thought of being alone in the car with him pulled at Iggy's guts. He could smell the man's plain soap.

"You've been walking all day," Valto observed, looking at Paganini. Iggy frowned as he pointed at his boots. "I know the look of a man who has been riding his thumb."

"I've been doing it for years," he confessed, setting down the guitar. "It gives me time to think about music." He wished the man would go. His head bobbled, thinking of a new beat.

Valto shrugged, though his jaw flexed. "That man seems to know you." He nodded towards the group of men.

"I've been gone for a while," he shrugged, rubbing the scar. Something familiar played at the back of his mind. Iggy had hoped his mother would come to pick him up. It was a long walk from Thadwick, but he had to talk to her. "It has been a little more than a decade," he stood, knowing it would be a long walk. He hoped the man wouldn't start a scene and attract more attention.

"A decade," he repeated, running a hand over his tie, "that was the time around the Nottingham Knob thing." His oily smile was slow to bloom but quick to die.

Iggy glanced back at him. It was hard to look at the other, but easy to dismiss him. "I can't recall," he muttered, putting a hand over his eye. A migraine had seized it, pounding with his heart.

"Yes, it was today," he shrugged. His eyes studied the sky. "I forget the details." He looked at the guitar. "I am trying to get better. I'm a picker, such as you, maybe not quite as skilled as you." Lip twitching, he stared at Iggy's guitar.

"You play," he dared to smile. Music always set him at ease. He forgot the world when he played.

"I do," he admitted, sliding his hands into his trousers. They balled into fists. "I would do anything to get better. I feel like I've hit a plateau in my skill."

"Be careful," he warned. Iggy thought of his plea that night at the crossroads, "Jimmy Johnson whistled up a devil that he couldn't put down, so they say." The blues singer had gotten more than he could handle. Guitar players still whispered his name, his disappearance.

Valto jerked. "Sounds like you may have some experience, and I would swear you played as one possessed." His eyes roamed over him as if the divine touched him.

"Oh, I just know there is no deal to be made," he laughed, shaking his head. "It is natural, and I practice every day for years." The daily practice had sharpened his natural skill. He had a gift, and he loved it.

The man in the suit and tie stared at him until Iggy shuffled his feet. "Very well, some would be happy to be... blessed," he nodded, looking away. His father said the guitar was a dirty thing for nasty boys. His eyes moved back to Iggy. "I heard of a boy; not quite a man, troubled, who played the guitar. Some used the word genius." His mouth worked, a curse in his eyes.

The young man looked away. It had angered his father. He had smashed his guitar. "I play because I love it," he whispered, looking away, "and I try to get better."

"You're incredibly talented," he accused him. He smiled, eyes flat. "I have to head back. I hope your business goes well," Valto extended a hand.

He shook it. Valto's hand felt oily, too soft, but held a steel grip underneath. "I hope you get better," he added with a slight grin, but the other's grip tightened.

"You too," Valto walked away.

Iggy watched him go, but his gaze slid away. A third man had joined the two. They glared at him. People crossed and uncrossed their arms. They exchanged murmurs, heads tilting, but none looked away from the guitarist. A group of women came to speak to them, and they finally looked away from Iggy.

He moved from the bench, while the men spoke to the women. The rhythm inside struck a fast, heavy beat. He moved into a department store, refusing to look back. He could make it to the back roads. It would be safer, he hoped. Years of hitchhiking showed him the different ways from Winter Rose to Lear County. Workers followed, watching his hands. He sighed. He placed his hands over his head, so they would have no excuse to stop him. Their manager waited by the door. He saw he carried nothing, just Paganini.

He strode out onto the sidewalk. Thankfully, no one else was out here. A few cars occupied the parking lot. Iggy moved, though kept it at a brisk walk. A man with his face gets the cops called. Lear County felt far. He stepped off the sidewalk.

"Hey Boy," a man bellowed, and Iggy looked back to see four men coming.

"Great," he cursed, letting out a breath. They always move in packs, lamented Iggy. They even did that in a school for wayward children, even in the joint. The men were broad and muscled, but he was used to walking. He could outrun them. It was something else with which he had plenty of practice.

He readied to bolt as a classic car rolled along. Its engine was a purr, a smooth, well-oiled machine. It was a white hue, like a bleached bone. The window rolled down. That is the old preacher's car, Iggy recalled. Valto looked at the men, who stared at the car, and its gold trim. They slowed.

"Are you gentlemen doing okay?" Valto asked, beaming. He ignored Iggy.

They looked at the Guitarist. The angry man approached. "We don't want him back in Lear County, in Meridian."

"If you have any concerns," he studied his fury, "you should call the Sheriff." There was a dare in Valto's smile.

"There is no need to bother Rutger," he begged, face burning. The other men looked at each other. The Sheriff was a fair man, but he was a hard one.

"Well," he looked at each one, "If anything happens to him, I think he'll have to know you boys were bothering him."

"I don't care if they let him out," he bellowed. Spittle flew from his lips. The others shook their heads. Rutger was a rough man.

"We can talk about that," Valto said, tone even. He looked at the Guitarist, "You should go, Ignazio."

Iggy nodded, turning turned away from the men. He ran. Had he told him his name? The closest back road was near, but only a single bridge crossed the Cumberland from this county to Lear. He thought there was the northern approach, but it would be morning before he arrived home. Maybe, this time, he hoped his fortune would be good. He wished there was somewhere else he could go.

The mall disappeared behind him. His heart raced. He slowed, staying clear of the main road. The music had turned down in his head, muffled by the headache. He withdrew the medicine, which kept the images at bay. It stopped the migraines, though it had been a long time since his last headache. He never missed taking a pill. Inside the bottle were several that would last a few days. Iggy wondered if the prescription was still necessary. It had been a long time since he had an episode.

If not for bad luck, Ignazio Ruffo would have none. If he fell, a boot to the ribs would follow. A wind, perhaps from an aggressive fall breeze or a speeding car, slapped the hand that held the bottle. It tumbled through the air, contents spilling. Deft fingers of the Guitarist snatched at them as they fell, but the medicine slipped through his grip. They struck the storm grate before disappearing into the dark. He pushed his fingers into the hole. They felt nothing but air.

"Please," Iggy begged, trying to fish out the pills. Nothing, they were somewhere below. He picked up the bottle. The La Voison woman had helped him get it. She believed his incredible stories. She had known how it felt to be an outsider, he knew. Sweet and patient, she spoke to him as a person. It had been a couple of years since he had seen her.

He looked at the pill bottle and then the grate. "I suppose I should have guessed," he grumbled. A long sigh blew strands away from his mouth. Better to accept it, and hope things get better, he thought. The night was coming. It wasn't smart to be walking around branches and hollows at night.

He trudged back to the road without a glance back. It was done. The music kept his feet moving, though the migraine stifled it. It dug deeper. It clawed into his skull and right eye socket. Even the scar burned. The X-rays showed nothing wrong. That never kept the pain away. He plodded on, though staggered, which threw off the beat of his song.

He moved over the streets, marveling at the changes. Pain stomped down his wonder. The sound of the traffic on the main road grew as he approached the bridge. Along the tree line, Iggy looked at the passing vehicles. I hope they moved on; he prayed. The guitarist moved towards the bridge.

"Okay," he blew out a breath, hands shaking. He tried to gauge the length. He was fast.

"Stop," a voice commanded. It was like a breeze given life.

A grip, light as air, jerked the Guitarist back. He fell on his butt, teeth clacked together with a click. "Hey," Iggy frowned. He winced. A teenage boy regarded him, eyes wide. The innocent face was too familiar. Iggy screamed as gray swelled at the edges of his vision. Beat of the music inside was riotous, which matched the beat of his heart. All thought fled his mind.

The boy jumped upon him, covering his mouth. His weight was light as a feather. "Shut up, Iggy!" He begged. The boy pointed past the tree line. A truck with an extended cab slowed, windows rolled down, and the four men looked about the road. They searched the tree line. A dark stillness lingered in their fury. They whispered to each other.

He breathed hard, wild eyes on them instead of the boy. They drove on and circled back towards the town's center.

Eventually, he looked back at him. "Page," sobbed Iggy. He hadn't said the name since that night.

The boy smiled, "It's me, Iggy, so be cool." He held his hands up as if careful not to spook the guitarist.

"Oh God, OH GOD," he moaned. "You're gone. You're," tears spilled, "this is impossible!" Gray turned black at the edges of his vision. His head felt light. The mustard clogged the back of his throat.

"I said to be cool," Page reminded him, holding his hands up. "You're going to blow a gasket!"

Iggy stared at him. He wore the same jeans and high tops as that night. The Forever Teenage boy's shirt had a picture of Einstein with his tongue out. It was still clean, like it had just come out of the dryer. No blood stained it now. The Guitarist saw and felt his heart split.

"Page, bro, I can't," he pleaded, shaking his head.

"Then turn around, Iggy," he frowned, unspoiled features cramped. Page rolled his eyes. "Never figured you for a coward," his blue eyes turned back, "not after standing up to your father."

Every man reached his limit, even boys. Iggy touched his lip at the memory. "And I suffered for it... the look in his eyes. I thought I would die." He recalled the sour tang of beer blowing over him. The memory was as real as Page. His old man liked to tune up on him.

"You looked like ten pounds of crap in a five-pound bag," he nodded. He waggled his eyebrows.

A quick laugh shot out of the Guitarist, "You are Page." His eyes searched his face.

"Who else would I be?" asked the teenager. "You were a genius on Paganini, but a bit slow at everything else." He shrugged, unsurprised.

"You could have been a doctor," he blubbered, recalling those old days. Iggy's eyes burned. "A lawyer, or a scientist, you had a future, man. You were going places." He shook his head, "You can't be you!" He produced the pill bottle from his pocket. "I ran out of that, my meds." He held it up as if the boy would disappear at this revelation.

Page opened his mouth and then closed it. His blue searched the ditch, thinking. He looked at Iggy, "You know Miss Booker, the Math Teacher?" He asked though blushed.

The boy blinked, "Yes." He hadn't heard that name in years. She had treated Page like some savant, an unparalleled genius. The woman paraded him around the class like he was her son.

"You were right," he admitted, blushing with a shrug. "She changed my grade on the test. It was a high B, and she bumped it into an A." He laughed a little.

Iggy's eyes widened, mouth worked, "I knew it." It was all he could say as the memories flooded back. No one scored above a B on the test, except Page. He knew he hadn't studied the night before. They had hung out and played around.

"I am here to help you," Page touched his leg, soft as a breeze. "Once you cross that bridge, brother, we are in it to win it." He trembled, feeling the words to be true.

"What if I don't go?" he pleaded. He had spent years trying to forget them. They had been his only friends. He terrified the other kids at the juvenile detention center. They had attacked him until he stayed away.

"We were your friends," Page reminded him, looking into his eyes. He had waited all these years, hoping. The others had given up, but not him. He knew one day his friend would return.

Iggy shook his head. Tears spilled, but the not-quite-a-boy and not-quite-a-man looked at him. "I waited so long to move on," he begged. All he wanted was to go home. He would move away. Life in Meridian would be hell, but it was all he had.

"So have we," he said, though his voice was gentle. Time was strange. They never slept, and days would crawl by, but then days, weeks, or months would pass. He sighed, weary. None of them ever shut off. There was no gift of sleep or rest. Sometimes he saw others, how they had changed. Everything became stranger, more distant.

"One more campaign," he wiped away tears. They were his only genuine friends. Less and less, he recalled them. It would be a laugh or a joke. He would smile until the memory of the last time he had seen them resurfaced.

Page laughed, "So, you haven't forgotten us." He marveled at all the changes in his friend.

The Guitarist stood up and brushed off his jeans. He snatched glances at the boy. Page rose, but nothing clung to him. He was like air or a shadow. He was there. Iggy swallowed, wringing his hands. His friend walked through the tree line, but nothing moved with his passing. After a moment to hum a tune, he followed.

The last time he crossed the bridge, it was in shambles. Ranked one of the ten most dangerous in the country, it was high above the Cumberland. Page walked close to him, watching him closely. That day began in Winter Rose like today. After watching a movie at the mall, they crossed the bridge. Swearing he could feel it shake; Iggy held his breath until one of them would nudge him. It would break under them. He had been sure. One time, he had passed out. Since then, they replaced the bridge with a federal grant. His chest tightened, but his old friend occupied his mind. Even the music fell to a low volume. The guitarist felt the migraine deepen, and he staggered. Page gave him a whack. It was like a puff of air. Iggy straightened as the teenager watched.

The migraine pounded like a sledgehammer against his skull. Each strike felt like his head would split. He focused on turning the page. His foot struck the pavement on the other side. Gone, his headache lifted. It was so sudden that he blinked. Iggy paused, bent over, and drew in a long breath. The edges of his vision blurred for a moment, then cleared. Music turned up as his shakes settled down.

Iggy looked at him, taking another deep breath. "Page, brother, did I do...?" he asked, refusing to look away. He had to figure it out. At Thadwick, he recalled nothing of that night. He had tried for years to figure out what had happened.

"I don't know," he admitted, shaking his head, "I didn't see anything." Page's eyes searched the world, finding nothing.

"Things are coming back." His brow furrowed. "I thought, because of my head," he hummed, touching the scar, "I would never remember." It was a constant reminder of what happened. It had taken a year before he could bear to see it in a mirror.

"Do you remember anything?" Page begged. They had tried to figure it out over the years. None of them managed more than bits and pieces. It felt like something was missing.

"I recall the crossroads," he managed, blushing, "and we walked to the mall and watched the movie. We came back." Iggy spoke slowly and then nodded.

Page frowned, "Wait... dude, did you go to the crossroad, because of that Jimmy Johnson thing?" More of that day returned. It felt like ghost ships sailing past him.

He looked away, shrugged, "You guys were going to college after high school. No matter how good I was, no one wanted to give me a chance. Even if I was better at music, just because my family lived out on Nottingham Knob Branch." He would have dragged them down. They wanted to help him prepare for college, but he wasn't as smart as the rest.

"I knew that girl from Duncannon getting that scholarship got to you," he hissed. Page popped his fingers, rolling his eyes. "Those spoiled, New Money brats were always butt kissers!" Page's blue eyes found him, "But, to go down to the crossroads, because of Jimmy Johnson, that is going too far." His face reddened. It was a stupid story to scare babies. No one believed it except for Iggy.

Iggy pushed past him towards another back road. "You were going places, dude," he moaned, brow drawing down. "You weren't the son of the town, mean drunk, and the town," he pressed his lips together. He hummed a quick tune.

As low as the town viewed his parents, both thought less of him. The townsfolk would grow to hate Iggy the most.

"You aren't your parents," he chided him. All these years, he was still on it. People were supposed to grow up when they got older. People held him up as special, and they held Iggy down.

"You know what that music teacher told me," He admitted, glancing back at Page. "She said it didn't matter because Mary's parents could get her through college. She said I would be lucky to keep a job at a factory, knock up some girl, and not drink myself to death." He stopped and shrugged, "You know what, she was right." Teachers told the other students they could be anything. They had to work for it. None bothered to put dreams in his head. They were certain where he would be, amazing talent or not.

"You just freaked her out," he reminded him, scowling. "Your music can feel intense, in a good way." It had affected most of the adults in a strange way. It was like they saw a ghost or whistled up a devil.

"I'll go back to see my mom, but I'll dust my boots off when I leave Lear County," he swore. Once he finished with Hemlock Hurst, Meridian, and Nottingham, he would never come back.

Page walked beside him, each step like he had springs on his heels. "At least we only saw that black truck once that day," he recalled. The image of it flashed. He kicked at a rock, but his foot only tipped it over.

Hairs raised on his neck, "Blue cars, man, you think about them, and you'll see them." He felt a memory prowl at the back of his mind. Something wanted to return, but it was too blurry.

"I don't know," Page breathed, looking back. He could feel them. They weren't as strong as him. It was harder for them to move far from their new home.

Iggy looked where Page glanced. "Oh, my GOD!" He froze, numb. Three shadows walked behind them. Run! a voice screamed inside, but his body refused to move. Instead, he kicked a clump of dirt with the heel of his boot. It bounced away.

"It is Mickey, Josh, and Brandon," Page smiled, lifting one shoulder, and then dropping it. "The Dud Gang is all here now."

Iggy could see only their outlines but recognized them. They distorted the air. "We came this way that night," he muttered, feeling the world disconnect. It looped in upon itself, he felt. Too old to trick-or-treat, he recalled, except for Mickey, who had tried for a month to convince them otherwise. He loved it, the costumes, the candy.

Page looked at a silhouette. "Yeah, dude, you're right. We should have gone out Sabbath Branch and checked out that Hill Witch's house." He nodded with a laugh.

"Don't call her that," he snapped, turning away from his friends, "don't be jerks." She was a sweet woman. His family disgusted the townsfolk. The La Voison woman frightened them.

"What are you talking about?" Page wondered. He frowned at the guitarist's sharp tone. "It isn't like you ever met her," he laughed, but Iggy looked away. "You met her!" he squealed. Everybody told stories about her. They said that she came from a long line of witches. Her daughter was one too.

He walked, ignoring the teenager, but the others gathered around him. "Fine," he threw up his hands, "she wasn't ugly or a monster. Bethany was nice." She had the most beautiful eyes. They were green, flecked with gold. He wished she were his mother. Bethany had hugged him more.

"Wow, awesome," Page breathed, "why did she talk to you?" He bounced around the guitarist, eyes large.

"The Sheriff Rutger, he asked her to talk to me," he shrugged. "It was about that... night," Iggy muttered, peering at them. He felt his heart drop. "They said something about strange circumstances."

"Did she say anything, you know?" he thrummed, bounced about. Page wondered if she had put a curse on Iggy. People said she did strange things in the woods at night.

Iggy opened his mouth, but her question echoed back to him. "She asked me if I had seen you guys," he whispered. They knew as little as him, it seemed.

"Bizarre," he blinked, mouth agape. He had expected more. Bethany must have waved her hands or chanted in Latin or something.

The Guitarist listened to the music, which was the clearest it had ever been. He paused, listening. Each additional step grew smoother, despite the ache of his heart. He whistled a tune, and the notes were sweet. Iggy's mind filled with memories like a half-formed song. Its discordance fell away. "I just can't put it together," he looked at Page and the shadowy figures. "Hey, man," tears filled his eyes, spilled, "did I, you know, did I do it?" He tried to look at him, but he couldn't.

Page's eyes filled. He cried, but the tears disappeared before they could touch the earth. "Like I said... I don't know," he shook his head, "I saw nothing but a flash, and there were a few moments of pain." His eyes searched the world, which had changed by degrees over the years. It was all he could recall.

Iggy turned away. He had tried to piece together that night or recall anything, but today was the first time he remembered anything. "You were my only friends," he trudged on, praying to be innocent. He didn't know how he would move on if he killed them. He wouldn't deserve peace. His friends hadn't found it in death, so why would he find it in life?

Page followed, trying to get his attention. The guitarist focused on his disjointed memories. "I remember finding you in the woods," he offered, but Iggy looked at the back road. A smile played across his lips. "I was joking when I asked you to play dungeon music." It had been an absurd thing to request.

The Guitarist burst into a gale of laughter. "That was the weirdest request I ever had!" He roared. His broad smile felt funny. He couldn't recall when he had laughed.

"You did it, Spooky," Page smiled, "I knew you were going places too." It was hard to play with his music at first. He was so skilled that everyone focused on him.

"Yeah," he said and chuckled, "going to straight juvie or a trailer in Owl Sticks." No one had called him Spooky since he had left Meridian. A teacher called him that after hearing him play. The other children picked it up.

"Hey dude," Page shook his head, "I would have probably taken over my dad's practice. But you, you were going to be a real legend!" He had listened to his dad's vinyl, trying to hear another as good as Iggy. There were none.

"I love it," he confessed. The guitarist walked with a smooth gait. The music played sweeter inside. "It was a challenge too," he bobbed his head, "and to switch it up as you guys played, fun." Every time they changed scenes, he had to write music for it.

"You could have played too," the teenager sprung up beside Iggy as they walked. He had wanted him to be the team's bard. Iggy was content to play.

"On a Jerry-can guitar I made," he added, smiling. Those days, playing for them was sweet. He had made one from a cigar box. A dark-colored vehicle ran over it, Iggy recalled. He didn't get a good look at them. It had almost hit him.

Before he could hum the tune to Page's campaign of Mad Max's Maze, the Guitarist stepped into Owl Sticks. Iggy's old man had moved them around the trailer parks here. That was before he found the ferryman at the bottom of a bottle. "Like a white trash hell, somehow sublime," he marveled, whistling a low, long note. It was spooky three notes. All the jobs were gone, he heard while in juvie. He looked at the long wall that separated the edge of town from the surrounding creek. It held the reek of drugs and sulfur from old, abandoned mines. Prone to flooding, the lack of rain over the last couple of weeks had left only a halfhearted trickle. Trailers and hovels beyond the fence peeked at him, most dark. The last of the day's light died, but the full moon had come. Its glow made the land horror haunted as the unsettled heart. Even beyond the low-end housing division, sour sweat washed in the cat piss stink of meth labs. He tasted the rotted egg stench. Children, parents too high to watch, roamed through the streets like feral packs of dogs. They fought or damaged the derelict properties. A house or trailer would suffer their joy and end in flames. The locals called them Devil's Nights.

"I walk through it sometimes, man," Page admitted, rolling his eyes. His dad closed his practice after his mom had left. They couldn't stand Meridian without him. "Like places with those creatures from a horror show; you know the things that shamble about," he recalled a movie they had watched at the mall. It was like a wasteland or sadistic dystopia.

"That was where I'm headed," he mumbled, recalling the terror that had bloomed in his heart. He would die here. The word Spooky whispered behind his back. He had heard those stories about Jimmy his whole life, and the man was a legend to all with a guitar. He considered the crossroads, where he had prayed for deliverance. His playing was the only thing that made him special. I could go around it, he mused, considering the dying light. He pushed away memories of the second time he visited the intersection of roads. Distant police sirens rose, but he heard only the tunes inside his heart.

He turned back to the road, stepping away from the desolation of rural life. The system of roads beyond the town spread out through the lowland. They were prone to flooding, but it was dry for weeks. Iggy preferred walking them instead of going back home after school. They wove through the forest. He ended up in an old home near the Blackberry Bog once. He saw two men lead another to the swamp's heart, while he hid, watching them. Men accustomed to the old ways sought justice in the muck where modern law failed. They would send them to the Serpent, he recalled. The Van Lear family atop the mountain used the mire when someone needed to disappear. Iggy had nightmares about the two men, faces shrouded, which would lead him to its heart. He dreamed of a serpent. A man with steel spurs, who smelled of hand-rolled cigarettes, would watch him swing. He was a deeper dark slash in the night.

Iggy shivered at the smeared face that leered from memory. It became clearer and closer. Page and the shadowy figures move about behind him. They stopped laughing and playing. Following, they huddled together. He walked, mind on the discordant image, and the music inside that had slowed.

He stopped. His parent's house stood before him. The years were hard on Owl Sticks, but it left the house untouched. Though the yard looked rough, it was the only place poorly kept. Iggy walked to the door, eyes moving about the property. Memories lingered, half-hidden in the bright moonlight. Dad wasn't much for work, even when he had a job. He obsessed over the yard. Once, after a bad day at the plant, the guitarist had found him passed out on a riding lawnmower. They could never afford it, but his father found the money somehow. It sat beside the porch he saw. Iggy frowned at it, stepping to the door.

He raised a hand to knock. Door ajar, Iggy felt an icy blade trace his heart. The music inside skipped. He looked back at Page. His friends had stopped at the yard's edge. The guitarist beckoned them, frowning, but they shook their heads. Over and over, the sour notes resounded. Their discord sent shivers through him. Bile rose in his throat. He called for her. Odd voices buzzed out from a speaker. They spoke in a monotone.

Still saying her name, he stepped inside. He hoped for a hug or told she loved him when he returned. A migraine tore through his head, and Iggy staggered. Its sudden return made his knees weak. The heat and humidity were hellish. In her favorite chair, his mother sat with her throat cut. The tableau was familiar. Just like them, his mind groaned. It whispered this dark knowledge with an eerie glee. The woman was slight. Her nightgown devoured her. It reeked of old food and urine. Blood turned the fabric black in the television's light. It swept over her in its muted hues. There was a symbol carved on her head. No blood dripped from it. The sight of it dug into his right eye. Exactly like them, a voice screamed inside. Tears burst out. The sigil was a tree of pain. It pounded in the mind.

"I'm a free man," he cried, vision blurred. "They found someone else's—" They had found additional evidence. There was DNA that exonerated him, an unexpected event. Some shy man living in Meridian had discovered the police acted inappropriately. They needed a perpetrator. They had planted evidence.

The scanner burst to life in fits and starts. He jumped back. Its buzz was alien and discordant. The voices of the police turned garbled and impish. They spoke to each other and dispatch, which came in quick bursts. They searched the town. A frantic edge was in their voice.

"How many are missing?" Rutger the Sheriff asked. His calm settled the others.

"We don't know," the dispatcher replied, "four, maybe five." The guitarist could hear the tears in her voice.

Iggy's head whipped to the scanner. She would never buy that, he thought. The rest of his mind was chaos and music. The number repeated in his mind. "Oh GOD," he grunted, staggering back. "IMPOSSIBLE."

He grabbed the door, unable to look at his mother. She never came to see him. Miss Ruffo never called or wrote, though he wrote to her every week. He wanted to say so much back at Thadwick, but couldn't find words now. It was too late. She was gone. Nothing of him remained, and one would think she had been childless. There were no pictures of him in the house. He stepped out the door. He wanted to tell her he loved her, but felt too little to lie. No one wanted him. The only people who cared about him were his friends and the La Voison woman. They were dead, and she had gone mad.

Beyond the yard's edge, Page and his friends stood. Symbols carved deep into their heads. They were trees of pain. They burned in the night. It was a hellish hue. The pain in Iggy's scar screamed. His hand slapped over his right eye. Image of them, the crossroads, played over the darkness behind the palm. He drew in a sharp breath. It was like he was a kid again.

"What is happening?" Page wept and touched his forehead. This had never happened through all the years of waiting. They never felt pain, but it seared him now. It was familiar.

"We have to go," the Guitarist rushed past. It was happening again. Like the songs in his head, life was a loop until you escaped it.

"To where?" he pleaded, running after him. Page shivered. All emotions were like echoes; memories gathered from life. He couldn't feel anything before but felt a wintry knife in his heart.

"The crossroads," Iggy moaned. He had answered without thinking. It was the truth. Something was pulling him to it again. It was a distant song, just below hearing. You could feel it more than you could listen to it.

"We don't go there!" Page stopped. His eyes were wide. Any time they grew close, darker things began crawling up from the earth. Some of them were once human, but that was a long time ago.

He paused, turning back. "I have to go, man." There was nothing left besides that distant, beckoning music.

There was unfinished business there, a voice whispered to him. Negotiations were underway. He had left it unfinished. It is time, boy. It is time we spoke.

"We can't go with you there!" Page begged, looking at the shadowy figures. They would come alive. They had twisted faces of pain and pleasure. These things dreaded their pain while loving it. Once, they had caught him. He had appeared again later, but he had felt dim for months.

Iggy walked to the crossroads. The townsfolk of Meridian avoided the intersection at Nottingham Knob. Don't go whistling past the crossroads unless you want to call up the Devil, people of Lear County said. People still came there for foolish wishes, desperate or fools. They threw a coin at the center, making the plea before it landed. The world was thin and spirits thick at such places. Things beyond this world could hear you. One could find many things beyond the Veil. It was how you asked and sacrificed. A few blamed the La Voison Women. They believed the Hill Witches conjured the hole in the world. The women allegedly prayed to an Ouroboros. It was the Great Serpent dwelling here.

Iggy had cared more about Jimmy Johnson. He was a master of the guitar. He had told the La Voison woman. Bethany had scowled at the name, disgusted. She told him Jimmy was a trespasser in the world. He had made a deal that no one should make. He had heard him play on an old record, but she didn't want to hear Jimmy play. It haunted Iggy since that day.

Although abandoned, the forest never reclaimed the crossroads. It hadn't changed at all. Iggy saw them, and another bolt of pain shot through his eye. The past overlaid the present. Page and his friends' spirits superimposed over the five boys. No sigil carved into their heads or throats cut. They shifted as if in the grip of nightmares. They called out for their mothers. Iggy glanced about the earth, rushing to them. He tripped. He crawled over to one, scrabbling at the rope. The boy's eyes sprung open with the restraints gone. As the teenager bolted, he turned to see the guitarist untying another. He came back. Both worked on the others until all of them were free. They ran, leaving the spirits of Iggy's friends.

The migraine dug deeper into his head. Only music remained, which played over the image of Page, Mickey, Josh, and Brandon. It filled the world. The Tree of Pain carved into their brows, above sliced throats. The ritual called for blood. It called for sacrifice. The night before finding them dead, he came to make a deal. It was the only way to escape. He had returned to find them dead. The blow came, merely a ghost too. The memory turned white, and the lingering pain passed. His headache was gone.

I don't know, cursed Iggy. I still know nothing! As the boys ran away, the night swallowed their sounds. The music inside him swallowed the world, but it battled another that lingered in the air. The low, wet rot of the Blackberry Bog came, and the tobacco of a hand-rolled cigarette lingered in the air. Sweat broke out over his body. Bitter bile rose in his throat. The strike of spurs was rhythmic. The guitarist frowned. These were no phantoms of memory.

Along the road, another set of boots had left their tread. They walked with a rhythm, too. Hairs rose on Iggy's neck. His skin pebbled. Warmth brushed the neck. His heart played a dervish. The music inside was smooth despite the speed. Through the tears and terror, the chords upon the wind called to him. They promised to keep playing. He listened. He followed the strum of the guitar, which beckoned. A dark promised slithered within.

The chords ensnared and entranced. His mind seized upon them and their melody. His gait shifted to the rhythm. Listen to an artist long enough and one would see their signature unique to the soul. Iggy followed, hands trembling. He needed to hold Paganini. He knew whoever played could have seen the kidnapper. They may have answers. Another part of him, a deeper one, knew the player. Artists were the only ones who could ever understand another of their kind, the rapturous obsession and joy. There was a merry darkness in the other musician's song.

Each step made the other's song grow. It teased darker emotions from the heart. Iggy stepped past the edge of the wall of willows. The house towered over the immaculate yard. It was an old plantation house. The paint was a pure white, trimmed in gold, and shocked the eye. It looked as perfect as the day, unchanged since built. No decay touched its perfection. Through the beauty, windows glared down upon this hidden kingdom. An old preacher lived in these woods; Iggy recalled. People said it, but he had never seen them.

A classic car sat out front, and the guitarist recalled it belonged to the man from the mall. It was a mirror of the house. He failed to recall his face or name. Some people are forgettable. The music rose, accompanied by the pound of his heart. It moved something inside. Between him and the source of the dire notes was a black truck with blacker windows. Hairs rose along his spine. It had followed them that day.

The door to the house opened. Iggy walked inside. It felt like a dream or nightmare, with every note resonating.

Everything was too real. He could touch, taste, or feel everything by looking at it. The notes flowed through the world. The ecstasy of playing was within and without. It wove its way through him and around. Nothing was outside the song. If creation was the perfect song, this was its antithesis. It infected everything. Page asked him to make music for their games, capturing the life of emotion. Whoever played hellish chords relentlessly raised the spirit beyond the flesh. The musician played to capture the soul.

Like a Faberge egg, all its beauty was skin deep. It was a paper mâché beauty that housed darkness within. Black paint covered the furniture, walls, ceiling, and floor. The former beauty defiled. A greasy, sweet air oozed over the skin. Destroyed statuettes laid everywhere. Snapped crosses rested. A bible, shredded, lie around the room. Sheets of music were everywhere. They were different genres of music, like they were deciphering a code. The Tree of Pain scribbled on them. The stains dark as blood. Among these were songs, none finished, all by the same hand. Over time, they had grown frantic, more unhinged, and obsessed. The half-completed song still played with its darkly sweet refrain.

Beside a book with newspaper clippings, a man sat with a guitar in his lap. Iggy waited for the guitarist to see him. His foot tapped. The jingle of steel spurs mixed with the song. The man's dark clothes were well-worn from travel, and his boots were like Iggy's. A hand-rolled cigarette smoke drifted up. The strange tobacco held a hint of sulfur. The song ended. Iggy heard his heart. The song inside was gone. Below a slouch hat, the musician regarded him like a master with a star pupil. Flames swirled deep in his eyes. Their light bled into the dark. The smell of scorched flesh seeped into the air when he smiled. Iggy's eyes went to the instrument he played. Strange symbols covered it, inlaid by the player. The man was familiar though his name escaped him, but the guitarist knew his instruments.

"Aleistar," breathed Iggy. He had dreamed of the guitar since that day at the crossroads. Its name whispered among musicians. Many whispered rumors said it made you're playing the best it could be.

"So, you know who I am," he returned. There was an interest in his amiable tone. He stood, spun the guitar by the neck, and then set it against the chair.

"Jimmy Johnson," he said, and the other smiled. This was a dream or nightmare. He denied the man ever existed; yet he knew it was true. He blinked. His skin felt too small as hot sweat broke out over him.

He bowed and tipped his hat. "I've been waiting to meet you for a decade." His smile was quick and easy. There was a covetous look beneath, a dark desire. It slithered over Iggy.

"You're not real," the guitarist swore, knowing it was a lie. He looked at a smashed picture. "This is that guy's house." Iggy looked around, but the man drew his eyes back. He thought he was a myth.

Jimmy laughed, "Yeah, you two are the differences between talent and genius. You can practice and get talent. Genius, brother, is in the blood: it does what talent can never accomplish. That is Valto's problem, down to the ground." He flicked his fingers at the other, lesser talent's name. A glorious prize was here for the winning. His Master loves the artist as much as the warrior. They both battled the heart as much as the world.

"Where is he?" asked Iggy, but his eyes fell on the guitar Aleistar. A truth gibbered at the back of the mind, but Jimmy's reality pushed out all other considerations.

Like a skin suit of darkness, Jimmy moved to the left. Tendrils stretched back to Valto, who had been inside. Caught in a snare of shadow, Valto looked at him. The man's eyes were wide, the color gone, and he could only stare. His body was under the other's control.

"Just another mediocre artist," Jimmy laughed, shrugging. He snapped back over at Valto, consuming him again. "He should've moved on. I don't make deals with people like him, but by Abaddon, they never get stepping." He smiled. It was broad and filled with dark knowledge.

The sweat that broke out over him had turned to ice. It pricked his skin. Sulfur settled on the tongue. Jimmy smiled at him, sensing his unease. "What Deal?" Iggy asked, his heart beating a heavy rhythm. Gray gathered at the edges of his vision. He knew the answer.

"The one I took," he confessed, looking at him. Darkness gathered to Jimmy, and flames swirled in his eyes. "The one you threw yourself on your knees for and begged for. It'll take you far away, away from drunken fathers, slut mothers, and a last name like a noose." He laughed. Black, abiding shadows hung in his throat.

"That wasn't me," he lied, shaking his head. Tightness gripped his chest. It was true. The words were right. He had sung them at the crossroads. The stories are straightforward on that part. It was all he needed to become a legend, along with a sacrifice. He would have given his life to be better back then. Hell could have it, a bargain. With time and patience, he saw his mistake. He had practiced every day since.

"Oh, Valto performed the ritual," he corrected. His shoulders raised and dropped again. "But I needed him to get us together. One could never make a deal with him. I heard your call, the music of another such as myself. That other fellow," Jimmy crossed his arms, "his father was right. He is just a nasty boy with nastier thoughts." Iggy had done one part while Valto had done the rest.

"My friends," Iggy breathed. Tears spilled. He hadn't murdered them, but he had done the next best thing.

"A sacrifice, a necessary one," he promised, picking up Alcistar, "once so we could meet. Valto done the deal, so to speak, and you can lay it all on him, if that eases you, brother."

He recoiled, lip curling. Iggy stepped back, "I don't—"

"You called, I came," Jimmy corrected him, stepping closer. Darkness deepened. It gathered to him. "There is a deal to be made, another legend born. Take Aleistar and I'll take Paganini. You'll step out of here. They'll come to find Valto dead. The world will know your genius, just like me." He made the deal as always. They had certain important details to discuss, but they would do so later. His Master wanted this artist.

"If I say no," he blubbered, trying to pull away, but he could only look at the swirl of flame in Jimmy's eyes. Everything else felt farther. His head grew heavy. His thoughts were music and black smoke.

"Like all veritable geniuses," he smiled and sulfur clawed the air, "no one will understand you. Maybe, one day, someone will find your work, and realize your worth well after you're gone, brother," Jimmy spat the words as a blasphemy. In every artist's heart, they wanted recognition above all. He would have died, starved to death. The ignorant people were too stupid to see his gift.

"People still say your name," he whispered. He saw the sigils burn on Aleistar, "Guitarists say your skill was impossible." Even hearing it, he felt it was unearthly. It was false, a fraud.

"Take her," Jimmy held up the guitar, a wonder of occult and craftsmanship. "Take her by the neck, and she'll show the world your genius." He watched the guitarist's eyes shift away. "Don't make your friend's sacrifice in vain." He smirked. The price paid, leaving acceptance.

Iggy's gaze snapped back, "Their sacrifice... no." Vomit rose in his throat.

"No," he repeated, scowling. He shook his head. "Trust me, one day, you'll accept the deal." Flames swirled in his eyes while darkness swallowed the room. "You'll watch lesser artists with greater connections get deals," he picked the strings of Aleistar with a laugh. "Only scorn, which will be your reward. Even if you're found innocent, even if all know, you still will have a stain." Jimmy played dark notes. "Always to play the villain, they'll whisper about Nottingham Knob. Or do you think people will suddenly become tolerant, understanding?" His smirk bled black.

Iggy looked into his eyes. "I would rather my friends were alive." Jimmy struck a sour note with a sneer. "If I took the deal, it wouldn't be my skill, my genius," he cursed, pointing at Aleistar, "because I would be a lousy cheat!" He had found there was no easy way. You practiced. You learned, but there was no quick answer or path. He had to earn it.

Jimmy put his hand across the strings to silence the instrument. The world went silent. In the darkness that hung about him, the screams of the dam rose into a chorus. He stepped towards him as sulfur thickened the air. Nails on his playing hand grew to a point. Swirls of flame opened inside his eyes to swallow up the guitarist. Iggy recoiled, but he stopped with a laugh. "I have all the time in the world," Jimmy confessed, laughing, and the world returned to its decayed reality. "Give it another decade, brother," he swore. He drew on the hand-rolled cigarette and blew out smoke. "If you make it," he grinned, pointing a finger at the doorway.

Iggy turned to where he gestured. Deputies piled into the room, and guns rose. The guitarist raised his hands in surrender, but Jimmy pointed a finger and mouthed the word bang. They fired at them. Each swore that the maniac musician would die. Iggy and Valto fell. Before he hit the floor, the preacher's son stared at the hell that waited for him. It welcomed him. All the horror of the pit twisted his face. Jimmy stood over them, tipped his hat, and walked past the cops, but only Iggy could see him. He winked, patient. Page, Mickey, Josh, and Brandon ran through the police to their friend as blood spread from him. They were brighter.

"Dude," Page squealed, face contorted by terror. Tears filled his eyes at Iggy's bullet wounds. He tried to cover them, but his hands passed through him.

"I didn't do it," the guitarist cried. A laugh seeped out. Tears spilled as a weight lifted. "I found him," he looked at Valto, "It was him." He felt distant, "Wait for me, Page. I'm scared, man. I'm scared!" The end was coming, but at least he was with friends. This misery would be over soon.

Page touched his hand. "Okay, we're here. We're here Iggy!" He wept. It was ending. He could feel it.

"I told Jimmy no," he grunted, half-choked. He grinned, though his smile marred by blood. He was no cheat.

Before Page could speak, the darkness came to swallow Iggy. It swept in from the edges of his vision. Somewhere, he could hear Jimmy's laugh and the guitar Aleistar. He played a death song for the guitarist. Hand-rolled cigarettes left the air thick with tobacco. Steel spurs struck odd chords. Twin whirlwinds of fire converged into one. Iggy tasted blood clogged his throat. As the blackness dragged on, the music that always filled Iggy returned. Nothing but a song greeted him.

The blackness remained. Time passed in this darkness. Iggy was alone. Finally, birds sang in the sun. Their song was a greeting to the new day. His music joined theirs, and Iggy opened his eyes. The blur faded with each blink, but it was slow to diminish. The sound of machines struck ugly notes. He peered at them.

"Mister Ruffo, Ignazio Ruffo," a polite voice inquired. He watched the guitarist stir.

Iggy looked at him, knowing a lawyer when he saw one. Do these guys come out of a factory? He mused. "Yeah, man, I'm him," he mouthed. He felt pain, though medicine tamped it down. It flicked about him from wound to wound. Page loomed in his mind. He searched for him.

"I know, Mister Ruffo," the man smiled, "I heard you may awaken, so I waited all morning." He had come that night but expected him to die, and then to never wake up. The recovery surprised everyone. Men lingered outside, but the Van Lear family name kept them from entering.

"I didn't do it," he promised. As if that matters, he thought. Even if I don't go to jail, someone will hang or shoot me. It was a matter of time before they got him.

"Oh, I know," he said with a smile. Iggy looked at him. "The ghastly man, Valto Miettinen, had all the evidence in his house. He is a perfect match for the DNA that exonerated you." If only all his cases were this easy.

Iggy's head fell back, tears spilled out. A sob slipped out of him. "Don't play with me, man," he begged, body shaking.

"It is true," he patted his hand. "I know. After all you have endured, it's hard to believe." He wore a practiced smile. It was the quickest way to get the man compliant.

"So, I'll be free to go?" He begged. Four teenagers stood outside his room. His eyes flew to them. Page and the others watched him.

"Of course," he picked up a briefcase, and opened it, "I'm here to represent you, free. Well, I cost money, but someone else is paying. The Sheriff's deputies shot you and almost killed you. I stopped Rutger from returning. The Van Lear family wants to see you receive justice." The Sheriff had been distraught. He had a gut feeling about Iggy being innocent, the lawyer recalled. It didn't stop his men from shooting the guitarist.

"All right," he breathed, studying his friends. The sigil cut into their heads was gone. They smiled at him, happy and unburdened.

"All you have to do is answer some questions," he looked through some papers. Alice Van Lear insisted he find out all he could about the crossroads, Jimmy, and Abaddon. They found the Tree of Pain sigil in the house. It had set the family on edge. The lawyer shivered at the thought of her icy gaze. Alice was the smartest of all of them and the cruelest.

"Sure," mouthed the Guitarist, and his friends waved. He waved back with two fingers.

They walked away with smiles to fade away. Light washed over them like water. Page was the last to disappear, bouncing. Iggy smiled, but a whiff of sulfur whispered to him. His friends had escaped the crossroads, but he was still alive.

Sleepwalking

"STOP CRYING," he bellowed. He struck the steering wheel with a palm. His face flushed. A vein bulged on his neck. Alcohol puffed out with every breath.

"I can't help it, Chris," Mavis whined, striving to keep the fuss out of her voice. Tears blurred her vision, and she stared out at the snow. "What am I supposed to do?" she snapped, pushing down the sound of her mother's voice. You should stand by your man. It insisted in a low yet insistent tone. Her mother had nagged her at home. She had nagged her entire life and was content to nag after death.

"I have a lot to deal with, Mavis," he added below a scream. "The plant is closing." Chris ran a hand through his hair, and the smell of whiskey filled the SUV's cab. The smell of sweat joined it. All he did was sweat, even in the dead of winter. They accelerated, and she grabbed onto the door. "It is hard to think with all that crying!" he wiped at his face. He cursed, unbuckling the seat belt.

"Our marriage is more important than the plant," she wailed. It was all he talked about. Leitch Industrial Company had been the center of their lives for nearly two decades. Their lives built upon years of work. Tears spilled, her face burned, but she slowed her breathing.

"It has to be Kayden," he growled low, rubbing at bloodshot eyes. They had hurt since the man came back into Sheila's office. What happened? He thought, seeing a haze of purple. Chris recalled lines thin as razors, and something squirmed inside. "He is behind all of this," Chris announced, nodding. Chris believed he had gone to the Van Lear family.

"What does he have to do with us?" she hissed. People talked in small towns. They loved gossip, and nothing is better than a scandal. You married him so he is yours for better or worse, her mother's voice observed. Mavis wished she would shut up. Her thoughts always sounded like her mother's.

"Who do you think told the Van Lear family?"! He barked, growing pale at the name. They were the oldest family in the community, and the county named after them. "The Queen of Lear Mountain has her people everywhere. Everyone knows they want Leitch out!"

I need to know what Kayden told them; he thought. They could end up in jail.

"One girl Brian abused told me what you did," she hissed. Mavis raised her chin. "You haven't denied it! So, is it true?" A small part of her prayed he would deny it so she could go on refusing it. She had worked so hard to make their house a home. Chris couldn't have betrayed that or her, she hoped.

Chris bared his teeth in a feral smile. "The Van Lear hard case came by to speak to me! Barnett, that psycho, came to the plant!" He had slipped out the back and drove around the town until he had left the factory. He had nearly shit himself.

I have to find Kayden, he thought, and prayed he could before things got worse. Once Barnett showed up, people went missing.

"Did you, do it?" she repeated, chin raised and jaw set. Mavis wished he would deny it. That would shut up the voice of her mother.

"CHRIST," he screamed at the windshield, "you never stop whining!" Chris turned bloodshot eyes on her, and his bulbous gut shifted. "YES, I SCREWED HER," he growled, and his face turned a dangerous shade of crimson. His eyes held a spark. "Do you want to hear that?" His knuckles turned white on the wheel. It was the first time he had enjoyed sex in years.

"I don't understand," she cried, chest heaving. She shook her head. All I've done, it means nothing. I'm still pretty! I'm not that old, Mavis thought. "Why Chris?" she turned to him, and the world felt unsteady. "Why did you do this to us, to me?"!

Chris glared over the wheel as they continued accelerating. People were correct, he knew. The Old Money, Van Lear Family of Swannanoa, had pushed out all the industries in the county. They had pushed most of the New Money of Duncannon out, except for a few. Wendal Swift dug in long ago. That old son of a bitch continued living out of pure spite.

"Between the Van Lear family, Leitch Industries, and you," he cursed. "It is too much!" He had known his job was ending. He thought about what he had done to secure a new life. The plant was closing. "I got us a house in Duncannon!" he barked, rubbing his temples. They pulsed. He felt like something slithered in his skull.

"We don't live in Duncannon," she spit at him. All he thinks about is that job, she cursed. "We live in Raven's Nest!" she screamed. Why was everything with him about stuff? He was always worried about other people's thoughts. Any rumor about him drove him crazy. He had fired people on suspicion of spreading allegations.

"I know where we live!" he roared, punching the SUV's radio until it flickered. Raven's Nest was technically within the Duncannon community's line. "You've heard the rumors about the Queen of Lear Mountain," Chris accused, but his eyes flew over the darkness beyond the road. His stomach rumbled as his gorge rose.

"Yes," she hissed, and part of her relished the tremble in his voice. Everyone called her Queen because she ruled the town like a monarch. People jumped at her command, except for a couple of families. She would suffer a cheater. She would cut his throat and throw him in the swamp.

"People have gone missing," he reminded her. He shivered despite the sweat that dampened his clothes. "You end up in the Blackberry Bog with lungs full of muck," Chris whispered.

"I don't know what you're talking about," she snapped, rolling her eyes. She hated rumors. They were petty and silly. Mavis rubbed the deep ache in her chest. "No one will kill you, because you're a pig!"

"This is your fault," he swore low. The company had offered him a higher position, but it would mean they had to move. Chris shook his head, "I should've left you here!" He grumbled. It was falling apart, and he would have to run or die.

"What could I have done?" she strove for a commanding tone, but it came out a plea.

Their life together kept flooding back in disjointed bursts, good and bad. She gave all the love, hope, and faith she possessed to him. It wasn't enough, Mavis's mother assured her, though dead for five years.

"Nothing was ever enough," she whined, covering her face. She wept. It was true. It was undeniable. He was a philanderer and a fool. Her mother had warned her, but Mavis had loved him.

Chris's lip curled up as if tugged by an invisible string. "All you've ever done is sit at home," he laughed, "while I done all the work!" The woman waited for him like an obedient puppy. She worried over his every ache and pain. She babied him. He could only imagine what she had done when he was gone. Mavis waits for him to come home, he guessed.

Mavis turned eyes on him, which had never lost their luster. She had turned down other men, better-looking men. "DID you like it, Christopher Peck, Pecker Head?"! she asked, but her chest heaved. So, she had been less excited in bed. How was she supposed to keep faking it? Christopher exhausted himself after a couple of thrusts.

He muttered a curse. It was the name the workers called him behind his back. "What kind of question is that?" Chris flushed. His eyes slid away from her.

"I was always there," she swore, rubbing her eyes. She hated crying, but she couldn't stop the tears. A dull ache centered on her forehead. No one would've believed Chris would become the Plant Manager two decades ago. She believed. Somehow, he had exceeded all expectations, even hers. She was so proud of him and his dedication. Things had gotten easier for him after he had become friends with Brian and Sheila. They had become like family.

"There at the house doing nothing," he said, and a nasty laugh slipped out. Mavis was an anchor around his neck. He didn't need her. He didn't need her encouragement because he had done it all. She could stay with the house if she cared so much about it. He was leaving.

Mavis turned back to him. "What does Kayden know?" she demanded with a smile. She grinned, satisfied at the look on his face. Chris talked about him every day. Kayden was smart, too smart for Leitch.

"I don't know what you mean," he looked away. Chris cursed the constant rumor mill.

"Does it have to do with that smarmy Human Resources lady or Brian? He is a bigger pig than you, and the Lady's Man has children," she added, fighting the urge to spit. Just his name was enough to leave her feeling ill. There were other rumors about Brian, but she had dismissed them until now.

"Let me worry about that," he peered at the road. They would take off if they were smart.

She watched him sweat, but old memories drowned clear the thought. "I don't know what Kayden knows or what you've done, but I hope he tells the Queen of Lear Mountain. I hope she sends that tough guy with the mean grin." She turned back to the window, and emptiness filled her. "I heard he likes to hit the fat ones," she mused aloud. "Barnett likes to make their guts shake." Mavis hoped Barnett would give Chris a beating.

Chris jerked as if slapped. He turned back to her with a snarl. "You know what, I did like it," he shrieked, and the smell of whiskey washed over her. He laughed, belly shaking, "I had forgotten what it felt like to enjoy it!" It was wonderful. He felt alive with her.

"What?" she begged, blinking at him. Mavis felt a hot dagger sink into her heart, but no more tears would come. This stunned even her mother's voice into silence.

"She doesn't just lay there like a dead fish," his mouth worked. Everyone else always had better than him. Chris shook his head. "And she doesn't act like she did me a favor." That was the worst of it. All those years that she slept with him, acting like a martyr. He had gained weight and gotten older, but he was rich now.

Mavis blushed. She had done her duty. All you can do, honey, is smile and pretend, her mother offered in her best sage voice. "I'm sure she loved your grunting and sweating," she sobbed. "She endured it to get something out of it."

Chris pushed the accelerator to the floor, and the SUV slid over the road. "When we get home," he boomed, "you can get your stuff and leave!" He imagined her standing in the snow with a grin. Maybe she would run back to her father. Mavis was just like him, always hanging around, ready to serve.

"What?" she blinked at his leer. Chris's eyes were flat. She trembled. The smell of whiskey on him was thick. His sweat hung below it.

"I'll move her in," he added with a broad smile. "Maybe she'll appreciate me." Chris savored the lie. He had to leave tonight, but he planned to burn the house. He hoped she stayed to watch it go up. All he wanted, he had stored in the pool house.

"I LOVED YOU!" she screamed. Her hand almost touched the wheel. How could it end like this? She did everything!

Chris brought down his fist, knocking her hand away. He lunged at her, and the slap caught her cheek. The SUV slid. He stared down at her, and the hand turned into a fist, "I'm warning—" The strange spark in his eye was alien.

"LOOK," Mavis pointed at the rail. Beyond, the headlights caught a tree.

The SUV slammed into the end of the guardrail, and the back of the vehicle rose into the air. Chris shot through the windshield. I haven't seen him move that fast in years, Mavis thought. The bedlam eclipsed memories. Her seat belt tightened. The coins in the cup holder bounced about. She watched him sail over the rail as a dime flew past. Her mother's voice was ever helpful, observing Chris had soiled himself. She caught the brief whiff of his shit. Pigs do fly her mother added. With a sickening crunch, his face slammed into the oak. The restraint jerked her back, but her head banged into the window.

Darkness washed over her, and pain pulsed in the side of her head. In the emptiness, there were no ungrateful, cheating husbands. Chris had papers from work. Once, she had sneaked a peek at them. She frowned, thinking of Kayden, but the ache persisted. It made the memories blurry and smeared. The urge to scream played behind her lips.

"Poor Mavis, bless her heart," she muttered. She spoke in her mother's sad but unsurprised tone. "She bought a pig in a poke and only got a pig."

"Why don't you say something useful?" Mavis countered. She knew her mother's voice was her, but she couldn't help it. Her father never remarried after her mother died. Who blames him? Who would want to go through that again?

"You saw more than you know, girlie," she whispered in an even tone, which always drove Mavis insane. "You chose not to see it."

"What does that mean?" she sighed. There was more. She had seen something. Mavis was great at ignoring the signs when it was hurtful.

"It means you hit your head," Rutger, Sheriff of Lear County, repeated, but saw the bump was small. His brow furrowed as she swayed.

"What," she blinked at the man, "what happened?" Mavis blushed. The Sheriff was a rugged man who was as hard as Chris was soft. The muscles in his forearms danced with the movement of his fingers.

"Honey, you were in a wreck," he shined the flashlight on the injury. Rutger drew in a sharp breath.

Mavis looked past him to Chris, who faced the SUV. The crotch of his pants darkened. Her mother was right, again. The blow against the oak's trunk had torn off half his face. It had killed him on impact. White teeth gleamed in the headlights. It had cost a hefty sum to fix his teeth. He is dead, she thought, but it was distant.

"He cheated on me," she breathed. "I loved him. He cheated on me." Mavis' lip quivered. She looked at the Sheriff, and then back to Chris. The blow ripped off her husband's eyelid. Something stirred there. She frowned. Did I see a purple light? She squinted. "Work stressed him out. Chris has been sleepwalking," Mavis offered, her eyes rolled. Her head grew light. She squeezed her eyes shut.

"Are you okay?" he asked, tilting her head up. He saw the streaks of mascara, and Rutger frowned. "Did he slap you, rough you up?" His face darkened as his heart stung. He never grew accustomed to the failings of men. Mavis was a good woman who suffered a wicked man.

She nodded, "Is he dead?" Mavis looked down. She knew the answer. The voice of her mother answered, but she ignored her.

Rutger sighed low, knowing it was best to be truthful, "Yes, but I think he felt nothing." He checked her injury. "I'll get you help. Make sure you're okay." There was nothing he could say to help her.

Mavis wept, looking at her lap. She nodded, but the cacophony of thoughts and images was a jumble. Time flowed in fits and starts. Another vehicle stopped behind the Sheriff's old jeep. Someone checked her, asking if she wanted to go to the hospital. She shook her head. Rutger came back after hearing Mavis was good enough to go home.

The Sheriff tried to talk to her, but she only cried. They drove to her house in silence. Rutger walked her to the front door. The Sheriff looked at the big house and then the small woman. Before he could help her further, Mavis told him she wanted to sleep. She had to mourn a man who didn't love her anymore.

Inside the large house, she leaned against the wall. The sound of his jeep's engine rose after a minute. She touched the lump, though the numbness persisted. Chris's face, half torn off, loomed in the darkness. It leered with a spark of light inside. She winced away. Images came in a flood. Another assailed her of him walking around the house, still asleep. Sleepwalking always freaked her out. She breathed deep, held it, and then released it slowly.

"I don't want to think, feel," she begged the empty house. Thoughts and images ignored her as they assailed the mind. A mirror hung next to the door, and Mavis saw her pale skin and vacant eyes. The smell of Chris's whiskey had sunk into her clothes. She could still taste his sour sweat.

She trudged through the house and picked up two bottles of wine and moved to the walk-in shower. Casting off her clothes, she was afraid to look in the mirror. Her mother's voice waited to critique her. The hot water filled the room with steam. It relaxed her muscles, which had filled with knots. The heat drove the cold away, except for the chill of the tile floor. One bottle of wine was already empty, though she was no drinker. It made her sleepy. She sat in the shower, letting the warmth wash over her. More tears came, lost in the water. Mavis drank from the bottle. Muscles relaxed, pain drifted, and she breathed slowly.

Despite her fatigue, the idea of sleep felt too far away. Mavis drank the rest of the wine. "Where did I go wrong?" she asked the empty bottle. Her lips curled at the whine in her voice. She always rolled her eyes at women, who cried over a cheating man. If they cheated on you, she once said, they never loved you. No more tears would come.

"Stop grumbling, girlie," her mother said inside. She would stay at least for the night in the battered chambers of her heart. "You already know what scared Chris."

She asked her mother what she meant, but unfortunately, she went quiet. Mavis shook her head, turning off the shower. It began when the Leitch Industrial

Company laid Kayden off . Brian had been behind it. Kayden had told Sheila about the quality problems. There were rumors that the women sent home that day were all Brian's victims. She frowned. That wouldn't get Chris killed by the Van Lear Family. They would have them beaten, or perhaps run out of town. The women got together, and someone had gone to the Queen atop Lear Mountain. Kayden returned the next morning, but Chris recalled nothing from the second conversation, except Kayden's odd gaze. The former Leitch employee's eyes were off.

"That is when the sleepwalking started too," Mavis mumbled to the empty wine bottle. Only crazy people talk to themselves, her mother's voice observed, but she rolled her eyes. "His eyes scared me," Mavis repeated Chris's words.

A wave of nausea flowed over her. Mavis leaned back against the wall. The darkness behind her eyes deepened. Her heart fluttered. The coppery tang of blood settled on the tongue. The beat of her heart echoed beneath the rasp of her breathing. Wet air carried the spice of Chris's body wash. Her honey coconut scent lingered below it. Alcohol numbed the pain, but the bedlam of her mind was more distant. Beads of water gathered on her body.

Black thickened about her. Something carried her back into the dark. Beams from the SUV cut through the darkness. She looked at Chris, who was lying on a table. The County Coroner had taken the body back, though it set where the oak stood. Mavis's heart ached, "I loved you," she whispered. Snow fell to the examination table. A finger twitched. Mavis's brow creased, a chill brushed her neck, and her face burned. Chris's arm jerked. His fingernails tapped the cold steel. Her mouth opened, though a gasp drooled out. Light burned deep in his eyes, and she saw his head had turned, while her attention was on his arm. Out of the shattered face, a moan leaked through the missing cheek. A leg jerked and slid over the side. His shoe fell to the floor.

Mavis flinched. She looked at the bathroom as the nightmare abated. She searched about the tiles. Her neck already stiffened. The rapid thunder of her heart beat against her palm. Fine hairs rose on her body. All the room's heat was gone. She stood, staggered, and looked at the wine bottle.

What do I do now? The question hung in the disquiet darkness of her mind. Although the cacophony had ceased, she could only think of Chris's mistress. One woman had told her all about it. It's her fault, Mavis thought, tasting the lie. "They did it in the pool house," she recalled. "IN MY HOUSE," she stood and then paced about the bathroom. It couldn't be true. There was no way Chris could slip that past her, but she hadn't been inside in a long time.

She huffed, stamping out before she returned. The two battles of wine had already passed through her, and Mavis used the bathroom. She dressed in a nightgown and robe, cursing Christ. She walked back and forth next to the bed.

"I should tell that low-class slut," she stomped her foot, "that she is a whore!" She wobbled, but straightened. She imagined slapping the tart.

No, I can't, she thought, fists relaxing. As other plants around Lear County closed, people moved away. Some had seemed to disappear off the face of the earth. The girl had disappeared too. Mary, one that Brian took advantage of, had told Mavis about Chris's indiscretion. She cursed, stomped her foot, and looked about the bedroom. A vase, a gift from her husband, set on a dresser. Unsteadily, she snatched it. It broke against the headboard, and the pressure in her chest eased a bit. She had never broken a vase, but it felt good.

Mavis looked for something else to throw. The phone rang, and she let out a squeak. Her eyes darted to the broken vase. She picked it up, "Hello."

"Yes, is this Miss Peck?" a gruff voice inquired as gently as he could manage. "This is Sheriff Rutger." He shifted, looking at his leg. Nothing like this had happened before tonight.

She blinked, cold dripped down her spine, and her stomach churned. "Yes, uh," she sighed, taking a deep breath.

"I don't know how to say this," he ventured. The silence filled the air. "Miss Peck, your husband is supposed to be at the coroner's place," Rutger rushed through gritted teeth. "I don't know what happened, but I'll find him. I'm sorry." The Sheriff closed his eyes, swearing he would put them in jail. There were a lot of weird people with strange ideas in Meridian.

Mavis shivered, and an iron grip of ice seized her heart. She stared at the phone like a venomous snake. The nightmare flooded back. "Are there any footprints heading out of the coroner's office?" she asked in a distant tone. Part of her was certain.

"Yes," the Sheriff replied slowly. He stared at the phone. Mavis's voice sounded strained, somehow distant.

"Is one of his feet bare? Did he lose a shoe?" she inquired. The phone shook in her hand.

"Yes," he replied, "What is it, Miss Peck?" Such a question would make him suspicious, usually, but she sounded strange. She had sustained a head injury.

"My husband has been sleepwalking," she sat on the bed. Gray crept into her vision. An image of him lumbering about the house played at the back of her mind.

"Miss Peck," he spoke slowly, "your husband is—"

Mavis set the phone back into the base. She wiped her hand on her robe as if she had picked up something foul. Blackness ate through the gray as the phone rang again. She ignored it, pretending it was the wrong number. She lay back as the world seemed to wobble. You shouldn't have drunk the Devil's Drink, her mother chided inside. Mavis groaned.

Snow drifted down in the devouring black. The darkness of the dream was complete, yet she could see a few feet. An ocean of black surrounded her. A streetlight flickered on. Inside their glow, everyone looked ghastly. Far away, it was an island of luminance. Its piss-yellow hue was repulsive. The streetlights turned on, one at a time. They had black lichen on them, which was throughout Meridian. It didn't grow at the top of Lear Mountain. It was everywhere else.

"I know this road," she whispered to the night. They had taken it earlier. Two pinpricks of light came up the gentle slope. Back and forth, they swayed. She narrowed her eyes. In and out of the islands of light, something moved. The sickly light graced the road's edge, but the walker stayed away. Mavis licked her lips, craning her head forward. She stepped back.

They came in meditative steps, wobbling to their left. Like they're missing a shoe, she thought. The sour knot in her guts turned to a putrid ice block. Mavis took another step back, head shaking in negation. Chris loped forward, eyes upon her. They peered through her. The light brushed him, and she leaned forward. His eyes focused on an alien horizon. Their pin-pricks of light pierced the night. Each time he neared the brilliance, its urine glow exposed more of his body.

"Red lines," she breathed, recalling Chris standing by the bed. He was asleep. I think I saw them, Mavis thought, eyes drifting away. They raced over his body!

The light bathed the ruin of Chris's face. His white teeth caught the light. Mavis jerked up and toppled out of the bed. The darkness of the dream was slow to depart. It clung to the edges of the room. Flakes of snow still drifted down as her heart raced. They faded.

"A dream," she breathed, voice shaking. Mavis assured herself the call and Chris were a dream. "Yes." she looked about the room, but all was still. Corpses don't walk.

I guess someone has a guilty conscience, her mother observed from the back of Mavis's mind.

"GUILTY," she snapped, jumping to her feet. Her face burned. "I loved him. He hit me! HE HIT ME!" She shook her fist. Her mother went silent again. She listened to the silence.

She stomped through the house. Muttering curses, her eyes flicked about the emptiness. Chris had hidden the pool house key, but she had found it one day of cleaning. Mavis had promised to stay out. Chris needed a place to himself. She cursed herself as a fool now.

"I thought it was odd," she muttered to the key. Its teeth bit into her palm, but she ground her teeth at images of their lurid embraces. Chris and some harlot cavorted beside the heated waters of the pool. They laughed at her in this dark musing. They mocked her crow's feet and the few gray hairs.

Mavis screamed. Her chest heaved, and she swayed. After stomping down to the house's side door, she stopped. "I'll burn it!" she crowed. "I'll go out there and burn the bed," she laughed, though another tear spilled.

She pulled on boots and a heavy coat over her clothes. Chris kept a gasoline can for the weed eater and lawnmower. "I'll burn it," Mavis hissed. "I have whore stink in my pool house." She grabbed the gasoline. She snatched a lighter he used to ignite the grill and stuffed into one pocket.

She stepped out into the darkness. Chill air slapped her, and her muscles ached. The temperature had dropped, and the air stilled. She paused, staring at a masculine silhouette, but it was only a tree. With an unsteady laugh, Mavis stomped forward.

How long did it go on? She wondered. Her head hung, eyes stinging. She looked at the pool house.

The Human Resources Manager had laid off any Brian wanted gone. "It makes no sense," Mavis looked at the Jerry can. "Are they up to something? Barnett, the Lear family pet tough guy, came to see Chris." She glared at the pool house. "Why did he think they'd kill him? Over a bunch of loose women, I doubt it!"

She shook off the questions. It was silly to care about it now. Chris was beyond their retribution. Brian and Sheila were still in trouble. "Let the Van Lear tough guy get them,"

Mavis barked at the darkness, and opened the pool house. They had to know Chris was cheating on her. She should have guessed Sheila wasn't her friend. The Northerner still acted high and mighty, as if anyone cared.

Mavis slammed the door, and the creep of chill cut off. Her hand slammed to her mouth. She had guessed they had cheated, but part of her still hoped it was a lie. Pictures of Chris and his low-class lover were everywhere. "He is old enough to be her father!" She wept. Her stomach churned, tasting the wine. Her eyes flew to pictures. They had gone on vacations and trips. "To France," Mavis yelled, shaking. "He was always too busy to take me! How did he even get the money?"! She wailed, dropping the can.

"Stop that crying," she snapped, and Mavis swore it had been her mother. She touched her mouth, skin pebbling.

She grabbed the picture of Chris and the girl in front of the tower in France. For years, she had begged to go. She flung it with a shriek. It shattered against the bottom of the pool, and the pressure inside eased. Another joined it. Mavis tossed mementos and cards. She snapped a porcelain bear's head off before it too joined the pile. Some ticket stubs for a movie, a stuffed rabbit, and a poem after she shredded it. She spun in a whirlwind of tears, curses, and bitter laughter. She tossed all their memories in a heap. All the sheets and linens covered the rest before she wrestled the mattress and box springs over. She grunted, sweat beading on her brow. It rested at the bottom of the drained pool.

Mavis opened the gasoline can. The fumes stung her eyes. Her hands shook, chest heaving. Gray returned to the edges of her vision. A ragged laugh escaped when she looked at the mementos of their passion. She couldn't recall the last time she felt anything close to it.

"I'll see you in Hell!" she promised, seizing the lighter. The fire would make it go away.

Sooner than that, a deep voice offered. She frowned. How long does it take? The walk from the coroner's office to here isn't that far. The deep voice pondered the question. Mavis paused. How long had she been out? How many times had she passed out?

She shook it off with a jagged laugh. Below the unsteady mirth of her joy, a clicking crawled over the floor, echoing in the drained pool. Mavis's hand froze on the lighter, peering about the room. Perhaps an animal, maybe a bird, which seeks shelter from the cold, she assured herself. Something is calling. Best to leave it out in the cold, away from the coming cleansing conflagration, she assured herself. A knock came, flat but booming.

"Might be a wild dog," she swallowed.

Yes, it had to be some poor puppy whose master had abandoned it. The Owl Sticks community was full of them. It wants food, warmth, and a loving hand, which I'll give it. I'll love it. Something thumped and scraped, and the wood creaked under its immense weight.

"Just someone from the Plant," she squawked, "or perhaps someone broke down. NO, it is the Sheriff, handsome Rutger!" she declared, but came out as a plea. An image of his arms wrapped around her came, and her face burned.

The frame about the door shifted slowly, popped, and snapped until a sliver from the door frame flew off. It bounced across the floor. Mavis peered at it and blinked. Something in the locking mechanism gave. Hinges whined as it opened. A dark figure filled the doorway. A rancid stink flowed inside. It was like blood fried in rotted mushrooms. His eyes burned with twin flames, purple deep as a bruise. Something inside them squirmed. Mavis's mouth opened. Her color drained to the hue of soured milk, and a flat huff passed between her lips. Her skin felt tight. The world felt as if it would unravel

"I hated you," he swore. The words drooled out.

She screamed, and the world took on a hazy white hue. Gray crept into the edges of her vision. If not for using the toilet, she knew, piss would have been running down her legs. She managed a few drops. She backed up a step, heels hitting the lip of the pool. Glancing down, she blinked at the heap. Chris staggered a step closer as if on strings pulled by a madman. His ruined form pulsed. Razor's thin lines opened and sealed on his flesh. One barefoot slapped against the floor. It was pudgy, with a patch of hair on the toe. The smell of a butcher's table pushed over the air. A coppery tang settled on her tongue.

Chris staggered another step. There was confusion in it, an unfamiliarity. Mavis tried to move her traitorous legs, managing a twitch. His broken body lolled; yet his eyes were alive, filled with an alien light. Something inside them squirmed. His bulbous gut, injured in the wreck, sloshed with a malignant ripeness. As his skin ripped, Mavis thought of the paper being torn. His intestines spilled to the ground, and he stopped. Like an old man's toothless maw slurping up spaghetti, it sucked back in with a wet pop.

Impossible, her mind groaned. "I'm sorry!" she cried. This was impossible.

Maybe I died in the wreck, Mavis thought with absolute confidence. I died and went to hell! She shivered at his gaze.

He lifted the barefoot and then brought it down with a limp slap. Chris raised his hand, but it fell back to his side. A nest of entrails snaked down to the floor through the hole in his cheek. Deformed teeth gleamed along its wet pinkness. The yellowed fangs clacked at their ends. They struck the floor with a splat before they felt about the floor. Probing the tile, it searched. The purple flame inside his eyes still seized her. Nothing of this world lived in them.

Nothing of this world was in the flames of bruised purple. The dead gaze held things that writhe and hate. Mavis felt its malevolence scrabbled at her mind with cruel little claws like a rat. Just a word, an utterance, from some unfathomable mind had eaten into Chris's brain like an acidic cancer. It bloated his psyche with ideas, dreams, and nightmares which would drive any mad. To hear the slight syllable of its insane tongue would undo the finite senses of man or woman. It was horrid knowledge in this bliss of ignorance.

In its eyes, she fell unmoored by existence. It was no demon or angel, but intelligence outside all concepts of form. Infinite possibilities of a word ran rampant inside. It was concept and meaning given sentience. They roiled and thrashed. Mavis recoiled from its intellect, which burned like a caustic darkness. Her mind clamored for a word to encapsulate its brilliance. She knew her attempts would fail.

Instincts, bred into the humans, screamed at her. A tendril, like a snake, dropped from Chris's mouth. It had a slick maw full of needle teeth and an enormous set of mandibles which clicked together. Mavis threw herself away in revulsion. The bruised purple flame in its eyes followed her, promising a fate unspeakable. He turned, guts sloshing. Lines, thin as razors, raced up his body. Whatever puppeteer him, it ran riot through meat and bone. Each step made the skin shift.

"I hated you," Chris confessed. The words bled from his slack lips. His last thought was all that remained of his mind. It was the guiding light for the alien reflections. He shambled after her.

Mavis's curse echoed about the pool house. Her face flushed. She had held her tongue for years. She whirled back. "You were always bad in bed! And, YES, I fell asleep!" she screamed with a laugh. A cackling exploded in her mind.

Chris raised an arm, skin pulled from muscle suspended by sinew. Veins like worms wiggled and writhed. Mavis's color paled, and the wine rose to her throat. Again, the gray returned with her fury spent. She dashed away, but the tip of her boot caught against the other. She slammed against the floor. Air whooshed from her lungs. Like some dumb bimbo in a scary movie, her mother offered. She was great at timing.

Mavis cursed, scrabbling to get up. Her legs buckled. She grabbed the top of a dresser, yanking off a box. Cash spilled out in neat stacks. She pulled herself up. Their bank account was healthy, she knew. Why keep this much cash on hand? They had money in a safe in the house.

Before she could consider the pile of money, Chris lurched forward. Skin peeled back from his arms and buzzed around his shoulders like an angry hornet. Veins probed the floor and wall like earthworms. The spill of tendrils from his ruined mouth waved across the air, serpent-like heads quested. Although Chris had a bulbous gut, the flesh had grown. The low hissing click boiled up from his bowels. It was insect-like yet feline. Mavis grabbed onto the wall to pull herself away.

The battered purple of his eyes grew brighter, and he threw his head back. Chris's throat opened, and all his guts rushed out. They shot from him like a frog's tongue. Eyes and teeth covered it. They writhed like a nest of skinned vipers tied in a knot. His entrails flew at her. Mavis threw herself to the ground. The mass obliterated the wall. Chunks of wood and plaster landed on her. The teeth along the insane innards bit at anything it touched. The hissing click grew to an ear-splitting whistle. She screamed, kicking a trophy at it—he had won it at a golf tournament, she recalled with an absurd certainty. She crawled away as an intestine slithered towards her foot. Mavis yanked a golf club down and slammed it onto the hateful sliver of meat. It snapped at the nine-iron, severing it in two.

She screamed, pulled herself up, and staggered away from the writhing mass of hateful flesh. Chris trudged behind her, but his body pulled back together. When he had expelled his gut, Chris's stomach had flattened. It was bulbous once moved. Purple flames in his eyes cooled, and the hissing click that boiled out of Chris's gut became low.

They stood in a bedroom. Mavis stared across the room at Chris. They stood next to doors, which went back into the poolroom. Her eyes went to the revolver. Mavis didn't recall him buying it. She grabbed it.

The first two shots went wild, and the drywall drifted to the floor. She winced at the boom pressure on her eardrums. Chris swayed back and forth. He was unphased by the gunfire. Mavis drew in a shaky breath, gray crept across her vision, which held an aura of blackness. Although her knees wobbled, the next couple of shots struck him in the chest. Hissing clicks escaped the holes before two serpent-like tendrils emerged. They waved in the air. Tears squeezed out as Mavis shot again. His head jerked back, his body tilting. Something held him up. Chris stilled.

Although Mavis's mother was gone five years, certainly not forgotten, she had a finite amount of patience. Whenever someone, always Mavis or her father, reached the end of her tolerance, she would give them a slap—both regarded as the act-right strike. Devoured by the horrific visage, Mavis froze. She felt a palm across the back of her head—she had received many at church when she had fallen asleep. She dived through the door, and the abomination crashed into the wall. The pool house shook under its charge.

She crawled backward. The shelves that had survived Mavis's fury toppled to the floor. A black bowling ball landed beside her hand with a heavy thud. She pulled away. Letters correspondence from Sheila and Brian spilled over her hand. Chris didn't want to use the company email. Her eyes caught the name of Kayden, but also that of Tracy Chaney. Even in her terror, Mavis still sneered at the woman's name. She terrorized the other workers more than Brian.

"I hated you," Chris bellowed. The words pissed out little mouths with teeth that ended in jagged points. His body shifted, tangled in the wall.

"Is that all you got, Pecker head?"! She hissed, feeling the soured wine rise to the back of her throat. Her heart raced, and her stomach felt icy. Gray turned to black, but she pinched her arm with savage fury. The black in her vision receded from the pain.

The eyes turned on Mavis, circle irises now rectangular like a goat. Its light blazed across the floor, touching her leg. Like little teeth or needles, the brilliance scoured her exposed skin. She tried to rise, but her leg buckled. She sat down. The tentacles ripped the door frame, growing tighter. Mavis cursed as a sob slipped out. Chris laughed. He lurched forward with a hissing oath of hatred. She threw herself away again; yet, her muscles felt like liquid flame. He flew past her into the pool.

As the slithering mass passed her, a tendril ensnared her ankle. Its teeth, like barbs, dug into her flesh. Mavis slid over the lip of the pool. An insect-like hiss boiled up, and its hateful glee pierced the ear.

Chris flopped and flipped with the unsteady heap beneath him. His shrill whistle of victory turned to tiny bellows. Mavis pulled her leg, but the teeth dug into her skin. She screamed, grabbing the rung of the ladder, but it sunk deeper into her flesh. Something in her coat pocket jabbed into her side. She ripped it out. Teeth bared; she stabbed at the snake-like flesh with the barbeque lighter. The trigger clicked in her grip. Sparks flashed. Flames followed.

Gasoline fumes caught fire. It raced over the heap of broken memories and mementos. Chris's body contracted, but it pulled the accelerant-soaked toys and papers in. The flames devoured him, and the tentacles of flesh let go of her leg. The alien light fueled the conflagration. Hissing clicks echoed about the empty pool filled with hate. The purple light burned brighter, filling the cadaver. His skin flapped. Veins snatched for purchase. Snake-like tubes of meat slapped, beat, and waved in the air. The flames grew, stained by the strange light.

Mavis tried to climb the ladder, but her leg would not support her. She crawled, stood, staggered, and threw herself away. The heat of the flames grew. The pool had a shallow end, where she could crawl out. She hobbled with little yips towards it. The room grew brighter with the purplish light, which made her head light and stomach twist. Within the stench of burned pork, an alien stink overpowered the smell of gas and trash. It was like rotting mushrooms. Higher and higher flames grew with the hissing click until she felt ready to scream. She may have cried, but the tumult consumed it. Her mind focused on each agonized step.

The purplish light turned on her as she staggered towards the door. "I hated you!" It bellowed in the voice of her dead husband.

Mavis opened the door, turning back to the hateful words. Inside of the conflagration, a geometric shape flowed in an alien pattern. A word made of burning, neon purple that felt like rotted flesh dragged over the skin. This representation of an idea scrabbled at her mind, and she could feel an insane hate, hungrily consuming. It grew greater in her mind. It swelled bigger than Chris, her, or this world. The weight of the infinite in a single utterance buried all, crushing it. White came, then gray, and black swept over.

She fell back into the snow. Mavis's eyes fluttered. She kicked the door shut. Unearthly screams battered the metal of the door from the other side. They quickly silenced.

Her arm had struck a metal fire firepit. She had knocked ash out on her. Snow covered it. Chris had used it to burn papers like bank statements or credit card bills. The small whip of the wind tugged a piece of paper free. It flew against her side. She sat up, cold, sinking into her robe. Glancing at the door, she held up the piece of paper. It was an invoice; she saw. Chris used them at Leitch Industrial, and this kind was for trash. Why would he be burning this? She wondered, thinking of the pile of cash in the pool house. There were more of them in the pile. He had burned them after someone went to the Van Lear family. She had watched him from the house.

"It was unusable materials," she breathed, as the purplish light bled through the cracks and window. All the invoices were for the same. Mavis looked at them. It was thousands of dollars' worth of junk inventory.

She wondered what he had done, looking back at the pool house. All inside her was numb, and she thought of all the years with Chris. Every little memento of her husband and mistress crashed into every sweet memory. His lies tainted every piece of their marriage. She felt no love searching her heart, but nothing remained.

What will you do now, girlie? Her mother's voice inquired gently. The voice was more like Mavis.

"I think I'll finally take that trip to France," she promised.

Call of Color's Folly

The rapid beat of the windshield wipers tore at her. They competed with the roar of the car's heater to annoy her. The ice storm raged above. The world turned to an icy glass outside. Sheila clicked off the radio, which spoke of the historic downpour. Rain was nothing new in Meridian. Despite the cab's heat, crystals formed at the bottom of the glass. She swallowed, peeking over the wheel. The sour, bitter tang of bile hung at the back of her throat. Mango banana air freshener was a tangy miasma. She tried to lower the window, but the ice had already sealed it. Sheila cursed. Her sweaty palms made the steering wheel oily. Her hands slipped. They shook when she released the wheel. Headlights did little to cut through the torrential downpour. The road snaked back and forth in a forest that shimmered and sparkled.

Although the compact car slid slowly, Sheila peeked at the small box beside her. Brian had called her and told her of Chris's death. They still haven't found his body, although the Plant Manager of Leitch Industrial Company had reportedly died in a car accident. Someone had set fire to Chris's pool house, and Brian suspected the Van Lear family. They wanted answers.

"Accident, sure," Sheila smirked, "a bunch of crazy hillbillies!" Everyone knew the Van Lear family ruled the town. They made people disappear. They also bought off the cops, she knew.

Chris dies in a car wreck, his body disappears, and then someone burned down his pool house. She chuckled with a shake of her head.

"That guy," Sheila shivered. Barnett, an enforcer for the Lear Family, had come to the factory's office. He was polite, but below, she felt a violence in him. She swallowed, recalling his hard smile under the trilby hat. She had dismissed Chris's and Brian's fear at first. That was before Chris's death and apparent disappearance.

No matter, she thought, swallowing. Sheila shivered despite the cab's heat. I'll be gone before they come to talk to me. Chris was a tubby idiot, and Brian was a lecherous fool. He never made it back from the war, not really. All I need is the box. I'll get out of the country. I have to get off Lear Mountain, she mused. Her knuckles popped on the steering wheel. Even if she had to drive at a crawl, all she had to do was leave.

She glanced at the box with a smile. It was her insurance policy. The car's headlights caught the sign, and Sheila whipped her head back. A curse leaped out, and she corrected the wheel. The car slipped.

"Am I sliding?"! Sheila bellowed. The compact car slid towards the road's shoulder. "NO, NO," she bounced in the seat, pounding the wheel with one sweaty palm. Bile rose, and she screamed at the windshield. Spit flew, splattering the glass. This was all she needed.

The car came to a slow halt. She blinked, listened, and peered about the road. "Okay." Sheila's shoulders rose and then fell. She pressed the accelerator, but the tires spun. She put it in reverse and tried to back up, but it remained in the same spot. Sheila tried again, but the car went nowhere. "ARE YOU KIDDING ME?"! She shrieked and slammed both hands on the horn. Its beep was petite.

Her hands shook as she rubbed her temples. Her flowery perfume filled the car, now tinged with her sweat. Sheila got out. "I hate this redneck cesspool!" she screeched. I've always hated it, she thought, lips puckering.

She pulled out her cell phone, praying for a signal. She let out a jagged breath. It had a single bar that flickered on and off. This minor miracle still soured on her lips. After running out of gas during the summer, Sheila kept the number as a contact. She dialed. Warren Haas answered, though his voice fell, and agreed to come.

Sheila hung up the phone. She swallowed, body quivering. A bruised purple flame reflected in the smartphone's dark screen. She frowned. It was familiar. His eyes had that color in them, she recalled. Kayden's eyes had been strange. She laid him off that morning, before the rest. They had work to do to cover for Chris. It had all come down about their heads after that. Someone had told the Queen atop Lear Mountain. She didn't understand, at first, why everyone spoke of them like royalty. She had learned. They had brought Kayden back the next morning. None of them recalled the conversation. Mavis, Chris's wife, had complained about her husband sleepwalking. Kayden had disappeared, but people from the Lear family were looking around the plant.

A hissing click echoed in her ears. It was only a matter of time, Sheila mused, and the myriad noises pressed on her, but felt far away. "Lady's man," she sneered, and Brian's face swam into focus. If he could have just kept it in his pants; she rubbed her eyes which ached. She closed them, but the brilliance burned through.

Sheila sat back, mind drifting through alien galaxies of light. Low grunts passed between parted lips and gritted teeth. She jerked, her body trembling. Her feet drummed on the car floor. Her mind became unmoored. All was purple flame. Among dead stars, she fell into the vast nothing. She held a hand up in this strange dream, and lines thin as razors raced over her skin. No blood dripped. It smelled of rotted mushrooms.

"Ma'am," Haas spoke politely, tapping on the window. His brow drew down for a moment. A purple light was on in the cab, but there was only the woman. "Miss Richardson, I am here," he ventured. She stirred inside. "Are you okay, Ma'am?" he asked, thick brow furrowed.

"Horse," Sheila mouthed at the distorted image of the giant man. She glanced at her palm. She hadn't felt like this since college. Everything felt loose and far away.

"It's Haas," he sighed. "I'll look at it." He walked around the car, stopping by the front passenger side tire. Despite the downpour, he kneeled. He returned. He asked Sheila to open the trunk. She pressed a button under the dash, and the trunk popped open. He stepped to the back, looking inside. The trunk closed, and he came back.

"What's wrong?" She demanded, feeling her stomach drop. Ever since she arrived here, she questioned the locals' intelligence. The simplest things escaped their understanding. Every day at Leitch, she had to deal with the backward yokels.

"Well, Ma'am," he leaned down. He towered over the car. "There are a couple of problems. You don't have a tire iron or a spare." His nose wrinkled at the rotted mushroom stink. She skipped a bath, trying to cover it with perfume. He pressed his lips shut at the thought.

"Don't you have them?" she snapped. "You are a tow person!" Sheila threw up a hand, nearing smacking his crotch. The man was a giant, and thoughts of him had filled the lonely nights. Maybe it was a con, a way to get her to pay another way. She blushed at her hope.

"Uh, no," he said, holding in his sigh. "I can at least give you a ride back to your house." He had a tire iron, but it was no good without the spare tire. It would do nothing to calm her, he was certain. Northerners had peculiar ways.

"I think that's the least you can do, Horse!" She wailed, adding a curse.

Why does all the help behave like idiots? She asked herself with a deep sigh.

"Sorry, Ma'am," Haas straightened. Dragons, he recalled, kept a princess captive in old stories. If she were in a tower, the giant serpent would be there for everyone else's safety.

Sheila turned off the car, waiting. She grabbed the box beside her. Haas opened the door. Ice on the vehicle had thickened. It tinkled to the ground. She slammed the door, as he promised to return for it. She stomped past him without looking at his hand to help her out. He moved fast to open the passenger side of his tow truck. Sheila almost walked in the door as he opened it. He moved to the driver's side, praying the sweet Lord above would give him patience. Rumors were ugly and cruel, but sometimes, they were correct.

Haas started the engine, "So, where do you live?" He forced a smile. All he had to do was get her home.

"It is at the back of Color's End Road," she sneered. It was the only house on this road. She studied the icy window. She prayed the storm would keep the Van Lear people away. Sheila gripped the box tighter.

He frowned, scratching his short beard. His eyes widened. Their blue was a light hue. He turned. "You live at the Black Priory?"! Haas blurted, shocked. He blinked, blushing, before the color drained from his face.

Sheila turned to him. Backward, she thought with a smirk. They spoke of crossroads, witches, and devils in hushed tones. "It looks like an old monastery, I guess," she admitted, covering her mouth to stifle a laugh. I can't tell if it's something in the water. Maybe that made them stupid, she mused. They're all just catastrophically inbred. Sheila laughed. She wished they were dead. It would improve the world, certainly the gene pool.

Haas shook his head. "It has always been called that," he corrected, swallowing. He started up the road. "It was here before anything else." His eyes roamed over the road, recalling the stories.

She crossed her arms. "I thought the Van Lear family was the first to settle here." Townsfolk spoke of them like saints or devils. They intertwined in the roots of the community.

"They were the first family to settle here and built the town," he nodded, shifting away from her. The rotted mushroom stink was unbearable. He swallowed. "The monks built it before the Van Lear family arrived. No one knows much about it." He glanced at her, "It is bad luck to speak of the Black Priory." Northerners always acted entitled.

Sheila shook her head. Country folk had long memories and many superstitions. "The rent is cheap," she admitted, shrugging. The price made it easier to put money back for her retirement, and no one ever came to bother her. At last, I know why now, she thought, pushing down the urge to giggle. "I guess someone saw a black dog after a storm," she tapped the box in her hands, "or whatever you people believe."

Haas blushed, clearing his throat, "An entire community goes missing, and that is no superstition." He huffed, "People go missing around that place and the Greene Community." He rolled his eyes. Why did he bother? She knew everything.

"Greene Community," she repeated. Sheila had heard the rumors. They ranged from the simple to the fantastical.

"Yup," he nodded, recalling Sheila was an outsider, "that was before you were even born, I'd wager."

She looked down at her lap, chewing her lip. "Do you mean those abandoned houses? I moved into the house in the summer. I didn't even see them until winter." They peeked out at first when the leaves began falling.

He nodded, drawing away from her. "It is an awful place." Haas recalled how the houses seemed to stare. His face and neck burned.

She blinked at him. He was enormous. Sheila pressed a finger across her lips to hold on to a smirk. "Aren't you the one who killed a panther with your bare hands?"

"Well," he shifted, blue eyes searching both sides of the road. "Yes, I did, but I didn't want to." Haas admitted, glancing over at her smirk, jaw flexed, "Rutger, the Sheriff, his father was the Sheriff before him. He came up here to this god-forsaken place, pardon my language. A town girl, Millicent, married Troy Greene," he glanced at her. This wasn't a pleasant story, but Haas wanted to wipe that smirk off her face. "She loved the boy, but the community had a reputation, even then. It was something about the Priory, paganism, and such. She got pregnant and wanted to leave, told her kin." Haas studied the road. His blue eyes searched the icy forest.

Sheila shivered, frowning at the hairs that rose on her neck. She shook her head. "And then what happened?"

"Clint, Rutger's father, came up to the Greene Community," he swallowed. "He brought a few men, but they found no one." The men with the former sheriff came back with stories.

"They found nothing," she said, brow drawn down. Sheila shifted. She could smell the soap he used, and the motor oil on him.

"Well," he glanced at her, shoulders rose, then dropped, "Clint said he had been there before, and it seemed bigger." His brow drew down.

"Bigger," repeated Sheila with a smirk, but felt cold creep up her neck. She had expected Haas to tell her the Devil rode after them. Nothing was just that, nothing.

"Yeah," he shook his head. "But that wasn't the last time something strange happened about the Black Priory." Haas clamped his mouth shut. His hand jerked, wanting to smack his forehead. A man couldn't speak anyway to a woman, and talk of the Priory was ungentlemanly of him.

"Really," she said, licking her lips, "what else happened?" Sheila managed a laugh, but it was jagged. She cleared her throat.

"There was the Preacher, Robert Delaney," he said slowly, measuring his words. His eyes searched the abandoned houses as they passed them. "He went mad, and jumped off a cliff behind the Priory," he confessed in a rush. Just because she was ill-mannered, this talk was unseemly.

Sheila blinked. "Is that why it is called Preacher's Jump?" Rural folk can be so literal, she mused. They lacked creativity, but the man was a superb storyteller.

"Yes." he stared at one house, which crept close to the road. "Rutger found him at the bottom."

"I thought people never found them." she looked back at him, but her smile was weak. That point everyone was clear on. People who go missing at the Priory never reappear.

"The body disappeared," he shook his boulder-like head. His lip curled. Sometimes, people mess with the dead. There was a rumor about one of the town cops.

Sheila jerked, thinking of Chris. "You people can't keep track of dead bodies." She imagined a crazed hillbilly with Chris' corpse.

"Ever since Color's Folly," he breathed, face now a shade of soured milk, "it has been a bad luck place with sick soil." They say that a star fell which cursed it.

Sheila trembled and crossed her arms. "This is all just stories," she whined, holding her chin up. He was trying to mess with her, she guessed. Sometimes, the locals like to tell tales to trick outsiders.

"What would you know?" he snapped. "You're just a stranger, a tourist. People like you come to our community because we smile and wave. But you demean us and mock us to our backs." Haas never understood why they came to a place they hated so much. They should stay with their kind if they are so superior.

Sheila's smirk turned into a sneer. "All right, fair enough, so you're right." She shrugged. She called her friends back home to tell them stories. They would have a good laugh.

They drove to the end of the road, and she stared at the forest. Where I'm going, there isn't snow, she thought. Thank the spaghetti monster no more cat piss stinks of meth labs. No more listening to the idiotic problems of a bunch of bumpkins. No more living in a backwater, where body odor and brain damage rule. Sheila smirked.

Haas peeked at the Black Priory, but his eyes snapped away. Sheila stepped out of the tow truck. He escorted her, face burning. Hunching forward, he was careful to keep his eyes away from the old monastery. He stopped a meter from the gate. He focused on his thick boots.

Sheila sighed, but a knot had formed in her stomach at the Black Priory's visage. "I can make it the rest of the way," she grumbled in her best professional tone. Haas was about to get her car and all.

"OH, I can escort you the rest of the way," a cool voice offered. There was a calculated laughter in it.

Haas jerked. He whirled, "Miss Van Lear, you gave me a start." He towered over the tiny woman.

Sheila jumped. Her eyes moved to the woman, who was too young to be the Queen of Lear Mountain. Although the other dressed for the inclement weather, she reminded Sheila of a high-priced doll. "I... Miss Van Lear," she mouthed, forcing a smile. She couldn't see another vehicle. "I wasn't expecting you," she added with a smirk.

"Miss Richardson," she smiled, but her eyes dissected the Northerner. "I've been trying to reach you. The cell service throughout the county is spotty, at best." She delivered the words in a smooth, Southern Aristocratic tone. "I'll consider that was the reason for you missing my calls," she offered, turning to the large man, who had removed his trucker cap. "Warren Haas, you are stalwart in your duties as always," she gave him a slight nod.

"Miss Van Lear," he shuffled his feet, "it is dangerous out here." Haas peered about, swallowing, "I don't want to see you catch your death of cold." He studied the shadows as if they would come alive.

"Thank you for your concern, Warren," she nodded. "May I call you Warren?" She asked. A ghost of her flowery perfume slipped to him on the wind.

"Yes, Ma'am," he smiled, blushing. Haas didn't like what her family had done, but that was before his time.

"I need to speak to Miss Richardson, so I'll see you later," she confessed, looking at Sheila. Alice vivisected her with her eyes. "And, Warren, there is no need to call the Sheriff about the wreck. Call Barnett. You tell him I told you to ask about compensation." She turned to Haas. "You're very devoted to come in such weather, and he'll reward you properly." She knew men like him were invaluable. It was unfortunate he declined work for her.

"Yes Ma'am," Haas backed up, put his hat back on, before he tipped it. After a glance at the Priory, face ashen, he retreated to his truck. He paused. It wasn't right to leave the women in such a place. He looked back, and Alice waved him on. He left, though cursing himself.

She watched his lights disappear. "Miss Richardson, I'm Alice Van Lear, but you will refer to me as Miss Van Lear," she commanded, smirking.

Sheila bristled. The other woman was smaller, and more delicate, but held herself like a noblewoman. "Well," she smirked, "you will call me Miss Richardson." Great, a pretentious hillbilly, she mused with a groan.

"I will refer to you as I please," Alice countered, "and you will wipe that supercilious smirk off your face." In her cold eyes, there was a dare, a hope the woman would disobey. Sheila was too poor in quality to make a proper doll, but there were other uses for troublesome outsiders.

She blinked, "You can't—"

Alice held up a hand. "Have you ever seen someone scream until their larynx burst?" She weighed the thought, letting the woman's mind create the image.

Sheila blinked, "I have not." Rain fell to the earth, and the world shimmered in the glow cast from the Black Priory. Each breath hung in the air. She tasted a low, musky grit at the back of her throat. The constant beat of the storm was relentless. Bile was bitter at the back of the throat. The eyes of the Princess of Lear Mountain cut through her with the dispassion of an undertaker.

Alice smirked. "I will be plain." She brushed off the ice that had built up on her shoulder. It snapped when it hit the ground with a brittle crack. "It has come to our knowledge that there have been some acts of impropriety," she spoke evenly. She laughed. It was like frozen crystal smashed on marble.

"I don't know what you mean," she countered, voice professional and distant. Sheila could outsmart this snooty trash. Money would never make her more than a yokel.

"I mean the women Brian abused," Alice returned, tone smooth but amused. "They came to my mother, and they were upset." She studied the woman's every tick. Her brow creased, smelling the rotted mushroom stench on her.

"It isn't within my control," Sheila sighed, "what adults engage in, outside of the factory." It wasn't her fault some women were loose in their morals. They could've quit or come to her.

"So, you know any in a managerial role," her eyes searched the Human Resource Manager's face, "who engage in such behavior, especially on or off the clock, do so with a threat?" Alice smirked. The woman's ignorance of power dynamics was comic but expected.

"I can do nothing without explicit evidence of wrongdoing," Sheila smiled, suppressing her smirk. "If a bunch of low-class women with loose morals use their assets to... receive certain benefits," she shrugged, "it is an indication of their character." Once a whore, always a whore, in her opinion.

Alice's eyebrows rose, lip curled, but her expression smoothed. "Miss Richardson, this seems to be a difference between New and Old Money," she observed with a nod. "The people of Lear County are my family's responsibility.

Those 'low-class' women's defilement concerns us," she stated, eyes assessing the other. "I don't care about your company's policies. The moral failings of the New Money are equally insignificant, especially one of their idiot servants. Your masters are crass and ignoble." She glanced at her, up and down. Her laugh was a sharp crack.

"Aren't your family former slave owners?" Sheila blurted, face burning despite the cold. "Didn't they execute—"?

Alice stepped forward, and she recoiled from her. "Know the Blackberry Bog never freezes. You and Brian are done. The factory will close." The coolness of her rage made the ice storm feel balmy. She gestured for Sheila to proceed. "If you are tired of living, by all means, go ahead," she dared. Something deep in her pale blue eyes slashed at Sheila.

She swallowed, shivering. Sheila shook her head, "You can't—"

Again, the Princess of Lear Mountain stepped towards her. "I can," she smirked, casting her eyes about the Priory. "The New Money of Duncannon needs a reminder of their place and role." She moved with an unnerving grace.

"I would appreciate it," Sheila swallowed, "if you left my house and property." She felt goosebumps rise. Alice talks like I'm some doll or toy. Her eyes were the worst. They moved like scalpels in a surgeon's hands.

"It isn't your house," she warned, looking at the Priory. "This place belongs to the family, Black," she waved a hand at the dark stones of the monastery. Eyes returned to Sheila, "You know anything of its history?" Her smirk flashed.

"I know a little," she confessed, fighting the urge to retreat inside. There were rumors about Alice, she recalled.

No one dared to say them aloud, fearing the Van Lear family would hear.

"You know people disappear from Black Priory," she tilted her head, considering the woman. Dark musings dreamed in ponderous measure.

"Yes," she replied, bile rising. Barnett scared everyone. She couldn't image him being worse than Alice. The Princess of Lear Mountain was colder than the ice storm.

"You have no family, no friends," Alice contemplated aloud, "except for Tracy Chaney, who is a friend to no one. She is a rat, who'll squeal to save her skin. Brian Weber is a fool who has betrayed his family, his blood." She looked back to her, "There is something else, though I haven't seen it yet. We have business dealings with your company, and when we shut you down, I'll personally go through everything." It was only a matter of time. Time and patience would always win the day.

"You'll find nothing," she shrugged, but her hands shook.

"No one will miss you," she offered. "Don't go anywhere, Miss Richardson. I'll speak to you more once I have more information. Maybe you'll learn some manners, and your New Money masters will throw you to the wolves, just for our approval." Alice turned around, indifferent to anything Sheila could say.

She watched the Princess of Lear Mountain walk away. Alice never looked back, and she disappeared into the storm. Sheila squeezed the box, body shuddered. I must escape! She considered, but fell back a step. She is crazy, but not stupid. Black Priory loomed over her, and she looked at it.

"Maybe," she whispered. I can hide somewhere inside if she comes back.

The Black Priory waited. She had planned to run, but tropical beaches would have to wait. Another night of the freaking rats, she thought with a curse. The days and nights were incredibly still at the Black Priory, even the frogs and crickets. Only the wind broke the silence until lately.

"It started about around that day," she paused. Maybe I just never noticed it before, Kayden. "His eyes." She rubbed her temples. "Red lines," she added. World drifted away though snapped back. "I hate rats," Sheila sighed.

Gray swept over her, and she sat down on a chair. A bruised purple bled over the floor, which followed her gaze. Some squirmed in the air before her, but no matter where she looked, it centered on the word. Kayden rose in her mind, across from her in Sheila's office. He had the smile of one who possessed a funny but nasty joke. His mouth moved, but her head felt full of worms made of razors. A dead galaxy of purple flames flowed around her. Muscle spasms seized her, and her feet drummed on the floor.

Gnawing, scratching, and scrabbling ate into the dream. Sheila floated in a sea, fathomless and boundless, unmoored from the body or the world. She frowned, and like the sea receding from the shore, the bruised purple fires of alien nebulas fell to black. She shifted; eyes fluttered, and an ache sunk deep.

Sheila shot up. The box had slipped out of her hands. I must have sat down and fell asleep. She snatched up the box, but the contents spilled over the floor. Everything she needed to ensure the others would never betray her. She even kept some of Tracy Chaney's correspondence. A rat is always a rat; she mused and cursed Brian for allowing the woman to be involved. Kayden had been snooping around, and rumors flooded the plant. He must have told the Van Lear family something. Alice may know everything but wants evidence or to play with her.

"I got to hide it," Sheila declared, chuckling. She stood and listened to the storm outside. The sounds of little claws and teeth moved throughout the Black Priory.

Although she had gotten a key, which opened some of the monastery's doors, most of the property locked. Sheila moved about the rooms, most updated beyond their original design. The structure was so sturdy that all the additions were easy to see. Every place she tried to place the paper was too obvious. She discarded every room's viability as the rats in the walls began their busy work. They moved to each room, almost hidden in the raging storm's tumult. Sheila's gaze retreated from the walls, shoulders hunched and goosebumps rose.

Soon, she moved in a hunched scurry. "I don't even know," Sheila threw up a hand.

Chris and Brian had handled the entire thing. She cursed. All I did was cover for them. I didn't steal anything, and I can't help some women who don't have self-respect. Could we have stolen something from the Van Lear family? If not for Brian, the Lady's Man, inability to keep his hands to himself, they would have closed the plant before anyone would know. No one got hurt. Sheila felt the world grow distant. Now, I have a lunatic on my doorstep.

She thought of the Princess of Lear Mountain, "I can't tell who is worse, her or Barnett."

Something writhed across her vision and swam across the dark stones. Purple light blazed in its wake. Sheila staggered a step. She leaned against the wall, which felt thin like a ruse. She fell to her knees. A hissing click filled her ears. Bile at the back of her throat was bitter. Lines, thin as razors, raced over her skin. Works of hatred echoed deep in the boundless space. A word in an alien tongue resounded, which was terrible and beyond the grasp of the finite. The box bounced once before the contents spilled over the floor.

Darkness swept over her, and Sheila struck the stone. She floated in a great nothing. Time was strange. She jerked. Eyes widened, flew over the floor, and spilled papers. There were gaps in her memory. I'll go to the Doctor when I'm far from this pit. About her, the sound of rats in the walls grew to a manic fury.

The scrabble of little claws stopped. She stood before the door to the basement, which opened with a heavy click. Sheila had only tried the door once when she had first moved into the Priory. In the darkness of the stairway, a light danced. It burned a greasy yellow hue. A spicy rot mixed with the musk of long, undisturbed dirt. Over her washed air, uncomfortable like hot breath. Despite this warmth, she felt icy needles trace her back. I guess Horse unsettle me; she assured herself. It is just a basement. The slight breeze cooled, and she doubted it had ever been warm.

"I found my hiding spot," she smiled, but it faltered. Her heart raced. Bile rose in the back of her throat, stomach twisting. Only the steady beat of rain, and her breathing answered. Sheila shifted and looked at the spill of documents, but her hands trembled.

She scowled. "Geez, I'm losing it!" She laughed.

Sheila smirked, feeling eased. He could give up the towing business. Horse could be a late-night horror film host. Like that little mutant zombie, or that redneck, she thought, though she failed to recall the names of the shows.

"Tales from the Grave," she mumbled. She tapped a finger. "Or was it the Creeper?" Her shoulders rose, then fell. "Whatever, it doesn't matter."

She stepped into the basement. The stone stairs cut into the rock. It had been down by hand with a zealous eye. Every wall gleamed and glistened, iridescent yet faintly luminous. A spicy smell of old meat crept about the room, which appeared blasted. The scorch marks seemed new. No rats clawed at the walls, yet a faint wind whispered through the dark. It almost formed a word, or it was a word given form. It was an alien utterance. The same symbol was across the pillars and floor. The skewered eyes on a three-tine fork watched her. Its solemn contemplation filled with alien thoughts. Sheila studied the arcane iconography, but it was strange. It unsettled the eye and stomach. She felt strangeness upon her, which judged. Among the bookshelves, alchemical devices, and religious accouterments, the shadows drifted over the skin like decayed parchment. At the room's center was a giant metal relief of the Orders or god's symbol, made to level out the floor, so it would no longer dip.

"They're too superstitious to look round down here," she observed, though a tremor crept through her voice.

She held up her phone. Its pale light did little to reveal the room. Sheila turned to candles, which burned though never lowered. Who lit them? The question hung in her mind. She moved the light about the room. She listened, but even the dull roar of the storm outside failed to penetrate the basement library. Sheila looked around the candles, but the layer of dust was undisturbed.

"Okay," she breathed, swallowing. "Yeah, I'm done," Sheila declared to the darkness.

Whatever they did, she thought, I don't care. I want nothing to do with the backward locals. I especially don't want to find out what a bunch of redneck cultists were doing.

She glanced about. A podium overlooked the symbol of their alien god. Sheila stepped over to it, careful to avoid touching its dark wood. She set the box atop a book, which felt like desiccated skin. Her lip curled, and she withdrew the hand, wiping it on her pants.

The sound of scrabbling claws, gnawing teeth, and thumping returned, though much louder. A rusty whine sawed the air as unseen stones shifted. Shadows moved, and the uneasy light from candles recoiled. The slow, ponderous steps were heavy, even on the stone floor. Each delivered with resonating booms, as if some belligerent giant rapped at a colossal door. Sheila's face paled, bile rising. Her eyes searched the darkness. She moved towards the podium to retrieve the box, but a tall, broad figure drew closer.

"Barnett!" she cried, falling back a step. She glanced at the box of paper.

That little psycho must have sent him! Sheila whirled.

She ran through the aisles of bookshelves. She snatched glances back, as the hulking figure moved in slow though fluid steps. The sound of rats, large ones, returned anew with manic fervor. A neon clover-green light burned over the iridescent walls. The stench of rotted meat left to molder for untold years thickened the air. Acid rose in her stomach. The darkness came alive, slithering into the black stones of the Black Priory. Between her lips, a low moan slipped, lost in the pound of footfalls.

She flew up the stairs. Sheila whirled and slammed the door. It refused to close. The silhouette moved below, silent as the wind, and the strange green light followed. Nowhere to hide! Her mind screamed. She rushed out the front door, and the dark figure filled the basement doorway behind her. It watched.

The ice storm still battered the Black Priory. It covered its stones with a thin layer of ice. Lightning lit the secluded community. These moments of brilliance were fleeting. More figures staggered along the road and tree line. Sheila clapped a hand over her mouth to hold in the scream, busting her lip. She stopped. Her feet flew out from under her. Crashing to the earth, she tipped. Her breath whooshed out, and she sucked in. Icy rain beat against her face. Each felt like a tiny needle. In another flash, the brilliance filled the world for a moment. They moved towards the monastery. People shambled slowly, heads down. Instead of a scream, a hot spray of bile shot from her mouth. She struggled to stand, despite the slick ground.

A house peeked at her with windows that caught the flash of light. Sheila recalled an entire community moldered in the forest. The Horse fellow had mentioned it. She crept into the trees. Her lip curled at the rotted mushroom stink that was everywhere. The shadowy figures moved, silent and slow. Her breath hung in the air. The rain beat it down. Even the thick coat dampened. Icy, rotted brush broke under her boots with brittle snaps like bone. The neon clover-green light burned in their eyes, all blazed at once. They connected, sewn together on some spiritual level. Sheila staggered, mind babbling half numb. No clear thoughts emerged in the bedlam of her mind. She struck a tree, falling on her butt. The figures turned. Their idiot gaze looked through the world.

She crawled, frozen earth jabbing at her knees. The flash of lightning turned the world to glass. Brilliance shimmered through the trees. Sheila saw the house, still half hidden. Among briars and brambles, it slept, though its windows watched. Each bolt of brilliance brought further revelations that shocked the eyes. It left an afterimage. Although it faded, pinpricks of neon clover-green sway back and forth in the questing, dark figures. Sheila recoiled from the alien gazes of eldritch flame.

She crept into the house, opening the door slowly. Sheila closed it, praying the old hinges would be silent. She frowned at the butcher's cleaver stuck deep in a post. It had rusted. She rested her head against the cold door and listened, and her stomach revolted. Bile rose, yet lowered after a few moments. The sounds of her heart resounded in her ears, but it faded. She felt the world settle.

Only the sound of the storm remained. Its brittle cacophony was relentless. Sheila listened. I had seizures. The thought hung in the darkness behind her eyes, which held spots of purple. This is all in my head! This is all just some misfiring in my brain! A jagged laugh slipped out. Her body quivered.

The scrabble of claws rose among the rotted timbers. They slipped about the earth below. Sheila froze. A foot dragged over the dust-smothered floor. Its rasp was ponderous. The clover-green light burned in the dark house, holding a profane life. She dropped low, peeking around the remnants of a couch. Dark stone made up one wall where she heard the scratching. Like the walls of the Black Priory, she saw. Gray crept into her vision. The black silhouette shambled into view, blocking the blasted rock. The eldritch flame burned beneath the eyes sewn shut. Upon their brow, in the center, was the same symbol in the basement library of the monastery. A hand carved it deep into the flesh. A brilliance fumed beneath. The bones of the cadaverous stranger snapped and popped in the sexless face. Lips peeled back, as teeth pushed forward into a pointed sneer. Their hands drew up to their chest, fingernails grew to points. From their bowels dropped a whip-like length of the intestine. Their blind gaze darted about the room.

Sheila's eyes widened. She prayed for a rational explanation, but the strange symbol repeated in her mind. It pressed against inside her thoughts. Bile rose in her throat. She choked, clamping a hand over her mouth. The dark figure hunched over, spine curving. She shook her head. Her mind emptied, body drawing up. She retreated to a corner.

Her wide eyes followed it through the door. Sheila's mouth opened to scream, but bile turned it into a choked gurgle. It dribbled down her chin. The phantom of shadow moved past, and she recognized the creature in the other room. Its actions predetermined like a play. It swung an arm in savage strikes; yet it held nothing. It moved through the house to act out old, dark deeds. With the performance complete, it froze, chest heaving. She swallowed, brow furrowing. Her mind blanked. The formation of dark memories turned, marching back towards her, and she shrunk into a corner. With a savage swing, it stepped out. Sheila saw the cleaver where it had swung. Old stains turned the wooden handle dark.

Sheila shook her head, crawling to the door. The neon clover-green flame moved closer. She opened the door, cautious to be slow, and slipped out into the tempest.

The eye of the storm drew closer. Bolts struck the forest. Their brilliance split the heavens. One hit an old, dead oak. It shattered the thick layer of ice, which smothered the dark woods. Brittle snaps rose in the wake of its destruction. A low stench crawled over the iced earth. Like rotted meat in a freezer, her beleaguered mind moaned. Her stomach churned. Things lurched amongst the trees. Eyes sewn shut burned from within. Sheila stopped. She pressed both hands to cover over a scream. A stalk had emerged from the symbol of their heretical god. It burned in the darkness like a lantern. Some cruel deity was twisting their form. Their long, crooked teeth chattered. Each slash of lightning revealed the horror of their misshapen bodies. So vile was their stench that it clawed at the throat. It was like a charred mushroom. More of them joined the hunt. Sheila saw them everywhere.

Two shades rushed at her, and she dashed away. She babbled an incoherent plea. Another house stood before her. The door was already open. Sheila threw herself inside, but the tip of her shoe caught the frame. She fell. Air whooshed out of her lungs. As the pair approached, she saw one had a round belly. She curled into a ball, but they passed through her. Is that Troy and Millicent Greene? She wondered. The figures looked back through the broken door at pursuers. Sheila peered into the dark, seeing nothing. The couple held each other.

They jerked suddenly. One looked towards the back door, and the other towards the front. The taller figure tried to shield the one with the swollen belly. Silent pleas still held hope. Sheila turned away.

The sound of scratching and gnawing crept from dark stones. Sheila thought of the Black Priory. The blasted rock was here. There was twice as much. Sheila watched the stones shift, and two mangled creatures slipped free. The shadow man figure knocked something away. They pulled the shorter one. They fled the house. Sheila saw the neon clover-green burn brighter. She rushed out.

The dark figures searched the Greene Community. Their net drew ever tighter. Sheila ran, but a line of the creatures had made a perimeter. Teeth chattered, hisses rose, and the stalks that protruded from their misshapen heads brightened. She screamed, slipped, and fell to the earth. They moved closer, and she struggled back onto her feet. They moved together. Shadowy figures, remnants of a massacre, alive only in memory, rushed away from unseen assailants in terror. Sheila ran past or through them, as they cut off every escape.

The Black Priory watched them. The storm's eye settled over the heretical monastery. Lightning crashed to the earth like heaven sought to smite the spoiled land below. The rain had soaked Sheila down to the skin. Her body was numb, except for the manic churning in her guts. A chant rose from the closing net of the mangled people. Their voices united in praise of madness. The shadowy figures closed on the couple, who had every escape cut off. Sheila looked back as they surround them. Ancient death and the low stink of insanity settled over the earth. A malignant fog had settled over the darkness, which held razor-thin streaks of neon clover-green. They burst through the mist like dead veins. This unsettling play of light gave birth to eyes, mouths, and little, scurrying things. They died as quickly as they were born.

She recoiled. The memory of death clawed at her mind. She turned to the Black Priory. Before her, another shadowy figure ran, and the memory acted out the last horrors of its life. Another had found the horrors of the monastery. They came for both.

The blind creatures followed, hissing laughter. They crawled on long claws, eyes like molten balls of tar. They burned with the alien green light. Elongated mouths rattled. In the unsteady light of the night, the lantern at the end of the stalks blazed. Its brilliance centered in her head, calling the purple light in her head. Deep in the glow, an awful truth eclipsed the mind. It wished to reveal something. The heretics came, lured by a call of Color's Folly. Whip-like intestines hung like tails. They ensnared others until they became one of many bodies. The Rat King of the Black Priory howled up at the storm above. It prayed to a secret god.

Sheila ran, forcing her gaze away from the blasphemy of flesh and madness. It gnawed at her thoughts. All that remained was the bruised purple in her mind, and the slither of half-hidden worms that crossed her vision. The blaze of the Rat King's lanterns grew brighter. She shook her head, denying its call. The hiss rose as teeth chattered, which was closer with each beat of her heart. The shadowy figure before her looked back. Their face twisted in mind devouring horror.

"Don't," she pleaded.

She threw herself through the Black Priory's front door. The fragment of the past staggered into the wall. Her numb legs buckled. Sheila fell on the dark stone floor. She glanced back, heart pounding. Her numb muscles refused to work. The boom of the Rat King resounded through the Black Priory. Its mass had grown too large. Only one passed through the door. The length of the tail stretched as the creature lunged. Claws scrabbled at the floor as it snapped back. It launched forward again. She screamed, scrabbling away. Her back struck the wall. Elongate jaws snapped at her. Misshapen teeth closed in the air next to her throat. Terror tore at her guts, bile shooting from her mouth. It splashed its face. It stopped. A nasty laugh seeped from jaws too malformed to close.

She lunged away. A claw seized her ankle, but Sheila kicked away the hand. She ran through the house, and the rest of the Rat King squeezed into the Black Priory. The box.

I have to get it; she thought. Alice or Barnett could find it! She ran to the basement door, but the Rat King drew closer. Sheila darted away from the cackling creature. She followed the phantom with a curse. It fled the monastery.

Sheila ran out into the storm. Rain blasted her. Bolts bashed the forest. Light danced across the glassy earth. More of the creatures, once men and women, searched the forest. Neon clover-green brilliance haunted the darkness, devouring the dark. She followed the fragment of a soul along a trail. It was another memory. Lightning fell from the cold firmament above to the frozen forest below. The world brightened. She saw the murky figure of gloom drop.

"Preacher's Jump," she cried, trying to stop.

Sheila's feet flew up, and she saw the long drop below. A flash of light unveiled the glassy depths below. She slammed to the earth. Air shot from her lungs. Her head slammed against the hard earth. A small groan passed between her lips. Icy rain stabbed at the exposed skin, and she slung an arm over her face. Purple light danced behind her eyelids. Each desperate suck at the air drew in wintry drops. She coughed. Dark stones shifted beside her as neon clover-green light blazed out of the unholy sarcophagus. An emaciated cadaver loomed over her. Their stained white collar caught a flash of lightning. They were ready to give the damned a sermon. Eyes sewn shut, turned down to her. She flailed, slipping on the slick stones. A lantern emerged from the symbol carved into its brow. Tremors ran through her. Her hands and heels drummed on the icy earth. A bruised purple galaxy drowned the mind.

It receded enough for her to witness. She watched the icy ground. It passed beneath her. Thin red lines traced her skin, and Sheila felt the world's thinness. Just past the veil of sanity, another reality waited. All that held it together was the frailest of threads. She listened to them chant. Their skin was rough. They carried her with prayers on their lips.

Sheila's eyes drifted up. The world shifted. Lines stretched and bent. Impossible angles and geometry assailed trees until they were an amalgamation of writhing madness. They swayed to a song, cosmic winds, which flowed through the fractured reality. Branches slithered, covered in razor-sharp frills. Boughs had mouths with shattered teeth, which gnashed at the dark. Sap bled as malignant tears. A warm stink of simmering infection clung to the fog. It spread through the fouled woods. A bolt of lightning became malformed when it struck a decayed oak. A hateful life was born in the brief existence. It licked all within its reach, tormenting with its caustic touch. Roots snatched and crushed. Ice congealed into glassy serpents with the faces of those claimed by the Black Priory. They swam through the air. The little legs along their bodies scrabbled. They moaned out their last words in life, pleas for deliverance. Green streaks of electricity flowed through the mist. It was like lightning in a storm cloud. It whispered to her as it flowed. There were many truths beyond the mind of the ordered, sane world. Sheila's mind, divorced of flesh, felt the strange will slicing at her. She wailed, and even the cry became a twisted parody of life. It formed. Her face leered back at her.

With great joy, they carried her into the monastery. It bathed in the glory of a heretical god. The lighting clouds clung to its crevasses and cracks. She saw Haas as they dragged her inside. He had returned with her car. A piggish squeal escaped her, and for a briefest moment, he glanced at the dark doorway. Haas paused. A shadow writhed, and he turned to it.

They ferried her into the basement. The monks retrieved her. Inside their robes, they seemed to float, as if in water. Skeletal hands were oddly gentle, almost reverent. The neon clover-green light roamed over the blasted walls. They set her upon the wicked mark.

Sheila looked at the podium, where she had hidden the box. The blasphemous bible was gone, and her evidence of the others spilled out all over the floor. All because of Kayden, she thought. Maybe, if I hadn't gotten his wife Jillian fired, this wouldn't have happened. She sneered. I'm glad that junkie trash died. I hope he dies face-down in a gutter!

An enormous shadow moved through the darkness and the vile eldritch light. Under the thick hood, three eyes burned. They saw more than this world. Long arms split into more until she could no longer count them. Sheila screamed. Countless hands waved before her. They sewed her lips shut, so no more could pass beyond them. They carved a symbol into her head. Runes on the heretical bible burned. Purple light glowed in her eyes. Deep in the darkness of the priest's hood, a smile contorted long dead lips. He beckoned. Her eyes pulled forward until they popped out. Like a lollipop pulled from a child's mouth, a mad voice considered. Optical nerves snapped, but she could still see, even as the lids sealed closed. Sheila's eyes floated up, and then burst into purple flame, as the alien word trapped inside released. This utterance of madness had infected her. The heretical priest offered it to his blasphemous god, as dark stones rose to make Sheila a tomb. She had become part of their community.

Haas moved Sheila's car. He listened, thinking he heard a scream. Silence greeted him. Although she had been thoroughly unpleasant, he regretted calling her a tourist. She lives here all alone; he knew. No one was her friend, except for Tracy Chaney. His lip twitched at the woman's name.

A little squeal escaped the Black Priory. Haas turned away from the car. His heavy brow turned down. Was that Miss Richardson? He saw the door was open. With a deep sigh, he stepped towards the old monastery. He paused.

"She hates locals," he muttered, face flushed. Haas was sure that she didn't want him around. Sheila didn't like his help, either.

Free of charge, he thought, shaking his head. Haas turned back to the tow truck. Maybe she needs a show of kindness from a local. We are no better or worse than anyone else. Television portrays us poorly. Hopefully, this may make her a bit nicer. Miss Richardson will see we are okay people. He smiled, pulling out of the parking lot.

Past the Veil
of Dreams

"Damn you!" Brian cursed, hands shaking.

He rubbed his eyes with a hand that shook. Brian closed one nostril, snorting hard. His boot struck a beer, which tipped to spread over the hardwood floor. It was stale. The smell was low and dull. Empty cans jangled in sour notes. His eyes burned and ached, no matter what he took. Cheri's light sobs crawled into his head with the persistence of a worm in a rotted apple. All she had done was whine and mope. His right hand flexed, relaxed, and he punched his leg with a savage grin. The pain cleared his head a little. His skin felt ready to unzip, like a jacket or coat. Acid rose in his guts, bringing the taste of whiskey and barley. The bruised purple light was a vibrant starburst behind his eyes. It waited for him to close his eyes.

The sands of that foreign land stretched out before him, in the darkness of his closed eyes. Part of him remained there. The same stretch of God-forsaken rock and sand always came when life was taxing. Every night for a year, less for years after, until it was a seldom. Now, it came when life became stressful. It always left him shaken and covered in sweat. Above, the endless blue of the sky became a bruised purple, as if an alien nebula cast upon cosmic winds. That was new, he noted. The event repeated, fate determined; yet he tried to choose another path. It was why he came back.

He shook off the image. Brian finished the whiskey, ignoring Cheri's low cries and tears. He could see it so clearly. Even the grit, which seemed to get everywhere, scoured his face. Heat rose above the earth. It seemed a feverish mirage. Sometimes, he saw faces on the stones. They were the faces of old friends and enemies. Different, somehow, he thought.

Part of him wondered if it was a combination of alcohol and drugs. He recalled the sardonic smile on his buddy's face. Those bitter truths always went down rough. Drugs and alcohol smoothed things, making them bearable.

"No blood for oil," Brian sneered. Everyone was for the war until election time came. All lies, he mused. "It was never about oil." The words drifted between lips in a broken sigh, almost a cry. "I killed and I killed," he confessed to the ghost, which was alive only in memory. He never trusted anyone once before or since.

"What, Dad?" Gage shifted with a shiver. When he talked about the war, he thought, he started drinking. He softened his voice. Any slightest hint of aggression would set off his old man.

Brian's eyes opened to slits, brow drawing down. His lip curled up on one side. "Opium, BOY," he growled, "it was about a cheap source of opium, probably sold to the Chinese. It ended up back in America." He laughed, face crumpling. Anyone who cared had found out later. You always discovered the truth later, when accountability became impossible.

"Are you okay?" he asked, wincing at the alcohol in his breath. Gage hated liquor. He would never drink. He had made the promise many times. Once his father had gotten drunk at the local bar called General's Shine, and it took a half-dozen men to subdue him. Mom had cried then too.

"I'm fine, Farley," he frowned, and the world wavered from his living room to that desert landscape. "They lied, and our friends died. Saving Democracy," he laughed, but his mouth worked like he tasted something bitter. It was what they told boys with star-spangled eyes.

"You're okay, Dad," Gage assured him, hoping he would calm down. He shifted from one foot to the other. "It'll all be okay," the boy added with a weak smile. He was a poor liar. He gripped his elbows to keep still. Fast movements could agitate his father.

Haas never acts like this, Gage thought. Their neighbor had served but never behaved like Brian. Why can't Dad be like him?

He laughed. "What would a little worm like you know?" he snapped, punching his leg. "Go get a pencil or something," Brian looked away. "I can't believe you're my son," he added in a distant whisper. The boy was practically a girl. For someone who barely spoke, he wrote a bunch of words down.

"Yeah Dad," he blushed, color high on pale cheeks. They never tanned like his father. His spindly arms were like pencils compared to his father's. Gage wished his father was smarter, or he was born dumber.

"Now Brian," Cheri chided, eyes fluttering and roaming the room. She picked at her lip. Her head nodded forward before it snapped back up. She frowned, unsure that anyone had spoken. "You're going to hurt him again," she mumbled.

He ignored her, punching his leg at his wife's words. "So smart, he is useless," Brian accused, gesturing at Gage.

Brian glanced at Cheri, thinking of Kayden. All of this was because of him. He ratted to those Grays. He thought and punched his leg. Kayden told the Queen of Lear

Mountain, and they're snooping. Chris and Sheila disappeared. They left me holding the bag. He cursed.

"Sorry," Gage apologized. He always apologized. He saw Moxie bound into the room and waved her back out. She blinked, shrugged, and whirled away with a graceful twirl.

Brian's eyes roamed over the living room, searching for the flash of a sniper scope. This time, I'll save the Corporal, he promised. The ghost of Farley asked him if he wanted a piece of chocolate or a cigarette. He held out a hand for him to choose.

"Why do you always try to give away your stuff?" He asked with a frown, smiling. Farley was a good man and a better soldier. He was the sort that could laugh anything off.

"I don't know," Gage peeked at his notebook.

In stories, he could escape. They never told you that you were weak or useless. If no one ignored you, then you weren't alone. Today was another day for a beating. The thoughts rushed through Gage's head.

Again, he searched for the flash of light on the glass, but the desert dissolved. The living room returned. Corporal Farley shook out a cigarette and offered it, but he faded. Brian scratched his arm as a red line traced over it. The razor-thin cut sealed. His eyes ached, and something swam across his vision. Purple light lingered. Brian blinked.

Chris and Sheila had complained about eye pain, he recalled. None remembered what Kayden had said when he had returned. "He should have minded his own business," Brian whispered. Kayden had found out that the women went to Sheila, the HR Manager, but she was in on the deal. I should've known he would cause trouble. The Van Lear family, who did business with Leitch Industrial Company, knew of Brian's side women. They had tried to speak to Chris and Sheila, the last he had heard. Tracy Chaney had discovered the little deal, but she seemed happy with the perks at work. She was also great at gathering information. Tracy was the first to come to him about Kayden.

"They'll send someone," Brian swore, standing. Despite all the drugs and alcohol, he barely felt a buzz. There was a hissing click, like a cicada crawled into his head, but it went quiet. He had thought it was a bug, but it was the wrong time of year for them.

"Who'll come?" Gage watched him stand. He looked for Moxie, but she was elsewhere with the shield he had reinforced for her. She had gotten interested in a comic book hero who used one to defend justice.

"The Van Lear family," Brian snapped, throwing up his hands. "Those filthy Confederate dogs, they'll send someone to TALK to me, probably Barnett."

If they see my lab, he cursed, they won't bother with questions. They'll kill me, one way or another.

"Because of those women," Gage frowned, blushing. Those women had said a lot of bad things about his father. Cheri had been crying since people started talking about his father and the ladies that worked under him. She had screamed at him at first. Brian had taken her to the bedroom, and she had shut up.

"BOY," he snapped, a hand rose. Brian saw the accusation in his eyes. They accused him like Kayden.

A wave of nausea washed over him, and Brian rubbed his eyes. He lowered his hand. The desert returned in a feverish haze, smothered in a bruised purple. Inside the infinite, a word whispered upon the scouring winds. This utterance filled the finite and crushed it with absolute entropy and chaos. Brian felt flesh unmoored from the world, though his mind stood in that desert. It solidified before him as the sky above parted to reveal a dead nebula of unfathomable dreams. This gibberish to the sane mind was a prophecy to the mad. It was both real and false.

"Give me your pencil," Brian ordered, staggering.

"I don't understand," Gage tried to steady his father.

He snatched at his son's back pocket and ripped the small notebook from the jeans. "BOY, are you good for anything?" Brian growled. He staggered. "I killed, and I killed," he whispered.

"Do you want me to help you get to bed, Dad?" He asked, eyes stung. Tears would only earn a beating, so he pushed them down.

Brian attempted to draw the alien symbol. The pencil savaged the paper. Blood ran from his left nostril, but he focused on the paper. It drew up into his head like a crimson worm. He cursed, kicking a bottle across the floor. It shattered against the wall. A child-proof lighter on the table next to the ruin wobbled.

"It's wrong!" He bellowed. He shook the notebook, ripped out the page, and threw it at Gage. "It... I," he mimed a cube with his hands, cursing in fury.

"A three-dimensional image," Gage ventured. He blinked. His father wasn't the sort of man who would know about such things. His father liked to work with his hands, on tools, on people.

"More than that." he shook his head, squeezing his eyes shut. Brian winced at a hissing click that buzzed in his ears. He tucked the picture into a pocket, though meant to toss it away. Gage blinked, but could only shake his head.

Brian opened the door but froze. A pile of river stones set on the porch. He looked about the yard, which had a thick layer of ice. Tracks cut through the grass, where boots had left obvious trails. He stomped outside, Gage behind, and kicked the smooth rocks off the deck. Brian reached inside the door and grabbed the shotgun. The late evening sun cast an orange light across the farm. He sniffed back something in his nose. He caught the scent of seared mushrooms. A bruised purple tinged the edges of his vision. He peered about the yard. They had left with the promise and threat issued. He threw a stone, bellowing a curse.

Gage peeked at the river rocks, hiding his relief. The men of the community were tired of his dad's behavior. Since the truth had come out, he had kept hope out of his heart. Things never seemed to get better.

"Do you want me to clean it up?" Gage walked over to the slick stones.

"No," he held out a hand and shook his head. "They can come teach me a lesson! Anybody who trespasses, they'll get a slug in the chest." Brian glared at his son, who shifted and shivered. "We need to get some stuff done."

"All right," he swallowed. Mom and Moe are at the house, at least.

Gage touched his scar, thinking of Moxie "Moe" Weber. He removed the hand as his father glanced back. Gage could still recall how the bottle shattered. I thought I was blind. The glass was everywhere. Better I'm hurt than Moe.

"Over to the back shed," Brian commanded, yet the vision of the desert overlaid the ice-smothered yard. Corporeal Farley's face sprung before him.

"He's coming!" Brian declared. Purple light burning from his eyes. It bounced and danced through the hoary grass.

"The Van Lear," he breathed, clamping a hand over his mouth, eyes wide. He watched him. Once, his father had a wicked spell. He went crazy, attacking things that weren't there.

"What?" Brian rubbed his eyes to dispel the bruised purple light.

"You said he's coming," Gage looked at his father, who swayed.

"I," he touched the pocket with the symbol. It stared into him like the eye of some malignant giant. "I don't know what you're talking about," he muttered, turning away with a shiver.

Gage frowned. Dad is afraid. The thought grew in his mind. Was the Van Lear family going to kill him? NO, Pa cheated, and they might send a man to beat him. He hated those Grays. Gage recalled how their family had fought for the Union. They had won; yet, the Confederates lived at the top of the mountain, looking down upon all.

"The Johnny Rebs," he ventured. "Those Slavers that live in Swannanoa, I mean." The one thing Gage was certain of was that the Van Lear family was evil to his father.

"Oh," he frowned. The world felt thin, as a cruel ruse upon an awful truth. "I've been meaning to talk to you, boy, about them," Brian turned a vicious grin on the Lear Mountain, which surveyed the entire county. They had a legacy, a war.

"Okay," Gage replied, bracing himself.

Brian moved to the shed but motioned for his son to stay outside. He dismantled the lab. "You know we fought for the Union," he said, "and we came here to uproot the Van Lear family. We failed, and people, ours included, died. Lance Van Lear, the Confederate General, executed his slaves. They're evil, through and through. We can't give up." He remembered the words of his father, tears welling up.

"Yeah Dad," he nodded, moving things around that his father set out.

"When I," he recalled the last time that they set stones on his porch, "made a mistake, I moved out here. I wanted out of town, a place to have a family, and to keep my business private." Brian looked up at Lear Mountain, eyes hardened. "Well, you might hear some things about money. I wanted you to know it wasn't for the cash like Chris or Sheila. I did what I did because someone has to stick it to them. They lord over this county like some royal family!" He cursed and threw an old brick. People called Van Lear's family matriarch the Queen.

Gage winced at the boom. "They are bad people," he ventured, nodding. He had learned his father expected certain replies. The Grays that remained loyal to the Van Lear family were odd, but he felt nothing about them. It was a bunch of silliness. It happened before any of them were born.

"I'm no saint," Brian admitted, wiping the sweat from his brow, "but I'm no Rebel scum." His lip curled. The Grays hung around the bar, griping about outsiders in Meridian. He liked to shut them up.

Once, a few years ago, Gage had asked why they tried to relive the war. Brian answered with his fists. He hadn't been able to walk for a couple of days. He learned tact regarding the Sons of the Confederacy. Thinking, he searched the ice-covered grass for the words vile enough. "Why are those," he held up his chin, "those Rebs bothering you?"

Brian stopped. The silence drew out, and Gage felt his guts churn. His father stepped out, closing the door. "We won the war. That is why they never let it go." The best feeling in the world was ripping down a Rebel flag when he was young. He had slashed Barnett's tires once.

"They're rich," Gage ventured, shaking his head. His father had voiced this opinion, but Gage didn't care about others' finances. It was important to his dad that the Van Lear family was rich.

"The one thing we have in common with them," Brian admitted through gritted teeth, "is we're both hold to the Blood. We hurt them, after the Civil War, and we should have hanged them! But we failed, and the only ones to survive were the La Voison women." He still had the journal from his ancestor, which had tears and stains on the pages. The Weber men handed it down from father to son. It was a reminder of the Van Lear family's evil. They had hung their slaves. The ex-Confederate General Lance would never let them go. "They wouldn't dare hurt those ladies, even then."

Gage blinked, "The Hill Witches." Most people never spoke of them openly. Some of the other kids whispered about them. They said strange things happened in Sabbath Branch.

"Hush that tongue, boy!" he snapped. "The youngest is gone, but I think she'll be back. There is too much blood of hers here. Miss La Voison, she dabbles in things no man should, but Rutger the Sheriff respects her." Brian paled, eyes darting to the forest. The women lived in this forest too.

"Sorry," he blushed. His eyes peeked at the tree line as if one of the La Voison women would appear.

"Don't tell me you're sorry," Brian shook his head, "I know you are." He withdrew the paper.

Gage searched about, desperate for any subject besides his failings. "What does that mean?" He pointed at the paper. "Words represent things, thoughts, and feelings," he tried to smile, "so, what is that supposed to represent?"

A tremor raced through his arm, and Brian squeezed his elbow. It felt as if it had a mind of its own. A wave of bruised purple flame passed through the darkness in his mind. It left a desert. The eldritch utterance formed as a whisper, like the death exhalation of the cosmos. It was a word given its true form. A finger jerked, and red lines, thin as razors, raced over the skin. Corporal Farley shook out a cigarette, and his face became a death's head. The eldritch flame burned in his lackluster gaze. Kayden had that spark in his pupils, his battered mind offered.

"I killed, and I killed," he whispered to that distant horizon. It tore open. He looked at the paper, which stared back. Even incomplete, it savaged the mind. His buddy grinned at him, world dream-like. He looked at the piece of chocolate and a cigarette.

"Do you want me to look at it?" Gage raised his hand, frowning. His father showed no interest in any form of writing. His lips curled. He caught his father's body odor. He thought of burned mushrooms.

Brian turned his head, bruised purple sparked deep in his eyes. "He's coming," he warned, gazing at the poor rendering on the paper, and then at his son. "Just like him," he accused. Cheri had dated Kayden before they got together. She had gotten pregnant soon after they started dating, swearing it was Brian's. He pointed at Gage. "You are too smart, and it'll get you into trouble one day." He told Kayden the same thing when he came snooping around.

Gage lowered his hand, "I know, Dad." He couldn't help his mind. He didn't ask to differ from his dad. He let out an inaudible sigh, bracing himself.

"Do you think anyone cares you're smart?" He demanded, and a nasty laugh jumped out. "No one cares," Brian sneered, shaking his head, "even if you're better than everyone else, it'll get you nowhere. They'll hate you more, truth be told." Brains never got Shy or Kayden anywhere. Alice was smart, but she was born into power.

"Yeah," he turned away. The teachers favored the kids from nicer homes, he already knew. They never disciplined the kids from Duncannon.

They punished me because of you, Gage thought, tears stinging. Everyone hates me.

"You need money or connections," he warned. The world spun around him. Brian bared his teeth in a snarl, punching his side to clear his mind. "Why can't you be like Moxie?"! Brian stepped closer, and a bloody musk hung over him. He raised his hand.

"I'm sorry," he looked down.

At least Moxie and Cheri were safe, Gage thought, and his hand rose to the scar. He thought of the broken glass. It had gotten all over him. He checked again that his sister wasn't around.

"Stop that," he barked, jerking his son's hand away from his face. "I would never hurt Moxie!" Brian turned with a curse. "GO, write your silly stories, or better yet, play with that stick." He walked back into the house. Brian listened to the memory of Farley. His buddy wondered if he wanted something. "He's coming, the Gallows King," Brian whispered in a lost tone of the damned and forgotten. He paused, casting a glance back at his son. Had his son just said something?

Gage frowned, closing his mouth before a question could pass his lips. He watched him stagger back into the house. "Gallows King," he repeated, thinking of the symbol Brian had drawn. A word inexpressible in two dimensions, and even three was insufficient. He would have never guessed his father capable of such thoughts. Gage had read that certain drugs could cause users to show mental illness-like symptoms. "Dad has been taking a lot of that junk," he muttered with a shiver.

"Who're you talking to, Sir Gage the Brave?" Moxie asked, kicking one of the creek stones. She watched it bounce with a giggle. It went a fair distance, she judged.

Gage jumped. "Moe, you gave me a fright." He laughed.

"Sorry, I was working on my ninja skills." She put her fingers together and bowed. "I have your sword, good knight," she presented a cured piece of pine, which was hand-carved. She marveled at her brother's handy work.

He looked at the house. "I better not." He would hate to get in trouble and scare his sister.

"I want to play," Moxie frowned, but slid the wooden sword into her belt. Daddy always came down on her brother. She didn't understand it. Gage was great. He was smart. Moxie paused, sniffing. She wondered if a cat had peed on something.

"We will, but," he looked back at the house. Gage considered his words. "Dad is behaving strangely."

Her pout turned to a smile. "What about a story?" She jittered, tutu flopping. "They're always so good!" Some of them scared her, which was good and bad. They gave her nightmares sometimes. Gage refused to tell scary stories after thinking he had seen her crying. Gage was sure she hadn't been crying. It was probably the dust or allergies.

"I read you the last one," Gage shivered. "I haven't even started on another since all of this happened." Her face fell. "Sorry, Moe," he smiled, "I'll try to start another one soon." He hated to disappoint her. His dad made sure he knew how much he was a disappointment.

"Will it have a samurai princess? Will she have a pet dragon and an unbreakable shield?"! Shaking, Moxie put her hands together. The story will be so good! Her big boots were an absurd pink. She crushed the ice-smothered grass.

"Sure," Gage laughed. "It'll be a challenge."

She threw her arms around him. "I love you." She wished their parents would say it to him. Moxie held him, but pulled back, eyes widened. "Did Daddy do something bad?" Everyone had been acting weird. Her mother had been crying and taking pills.

Gage's eyes moved from hers, for the hope there was unbearable. He wished he could lie. "Yeah, he did something bad, Moe," he patted her head. Moxie was smarter than his parents knew.

"It hurt Mommy, didn't it, Sir Gage?" her eyes filled. She held her chin up, defiant. Moxie willed the tears to go away. She was no damsel. She was a super samurai hero.

"Yes," he admitted. Gage blushed, feeling his eyes sting.

"Daddy didn't just cheat on Mommy," Moxie held her chin up, defiant but tears fell, "he cheated on us!" She didn't understand as many big words as Gage. She understands good guys. Good guys didn't hurt people because they were mean. They stood up to bad people even if they cried or if it's scary.

Gage studied her face as words failed. "Yes," he whined, wiping away a tear. "I'm sorry," he added, shifting. He wished he could lie to her. Everyone fibbed to his sister, thinking it was kinder. It always hurt her more.

"I won't forgive him!" she declared. Her brother tried to hug her. Moxie jerked away, disappearing around the house.

"I'm sorry, Moe," his heart hurt, and he wiped away another tear.

He knew Moxie would go to Castle Bubblegum, a severely pink playhouse until she stopped crying. At least there is no way Dad can hurt her there; he thought with a prayer.

Gage glanced at the house. Gallows King, that is what Dad said, he thought. The name hung in the mind. The hairs rose on his neck. He shivered. Something stirred in the darkness at the back of the mind, slithered and curled. It scrambled at his mind. He pushed the name away, and the image of tiny claws vanished.

"I need to check on Mom," he declared, peeking inside. He pinched his nose shut, looking for mushrooms and cats. Gage pulled away from the shadows. Brian allowed no one in the shed.

Back inside the house, the smell of spilled whiskey, beer, and drugs choked the air. Gage coughed. Heat seared the room, and Gage saw the thermostat turned up to its max. No one dared touch it after his dad had seen it turned back to seventy-five degrees. He had turned it back, cursing the desert's heat. Brain cussed from the master bedroom, and Cheri sobbed from the spare bedroom. The creak of ice-covered branches crept inside, and the roof groaned from the weight. The ice storm had given the world an ephemeral beauty like delicate glass. Gage crept past the bedroom. His father's absence eased the tension. A pile of dishes set in the sink, and he sighed. It was more work for him. Water dripped from the faucet, which dribbled down to other bowls and plates. He pulled his shirt away, sweat sticking it to his skin.

"I killed, and I killed," Brian whispered, and it haunted the hall. His distant words were a curse, prayer, and confession.

Gage swallowed and opened his mouth, but shut it. He hurried past the master bedroom, eyes adverted. The spare bedroom was further down the hall. He listened. Only silence came. Even the sobs had stopped, for which he thanked God. He knocked, though kept it low. Nothing. Gage tried again, but louder than before. Cheri was silent. He tried the handle, and it turned in his hand. After poking his head in. She didn't tell him to go away. His mother sat against the headboard, hands in her lap. Her head turned slightly, as if in thought.

"Mom," he mumbled, crossing his arms over his meager chest. "I just came to check on you. I was worried." Gage crept closer. No words came, which could soothe Brian's betrayal. "I just wanted to tell you something, and then I'll leave you alone." He considered turning on the lights. She had turned them off because of the brightness. "It isn't your fault, and we, me and Moe, love you. It'll be okay." Gage assured her, though blushed at the lie.

He listened to the silence, hoping. Cheri didn't raise her head. Gage braced for a rebuke, gentle though firm, but still an admonishment. His mother's chiding was soft, but it always hurt deeper than his father's. Gage had always expected a reprimand or disappointment. Her eyes were open to slits. He waited for the tongue-lashing, always his reward.

"Mom," he whispered, fearing to wake her. She looked sleepy. Gage came closer. The red of the alarm clock splashed across her face. Its crimson hue was gaudy and bloody. Although Cheri was present, something in her felt absent. "Mom," he repeated, stepping closer. He touched her leg. A bottle of pills in her hand tipped out. White dots turned sanguine in the light. Little beads of sweat rolled down his spine. They turned to ice despite the heat. The high tang of piss cut through the air. There was a wet patch on the covers. As the question rose, his mind slammed shut, crushing it. Gage shook his head. "Momma," he blubbered, and the world wavered through his tears.

"No," Gage grunted. The question crept closer, though he denied it. He wished his mind to empty. Gage shook her leg, which was cool. Cheri's head tipped forward, chin on chest. He held a finger up to her nose, but nothing. Her chest was still. As his head shook in negation, his body trembled. Beside the bed was a small mirror. He grabbed it, holding it under her nose. Her breath didn't fog the glass.

Gage's knees buckled. The question answered. He buried his face in her lap. Small bumps dug into his face, and he pulled back. The world wavered before him, stained crimson by the alarm clock's glow. He dashed away the tears, seeing what had stuck to his skin. Pills had spilled across her lap. All he knew was they made his mother slow and stupid, distant. Cheri felt better because she felt numb, he knew. Once, he had considered taking one, so his father's barbs would sting a little less. His eyes locked onto it. Something so small held all mother's love. No matter what he had tried, she had loved them more.

"Is this," he cried, holding the bottle up to Cheri. He shook it. Her face wavered through the veil of his tears.

She had grown cooler. Was this pill worth more than me, Moxie? Was it better to exist, or die, upon an island of stupefaction? To feel numb, the entire world a haze of disjointed sensations was better than her children. What could I have done? You can't abandon someone you were never there for, he thought, crying.

Gone, the word echoed in the heart as a stone tossed in a well. It was true. Goosebumps rose. A shiver coursed through him. The hope that one day she would love him as he loved her was gone. Abandoned to the megrims of his father, he knew. She had left a long time ago. Gage hoped Cheri would intervene on their behalf. Children at school, whose fathers hated Brian, would make their displeasure known, but she never came to his rescue. Once, when she had taken a bunch of pills, she had called him Kayden. He was adrift in her heart. Maybe her son had a place in her heart, but it was far behind the pills.

His head rested in her lap as the comforter muffled his cries. He trembled. Gage pulled Cheri's limp hand onto his shoulder. At least now she held him. He pretended she said that she loved him. In his stories, mothers loved their sons. He would write her into a story. She would be affectionate and listened to him. Maybe it would be good enough to make him feel it was true. In stories, he chased those pretty lies. He offered a prayer, though it seemed even the Heavens ignored lonely children. It ignored Gage so far. The dream of seeing pride in her eyes melted away. It was a foolish yearning. Any hope of their family being whole became dashed. Very few pillars held up the world of a child, and he already lost his father. No one is coming to help, he cried.

Tears always failed to capture genuine sorrow, for they would eventually run out. Gage's eyes ached, and he wiped at them. Bloody light still washed over them, indifferent to his pain as his parents did. Moxie, he thought, and his stomach twisted. I must protect her. How do I tell her?

"Dad," he muttered, and his lips pressed together. He was the parent. It wasn't always him who had to be the adult.

Brian's face rose in his mind. His slack, stupefied features held the directionless anger, which always fell on others. No matter his failure, it was someone else to blame. He did this to Mom, and us, Gage cursed. Momma found her freedom! She is gone.

I should tell Dad, Gage thought. Nothing could save him from his father's fists today. "He can go to the Devil," he muttered. He clamped his hands over his mouth. His wide eyes searched the room. Cheri offered no word of reproach, and his father was still in the master bedroom. Brian's prophetic apocalyptic proclamations seeped through the walls as though were unintelligible. They had all the charm of a mad prophet stewing in their excrement. Gage's body quaked, but he felt a bitter ease.

"I love you, Mom," he whispered. He waited, hoping she would say it back. Death changed a little.

He slipped out into the hall. It was empty. Moxie sprang about in another part of the house while swearing to uphold justice. She swore oaths to champion the weak. Below her words, the house creaked and popped under the weight of ice. The last of the day's sunlight splashed across the hall's end. The dark about it deepened.

"I killed and killed," Brain swore, and the words drifted over the still air. He had killed. They had told him who to hate. They had taught him to butcher.

Gage shivered, slowed, but drew closer to the door. He raised his arm and paused, but he let out a long sigh. His hand shook when he knocked, so knuckles scrapped the wood. The pathetic rasp was low. He rolled his eyes, but a shiver pranced up his spine. The next knock was still low. Nothing, blasphemous utterances mangled the silence in return. As he raised a hand to try again, a liquid laugh bubbled through the wood, a disjointed garble.

"Dad," he gasped. Gage swallowed. "Dad, I have something to tell you," He whispered, tears spilling.

"Farley," Brian growled, lost in the desert. Red lines raced over his skin, though no blood dripped from the razor-thin cuts. They sealed shut. The bruised purple light cast across the ceiling everywhere he looked. Something slithered across his vision. His eyes no longer ached, but they roamed of their own volition. Alien thoughts moved them. Brian gazed out on the desert in his memory. The sniper eluded him. "That shooter is out there," he observed in a slow, measured tone. "Just waiting," he warned. Farley muttered something about his brother.

"Dad," he stammered, "it is Mom." He sounds like he is gargling with a throat full of worms. Gage shook off the image.

Brian frowned, looking about the empty land. The dream was so real. Corporal Farley smiled, holding out the pack of cigarettes. He shook one out. Brian took it, and Farley lit it for him. Although his body was in the master bedroom, his mind was in the arid lands. "It was never for oil," he confessed, considering his hands. "I killed, and I killed," he looked at the Corporal, "and it was for opium." The words squeezed out of his throat, pinched off by his lips.

Gage stared at the door, lip jerking up in a twitch. It doesn't even sound like him. "I... Dad, it is Mom," he willed himself to be still. No matter what his dad did to him, he had to tell an adult. His father had to do something.

"It flooded the streets," Brian revealed in a hushed tone, swearing he heard someone talking. "They flooded our land with cheap opioids!" he laughed. Corporal Jessie Farley smiled and nodded, but he was long dead. Brian had tried to speak to his half-brother. The boy had gone crazy at the news of his brother. "We got Star Spangled Eyes, wanted vengeance," he wailed, "and they sent us to the meat grinder. Came back, and called us baby killers and fascists, but they broke us! I escaped! But I... didn't. They got me too. This is the Grays' fault! All of Lear County rotted down to the foundations, the roots, man, and those Grays still live at the top. They look down on us!" He looked at Jessie, whose face leered like a skull.

"Dad," he pleaded. His face paled. Gage listened to his father. He thought about the last time Brian talked about the war and drugs, touching his scar.

Brian's skin pulled from muscle. There was no pain, only relief. He frowned, but only the desert remained. A flash of the sun on a lens glittered in the distance. It was the sniper. He moved, yet like all nightmares, it was always too slow. The right side of Farley's head exploded. It vaporized in a fantastic spray of bone, brains, and hair. Like a bloated, long-dead animal on a road filled with gases, it blew apart. Inside the rotted skull were nasty little things that squirmed. They glowed with an eldritch, bruised purple light. Blood splattered across Brian's face, though it was too thick and congealed. The Corporal fell back, yet his body stopped inches above the hot earth. Like a puppet on strings, Farley stood back up. Purple light blazed out of his one good eye as he clamped a companionable hand on Brian's shoulder. He laughed. The strange maggots fell to the earth with human screams.

"The Gallows King comes," Brian muttered, "the Riotous of Violet."

Gage recoiled. This low utterance from Brian profaned the air. Goosebumps broke over cold skin, and gray brushed across his vision. Gage's chest tightened as the world wavered. He pinched his arm and felt the world grow solid.

"I," he pleaded, looked for Moxie, but she was still in her playhouse. Please, this one time, let someone help me, Gage thought.

Skin held Brian above the bed, and his veins hooked into the veiling. His muscles crept over the bed. Little eyes stared out in hate from the man's flesh on the mattress. Mouths opened in the meat to whisper mad blasphemies. His eyes melted, and the bruised purple flame flowed out in a tendril of eldritch light. Inside the glow was the word, which Brian had tried to recreate. The paper disintegrated into a plum-purple ash.

Flames and flesh crept into the floorboards. It melded with the house. It grew and expanded. Veins pulled a loose board open. It squeezed beneath the house. It groaned as

Brian's body clung to it. Through the walls and spaces, the cosmic utterance crawled into a baptism of discolored purple brilliance. Gage peeked about the hall as the house shifted and groaned. The man became the house, flesh melded with timbers. Brian's meat bit of metal, and the alien glow spread into every corner. The abode awakened.

Blood and earth were in the heart of all the countryfolk of Meridian. They sacrificed their body, breaking themselves. It ended with burial. Some worked the fields, which fed them. Others defended it. They gave all, so some may enjoy peace and prosperity. Brian had served. All the Weber men had joined the military. It was a tradition that went back to the American Revolution. Brian had worked the family farm after serving. One day it would pass on to the next in line. Brian had doubts about his son, so decided it passed on to Moxie. She had more grit in his estimation.

Nothing remained of Brian's mind except a confession. It infused his body as it possessed the house. "I killed, and I killed," he moaned in a rasp. Lost in the buzz that vibrated through the timbers, muffling it. It rose from every vent and fell from each ceiling as putrid tears. His hate-filled heart was in each repetition of the words. Contempt burned in the whispers, which lingered in the still air.

The alien abhorrence remained with its condemnation. Like a viral cancer, it had eaten the man. It was on a thousand cursed lips. It repeated the words I killed, and I killed in stupid fervor. Singing, it hummed in every piece of lumber and nail. This confession prayed to the ugly intelligence. Its desires were also hideous. This flesh, once Brian, hated the sanity of this world, its order. Slobbering idiot malevolence oozed from every repetition of the phrase. It desired entropy. It lusted for pain. These entreaties were oaths and sworn to the intelligence of riotous flame.

Gage's eyes moved over the walls. His head tilted, but the low words were indecipherable. "Dad is no help," he moaned. He wiped away another tear. The doorknob would not turn, but he tried only once.

"What do I do?" He prayed, glancing up, but no one answered. Gage hadn't expected an answer, but wished for one.

I can't tell Moxie. He listened, hearing the front door open and then close. She bopped through the living room. Gage sighed, which turned into a sob. Brian had gotten himself into a stupor, needing time to sober up. He was in charge again.

Gage trudged into the living room where she studied the shield he had made her. On its inside, Moxie had placed stickers of unicorns and rainbow cats. He considered the truth which lay in the spare bedroom. He blushed. The image of his sister's heart-wracked wails stung his heart. Gage wrung his hands, bopping from foot to foot. He sat on the couch. His head ached, eyes felt full of grit and puffy. The light tang of his mother's urine clung to him.

"Sir Gage the Brave," Moxie proclaimed, hopping over to his brother. Her eyes had a reddish tinge. "My shield has been... uh, reinforced," she showed him the stickers. "Nothing can withstand the power of kittens." She nodded at this self-evident truth.

His lips twitched. Her sincerity was refreshing with the adults. Teachers and parents or any adult seemed to have forgotten it. He smiled. Solemnity exposed part of the heart, leaving one vulnerable.

"I should've thought of that, Moe," he nodded, attempting to be grave.

"You're the writer!" Moxie observed. She cocked her hip to one side, rolling her eyes with a giggle.

The move was Cheri's when she was happy. He had almost forgotten it. Gage felt a slash across his heart. "I'll do better," he smiled, though his eyes stung.

Moxie smiled, studying him, "Pain stays with you a long time, Bub." Her brother looked away. "You're great," she added, mouth drawn up on one side as eyes searched the nicotine-stained ceiling. "I love your stories," her head bobbed. She bounced with a grin.

"Thanks, Moe," he felt the weight lift, which always felt ready to crush him.

She looked at the carved stick in her belt. "Are you sure you don't have a story?" Moxie smiled. "It can be a short one," she hastened to add.

"Yeah," he glanced at the wall. His mother sat with all she cared about clutched in one hand. Had she thought of her daughter?

"Sucks," she mouthed with a pout, but the smile arose fast as it had failed. "Soon. Will you write one soon?" Moxie knew he always had one in his head.

"Yes, Moe," he wiped his eyes. "I'm not trying to be mean, but I feel bad. Mom and Dad want to be left alone too." Gage considered locking the door to the spare bedroom so she wouldn't find Cheri.

"All right," she agreed with a shrug. Moxie withdrew the hand-carved sword in a fluid motion. She bounded across the floor, ready to defend justice. It was an unending endeavor, she judged.

Gage sat back against the couch, head falling back. In stories, he could escape, but it would be a while before he could write. He felt a wall around it in his mind. Without Cheri, he and Moxie would carry her share of abuse. Brian treated his daughter better, but that was a low bar.

"Hello," she warned, "my name is Moxie Weber. You stepped on my kitten; prepare to cry." She held the sword up to pretend ninjas. The stealthy warriors were no match for her.

He laughed, shook his head, "Get them, Moe." He had tried to get her to write, but Moxie's energy kept her moving.

She blocked, parried, thrust, and slashed. After a smooth roll, Moxie leaped forward with a broad stroke. She circled. A bloody stench crawled up from the vent with a flicker of purple. "Yuck," she turned, looking about the kitchen. The room connected to the living room, though no wall separated them. She raised the wooden sword. Gage had read a book, which detailed swordplay, and had taught her. She had asked for more of the books. "Your stink has no power here," Moxie declared. "You shall bathe!"

She held up the shield to bash the pretend ninja. She imagined them everywhere. "The Shogun shall never have control of the Cherry Blossoms. Their beauty belongs to the people." Moxie held up the shield. "Feel the power of KITTENS!"

Imaginary bad guys assailed her, though she was resolute. Again, a puff wafted up from the vent, cast upon a whisper. "No," she coughed, "you've used the fart of death!" She pitched forward. Moxie coughed, flopping on the kitchen floor.

A tremor ran through the wood. She stilled, brow furrowing. Whispers echoed through the vents, just below intelligibility. Their confession repeated, and Moxie listened. The stink of rotted mushrooms pushed through the floor. She crept towards the source, listening. It came from different places. A chuff and snort came from the corner, where her mother kept a small trashcan. She adjusted the grip on her wooden sword. The plastic trash receptacle shifted, and a low whisper oozed. She crept closer, holding up the shield. She peeked over it. Gage's sword shook in her hand.

"The Shogun has sent assassins," she breathed.

The trashcan shifted, and a low squeal squeezed out of the shadow. Moxie pushed it with the hand-carved stick. Eyes rolled up to her, too human in their terrified hate. Bruised purple pinpricks gleamed deep inside them. Molten flesh writhed as if boneless. Its pushed-back snout drew in the air as it dripped a strange ichor. The curse remained on the flabby lips. It spit a venomous curse, though it was incomprehensible. Tusks framed the ruined mouth, which reminded her of Brian. It hissed. There was clicking inside that squealed like cicadas boiling alive.

She recoiled, holding up the shield. It retreated into the darkness. Moxie peeked at her brother in the living room, but his eyes were closed. Gage warned her to never touch strange animals, especially if they were sick. She slid the wooden sword back into her belt.

Gage jerked. A gentle finger prodded his leg. "Yes, Moe," he mumbled, rubbing his temple, "is everything okay?"

"I think there's a tusk hog in the house," she pointed to the kitchen. "You told me not to play with anymore wild animals... after the polecat," she reminded him with a pout. Moxie's face fell with the memory of Stink Kitty. He was a pretty skunk but didn't warm up to her family.

"You can't have a skunk as a pet," Gage recalled her last forest friend. He rubbed his eyes. The country vernacular bounced in his mind. He frowned. "Did you mean a boar?" His eyes widened.

"Yeah," she placed fingers on both sides of her lips, sticking out her lower teeth. Moxie found that visual aids hurried things along.

"Where is it?" he stood up, listening, but the master bedroom was silent. All he needed was another incident like the Stink Kitty.

Moxie led the way, sword and shield at the ready. Her big boots clomped with each step. Gage followed. He shivered. She pointed at the dark corner. He looked, seeing nothing. The trash moved.

"See Moe," he muttered. He took a flashlight from a drawer. The light caught nothing in its beam.

Moxie peered down with a scowl. "It must have crawled down into the vent," she guessed, shrugging.

"Well," Gage said, softening his tone. He switched off the light. "It is gone, now," he assured her. When his sister's imagination was active, she told some wild tales.

Gage put the flashlight back in the drawer. The bright memories of his mother played in his mind. Every smile came with a slash of pain. Misery would fill the days ahead, but most people brought light into others' lives. Maybe she finally escaped what hurt her, he hoped. I wished I could've loved her enough, so she'd wanted to stay. The thought came with more tears.

Moxie looked about the kitchen, brow drew down. The clang of metal and the clack of dishes were sharp. She glanced back at her brother, who went back to the couch. Again, the stench clawed at the air. Its rancid stink tore at the sinuses. Little claws clicked on the floor. She listened, creeping closer to it. They kept dishes under the sink. They clattered, and some broke. Gage sat up, frowning. His eyes flew about the room. Beneath the sink, one of the cabinet doors popped open an inch.

Moxie jerked, "I'm not scared," she swore. Her brow drew down with a pout. She didn't want to hurt it, but it couldn't stay in the house.

The sink cabinet door jittered, and she used the tip of the wooden sword to pry it open. The creature burst out, hairless except for little tufts. Its molten skin was pinkish, scarred, and shifted under the surface. Moxie's eyes devoured it, recoiling. Its form defied coherence. Her eye couldn't fix its form in her mind. Too human eyes rolled independently of the other. Just like a tusk hog, she thought, mind reeling. She recalled her father's eyes. It squealed. It was a shrill whistle filled with insectile clicks. Gage shot up, eyes wide, and she pointed at the foul little creature.

He leaped up from the couch, scowling deep. Moxie stepped back as it scrabbled away. Gage rushed into the kitchen. His wide eyes swept back and forth.

"What is that?" He demanded. Gage blinked.

"This is a different one," she realized, holding up the wooden sword.

Gage thought of Brian, shaking his head. He listened, creeping closer to the clicking of nails on the floor. It popped out. He recoiled. The molten skin was pinkish like a badly burned pig. A raccoon, he mused, though frowned, a mangy one that has been severely scarred. He drew closer to the creature, but it slunk away.

"Is it a Hunky Punk?" Moxie shifted, eyes widening. Her brother said monsters were always figments or misunderstandings. "Monsters are afraid of fire," she added, hoping it helped.

"Don't be scared," he whispered to her, holding up a hand.

"I'm not scared," she countered. Her brow drew down, hand resting on the wooden sword.

They followed the sound of its claws and labored breath. It muttered in idiot tones. "I have to get it out of the house," Gage moaned. He took the wooden sword from his sister, who curtseyed. He smiled, feeling his stomach ache. Asking her to move, Moxie slid over at his request, and she held up the shield. She was ready to defend him. Gage leaped out with the stick. He flinched at the creature before him.

"MY GOD," he shouted.

The canine-like creature screamed, voice high as a woman during impalement. Between the four legs like a dog, another two sprouted from its ribs. Too human eyes rolled at him, and he thought of Brian. A bruised purple flame glimmered deep in its eyes. Gage's mouth opened, but only a squeak escaped.

"I killed, and I killed," it swore in the rasp of his father.

"Gage," Moxie pleaded. Her head lowered, still peeking over her shield.

He held up the sword, though it shook in his hands. It rushed through the kitchen. Gage blinked, glancing at his sister. He forced his feet to move. The creature's hateful screech peeled out of its rubbery lips. He followed with Moxie behind him. It squeezed into the vent, where she had seen the other retreat.

"I better tell Dad," He sighed, swallowing the bile in his throat. Gage paled.

"Why was it talking?" she begged. "What is wrong with it?"! Moxie had never seen such an animal. It stunk too.

He shook his head, walking through the house to the master bedroom. Better to just act, he thought. Gage knocked, but it was silent. He tried again, but only the pounding of his heart greeted them. Moxie bopped about behind him. She whirled back, holding up the shield, but saw nothing. Before he could try again, she pounded on the door. Both stared at it.

"I'm going to wake Mom up," she declared. Moxie was tired of her crying. She never cried as much as her mother, and she was a kid. She stomped down the hall as the house popped and groaned.

"Wait," he dashed after her and touched her shoulder.

Moxie turned back. "What is it, Sir Gage?" She held her chin up and back straight.

His head fell, face pale except color high on his cheek. "You can't wake her," Gage admitted, wiping away a tear. He opened his mouth to say more. He wheezed out a sob.

"What do you," she studied him. He had the same look on his face when her cat died. Her brother hid things from her that would hurt her. Moxie's eyes widened, "Is Mom like Tipsy?"! The words came out in rushed blubber. Tears streamed down her face. She danced from foot to foot, shaking the shield.

"I," he looked at the question in her eyes, but failed to say a comforting lie. "She is gone," Gage breathed low.

Moxie's eyes filled. Her lip quivered, but she held up her chin. "It was that junk, wasn't it?"! she demanded. She saw her mother take pills.

"Yes," he muttered, shifting. He knew his sister was more perceptive than the adults gave her credit for.

"She loved us less than that garbage," Moxie accused, tone flat. Her body quivered. She kept her chin high in defiance.

Gage felt the tears spill. Their warmth left a cold caress. "I don't know," he admitted, though he had suspected it. "I'm sorry," he offered, for nothing else came to mind.

He blushed. Dad is right; I am useless, Gage felt with a curse.

"What do we do?" she asked. Moxie thought he was more of an adult than an adult.

"Dad had cut the phone cords." his eyes fell to the floor. Men called. The truth was no longer an open secret. None would act on rumors. None would tell the truth until Brian had those women fired. Their mother had answered without thinking, and she had screamed. Cheri had cried. Their father had given her more pills.

"Maybe we should leave," she ventured, chin still high in defiance of her tears.

"The closest farm is Haas's place," his head bobbed. Brian had met the other man at his property line with a shotgun once. Haas saw the gun, but his eyes had gone hard and cold.

"Why did it sound like Dad?" Moxie shivered. The words played again, and she was ready to use the potty.

"I think we just heard him in the other room," he mumbled, eyes sliding away from her. The question of why or how always destroyed his resolve. He would get bound up in them.

"We should leave," she repeated. The answer to her question was too great and terrible. "We can open the lock to the master bedroom," Moxie added.

Gage nodded, "We should try to rouse Dad." His face fell. This was too much for them. Without their mother, he feared how his father would react.

They moved down the hall as the house shivered and moaned. The whispers were deep and blasphemous. They coiled about the air, slithering into the ear. Gage grabbed a small screwdriver, which could open the door lock. It slid in and the door popped open. Both stared at the bed and then at the ceiling. Something had wrecked the vent in the room's corner. Shredded clothes rested atop the bed, which was also torn to pieces. Moxie's sobs were low, but Gage frowned at the bedding. They blinked at the carnage.

"No blood," he observed, and she stopped crying.

"What happened?" Moxie held her chin high, eyes reddening. She would not be afraid. She swore she would not cry.

"I don't know," he frowned. "Dad had to have torn up his clothes because there is no blood."

She scowled, lips pouted, "Did he crawl into the vent too?" Adults could do funny things.

"I don't know," he studied the torn-up floor, where dark utterances bloomed. "He probably did some of that junk." he looked at the deep shadows. "It is nighttime, and we need help."

Moxie nodded and followed him with her shield raised. Silent tears fell from them both. Meridian was a savage place for abandoned children. Bruised purple light traced their steps as low curses followed. The reek of rotted mushrooms stalked them. It festered at the back of their throats.

Gage turned the knob, which moved with ease. The door held firm. He frowned, pulling with both hands. It finally gave with a rip-like adhesive being torn. Both frowned. A thin membrane stretched over the frame. Its blood vessels shimmered with bruised purple light.

"Gage," Moxie pleaded, voice trembling. She held up the shield.

Numb, he lifted the wooden sword. It pressed against the membrane, and the house hissed in rapid clicks. Bruised purple light shimmered over the thin layer of flesh, which made his head feel disconnected. Teeth, jagged and yellow, formed around the carved stick. Like a man who dips, Gage's mind whimpered. The hateful little mouth bit at the practice weapon's tip. Gage screamed. His sister, too proud to yowl, let out a long whistle. Both rushed away, minds numb.

"I killed, and I killed," it called to them, threat and confession. The whisper haunted the air with its alien rasp. A musky, decayed air vomited from its lips.

They flew to the back door. He led her by the hand. They cried as the house shifted. A dead laugh crawled up from below. Words uttered by the wall of skin rained from a thousand mouths. Alien threats and sacrileges showered them. Another membrane stretched over the door frame. Gage pulled her away. He tried to think of every exit.

Riotous, vile flesh covered every means of escape. They mocked and jeered. Each proclaimed the same mantra, a prayer to a hidden god. In the walls, ceiling, and floor, the bruised purple light slithered just below the surface. Blood crept out of the cracks. Its gentle stink was a kiss. Although the heating and cooling unit had ceased, a balmy heat filled the rooms. Clicks vibrated through the walls. Inside of timbers, the hiss resounded. Sweat broke over their skin, cold as pins of ice. The angles of the room bent before the eye. It remained unchanged after a blink. Like a fun-house, Gage's mind groaned. Everything felt tilted or flipped. Their vision reeled from the banality, turned insane. Space stretched, then snapped back.

"It is all locked," Gage groaned. His eyes rolled, vomit rising at the back of his throat.

"What do we do?" she held up the shield, but a tremor ran through her legs.

A croak popped up behind them, garbled like a man choking to death on a spit. Both turned to the small creature.

It hopped on legs like clawed thumbs. Eyes covered the top of the frog-like abomination, which rolled in every direction. Its wide mouth encircled nearly its entire body. Cruel lips misshapen.

"I killed, and I killed," the creature swore in the voice of their father. With a small hop, it came closer to them with another of their father's curses.

"I told you that Hunky Punks were real!" Moxie groaned. No one listened!

Gage kicked. It flew across the room, striking the wall with a pop. Eyes splattered across it. They crept down. Its legs kicked. Ichor held a shimmer, purple and eldritch. A hissing cut up from beneath, and the buzz of clicks vibrated through the house. Moxie kicked one of its legs away, which still moved. Every part held a malignant life.

Moxie's lips curled. A low laugh squeaked out beside her, delight cruel as an imp. Like a corrupted fruit, there hung an insignificant creature of molted flesh. Only an idiot god of disgusting mirth could produce such a failure. It shared its creator's vile glee. Body like a pudgy baby, its warped face leered with bulging eyes. Crooked teeth in a sideways mouth gleamed at her with alien desires. Three fingers gripped the wall with eyes the same color as the misshapen frog. They were the color of their father's.

Despite its frail body, the vile homunculus leaped through the air. It flew at her, mouth wide in devilish delight. Moxie had practiced with the shield, and her brother had mixed training with play. Although all her mind could see were the horrid teeth, she swung the reinforced toy. The small man splatted against a defensive blow. It slammed into the wall. Once, she had stomped on a water balloon. Moxie recalled it had splattered like a rotted grape. The memory made her guts turn.

Moxie's mouth turned down. Her tongue poked out. "Yucky," she squeaked. She stepped back from the little man, who still squirmed. Arcs of bruised purple light flickered over the ruin of flesh. Life refused to leave it.

Gage stepped over, and the other creatures crept out to glare at them. They laughed. Some repeated their father's confession and curse. Others crept closer with dark grins of blacker thoughts. More congregated before them, and they stepped back from the gathering horde. He held up the wooden sword. Moxie stepped up beside him. More of the abortions of a disturbed mind trudged out to laugh. The house trembled under the mirth.

He pulled Moxie, who braced herself to block oncoming attacks. They ran through the house. The amalgamations of flesh followed. With laughs and curses, little goblins of meat cavorted behind, and the house shifted. Ugly little teeth gleamed. Rasps oozed from limp mouths, full of vulgarity. Bruised purple light squeezed through the walls as it moved about the timbers.

As they ran, the menagerie of flesh homunculi frolicked in mad glee. Gage pulled his sister along. The house had a loop with the bathrooms at the center. Around and around, they ran with the horde of misshapen homunculi in pursuit. It felt longer and appeared to stretch. Hallways lengthened, as the house dreamed. It consumed Brain's mind, yet pieces clung on like scum about a drain. Every angle bent before the eye. Whispers dug into the ear, burrowed in the mind. Inside the nightmare of a dead man, the world between conscious and unconscious blurred to nothing. Each lap took them a step farther from the world. They grew closer to another dimension.

A bruised purple light blazed down upon them. It crawled over the flesh. Gage kicked a rock, which bounced and jumped across stones. Sand choked the earth. Gage pulled his sister. The force of Brian's nightmare split the house. Outside, the dimensions of the home remained the same. Inside, it expanded. Dreams had no measurable restraints, guided only by the dreamer. Dead brains still clung to pseudo-life, fed by arcs of purple. Part of their father never left the desert. It refused to let go of his half-death. Dead friends and enemies lay strewn about, bodies blown to bits. All wore the horror of their last moments. The rictus was half surprised and half horrified. Among a pile of bones, a throne made of a skeleton, sat Corporal Farley. His empty stare swept over the ruin of life, and Gage's family home. Inside his eyes, flames swirled from alien stars out of insane dimensions. It was another form of life.

"Where are we?"! Moxie wailed. She felt like she had run into a nightmare.

"I don't know," he barked, eyes searching for an escape. A bottle of whiskey was in a pile of bones, next to a table. Gage recognized it from the living room.

Doors to other rooms in the house blew from their hinges and lay half-buried, and tilted. Gage stared at the one which led to the spare bedroom. Like a bad dream, he thought. This is like being inside Dad's rambling. He pinched himself, but the world only grew. They fell deeper into Brian's nightmare. They were adrift in its broken fragments of past and present.

The knob to the spare bedroom jiggled. Both children turned. Both hoped their father would emerge, for once, to save them. Gage felt his guts twist. Moxie swore she would forgive all if only delivered from this madness. The door opened slowly but in little jerks. The darkness beyond the frame was the world of cruel fathers and broken mothers. Inside of shadows bathed in the crimson of the alarm clock, a figure stood. Their head lolled, but something tugged it straight. It tilted to the other side. A single tentative step was unsteady and unnatural, and the body appeared to float. Tendrils rose from the silhouette, which tugged them into motion.

Gage and Moxie stepped back. Cheri stalked out of the room's darkness. Some strange power operated her like a marionette. Grotesque flesh covered her. It moved her corpse. A web of eyes covered her face from the nose up, except for one sleepy eye. They stared in different directions. Shreds of skin hung from limp shoulders, covered in mouths. They lifted their voices in prayer to a far god. Draped over half her chest was the face of Brian, twisted in hate, and filled with an insane rage. Ribbons of flesh moved her along in a bouncy approximation of life. She shambled towards them.

Gage's eyes filled with tears. He felt his body go numb, but the puppet of ruination was all he could see. Moxie wailed, though it seemed to come from a world over. Cheri trundled closer. Her body shifted. Whispers rose from the lips draped about her. From the gazes of the veil of eyes came a bruised purple flame. Into his mind, its light pried gentle as a sigh, undeniable as death.

"I killed, and I killed," they assured him.

"Hey," Moxie squeaked, pulling him. Tears blurred the world. Her brother stared into the blaze that burned in the eyes that adorn Cheri's body. She turned to the light, but her head hurt. Moxie jumped onto her brother. She held up the shield to cover Gage's face. Tears streamed down her face.

"What?" he whispered and stared at the stickers of kittens. Gage blinked.

"RUN," she screamed.

He stumbled away as the corpse of Cheri followed. Gage blinked, but a word bathed in bruised purple hung in his mind. Three dimensions failed to capture its complexity. Beyond the sane constraints of reality, the single utterance tore at all within its reach. Alive in the terrorized horror of Brian's nightmare, it sought to consume them. The human form would be a riot unrestrained by the banality of normality. Meat and bone torn asunder, reforming in the image of hateful insanity. Moxie pulled him away as his mind reeled.

They ran. She guided him through the decaying nightmare. Parts of the house sagged like an over-inflated balloon that had lost all the air. The bruised purple light diminished, though it strove to stay aflame. It writhed inside the corpse of Brian, hate in full bloom. No matter its unsteady step, it gained on them, alien curses upon lifeless lips. Tendrils of skin lifted from Cheri's arms to grab Gage, but he slipped out of her grasp.

He looked back at his mother, as his father's voice cursed him in idiot repetition. Cheri's one exposed eye was heavy-lidded and appeared as one upon the edge of sleep. Perhaps she was in her eternal nightmare, one deeper than this, a dark voice mused. Death had taken her, but that drowsy eye promised one last loveless embrace. She would drag him to the deepest depths, no doubt, as Brian cursed. Heaven may ignore abandoned children, but Hell loved them. The darkness in her gaze promised. Let me hold you, her slack face implored, so you may see where I've gone. There is darkness here, and it is far from empty, this voice added.

Gage felt part of him wished to gaze into the eldritch flame, so all became devastated in the infinite. In the boundless, there was no self. If there was no self, there was no betrayal, indifference, or heartless shepherds.

"Just fall inside the numbing light, and all will be nothing," the flames implored.

"GAGE," Moxie howled through tears. She stumbled. Her legs were full of knots.

He turned, mind and body disconnected. The front door was before them, still ajar. A bottle of whiskey set in the sand propped up by bones, and a lighter set atop the table. Monsters are afraid of fire. Moxie had said that, and his mind gnawed on it. She snatched up the bottle and doused the membrane with the liquor. Little mouths formed to curse them. She snatched up the lighter, but little thumbs could barely strike it. Brian had bought child-proof ones after she had tried to use a flame to ward off Hunky Punks.

She pressed it into his palm. "Please," she cried in his dazed face.

The nightmare faltered. Corpses of friends and foes rose. Corporeal Farley, still upon his throne, watched them with dispassion. He had ruled Brian's heart and dreams. Above, the endless sky split. A hole opened to a reality unchained by all notions of sanity. Something drew closer.

"Monsters are afraid of fire," Gage bellowed.

He pressed the button and pulled the trigger. A flame danced out of the lighter. Gage stuck it to the membrane. Fire devoured it. Moxie darted through as the skin retreated in agony. She grabbed his hand, and both stumbled onto the porch. Brian's voice cursed them, though a cat-like hiss bathed in insect clicks thrummed through it. The cacophony was like a horde of cicadas tossed into a furnace. Her hand slipped when they stepped into the yard. Moxie ran, terror kept eyes from the house.

Gage stopped. The haze of his mind covered thoughts like a heavy fog. Gage turned back, perhaps to see his mother still under the control of his father's malignant corpse. She still held her arms out for an embrace. Above her, the sky tore open in Brian's nightmare. Closer, something came, enticed by the promise of flesh to defile. Bruised purple light blazed behind it, like some darksome saint or a god of consuming flame. Its brilliance shined upon him, driving away the entire world. This cloaked figure's form was a lie, told by the mind. All within its darkness writhed and cursed. All within its power were riotous and hateful. Truth beyond the finite mind crashed into Gage.

Moxie stumbled onto the road. She bent over, sucking in the air. The world grew distant around her. She coughed. Only she stood by the road. "SIR GAGE," she cried and looked around.

The headlights of the tow truck struck her, and she turned. Moxie held up the shield. It came to a halt. Haas peered over the wheel before stepping out. His eyes flew around, searching for her parents. He left it running to keep the heater going. He rushed over.

"Honey, where are your parents?" he asked, knowing Cheri and Brian were addicts. Haas tried to soften his voice.

"I want my brother!" she commanded. Her chin high. "He is brave, and he protects me! He doesn't know that I know, but I know!" Tears streamed down her face, and her chest hitched as she tried to hold back.

Haas kneeled. He was afraid his size would scare her. "Don't be afraid, sugar," he smiled.

"I'm not SCARED!" she wailed. Moxie stomped her foot.

"Sorry," he held up his hands, "I meant I'm scared." Haas wished the Misses were here. She was better with little ones.

"Oh," Moxie rubbed her eyes, and the tears slowed. "It's okay. I'll protect you."

Haas smiled, "Thank you, I appreciate it, Little Miss." He sat down to further reduce his height. "You're looking for your brother?" He asked softly, as he could manage. A low rumble was all he could manage.

"Yeah," she nodded.

"Do you know where he may be?" He took off his coat and put it around her. It swallowed up Moxie.

"I saw him at the house," she recalled, glancing back. "I left him because I didn't want to look back!" Moxie confessed with fresh tears.

Haas held up his hands. "It is okay. I'll fetch him." He stood, "I want you to get in the truck, where it is warm."

"I have to pee," she sniffed, and he ignored the wet patch on her pants. She shook.

"I'll hurry," Haas promised. If Brian and Cheri wouldn't straighten out, he would make them. Parenthood blessed them. This was how they treated their blood.

He drove the tow truck to the house. His knuckles popped on the steering wheel. The headlights cut over the smoking timbers. Haas frowned. It had collapsed. Like everything had pulled to the center as if it had imploded; he guessed. He stepped out, and Moxie stood to look out the windshield. Gage lay on the ground. Haas rushed to him. Checking for a pulse, he let out a sigh. He carried the boy back. Moxie took off the jacket and put it around her brother.

"Where are your parents?" he asked, looking at Moxie.

"They're gone," she whispered. Moxie hugged her brother. She hid her face, crying.

"I'll take you to the Misses," Haas promised with a nod. "She'll know what to do." He thought of the Van Lear Family atop the mountain. They were coming for the Weber family. Brian and Cheri probably ran, so they wouldn't have to answer for anything that happened at the factory. He was unsurprised Brian had left the two little ones. He hated getting into others' business, but he had left a stone on their porch.

There was nowhere they could go to escape, he thought. Alice will find them.

"Sir Gage is a writer," she revealed, wiping away tears.

"Is that so?" he smiled. "That is great! I could never write a story," Haas admitted. He peeked at her. "Sir Gage must be very talented, and to be knighted at his age is rare."

A long memory cursed her brother. She wondered how it bore it. Gage's mind drifted, drawing closer to his body as they moved along the icy road. The cloaked figure descended in a halo of purple flame. Moxie would remember nothing. Alien intelligence ate away at the mind until it was gone. He would have nightmares for a year. Sometimes, he would think of a hooded figure, failing to remember. The worst was the sunset, when it turned a vibrant, bruised purple. A broken memory would bite into his mind. Gage's heart would race. He would hide from the dying light's brilliance. Something, a word, failed to form in his mind. It was too much to recall or imagine.

Moxie pulled the coat tighter around her brother, who seemed to be in the grip of a nightmare. She patted him. She would quickly forget in the coming days. Bad dreams came that night but were gone afterward. Haas and his wife fell in love with her energy and quirkiness. Her brother's talent astounded them, too. With nowhere else for the children to go, they stayed with them until they adopted them. This night was gone from Moxie, never to return.

Rebel Heart

"The South Shall Rise Again" blazed in blueberry and cherry-red neon against a rebel flag. Blaze of neon warred against the dark. Spit and beer smeared the sign's bulletproof glass, old scars of gunfire invisible at night. Every son of the Union entered after spitting on the gaudy standard. The door opened and closed to allow the smell of fresh beer and food. It was no mere slaughterhouse with sawdust on the floor. The General's Shine was one of the best restaurants in Lear County. Music of the hills and lowlands passed beyond the walls, and the dark heart of the rebel bled through every cord. It was a gloomy lullaby to the drug-ravaged town, a dirge for the damned.

Unlike the rest of the town's buildings, it was the only one in fine condition. Since Prohibition, the General's Shine had sold spirits, though their famous liquor recipe was much older. The bar had weathered the years. It became a neutral territory. When the children of the Blues and Grays needed to reach an accord, they reached it within the walls of the General's Shine.

Leah's lip curled at the Confederate Flag, but her mother's stomach growled. Both sides treated the General's Shine as hallowed ground. The Sons of the Union and Confederacy had fought since the Civil War. Neither side wished to break a truce. It was the safest place in the county, but both sides were harsh on any infraction. Anyone starting a fight on the property marked them as open to any insult without reprisal. When you ended up in Blackberry Bog, the talking stopped, she knew. Tracy had crossed the Van Lear family.

"We'll order something," Tracy grunted, wiping her brow. Leah's mother never stopped sweating, even in the heart of winter. It soaked her frumpy clothes. "He is coming soon."

"Maybe I should stay with Dad," she mouthed, crossing her arms.

"He left," she groused, color high on piggy features. "You'll be fine. No one would dare start a fight inside." Tracy's mind riffled through the myriad dishes of the General's Shine.

Leah opened her mouth, but the guitar chords cast a spell on the air. They were frantic and transcendent. The door flew open and then closed slowly. A thin man played the guitar on stage. She shifted to see his instrument.

"I heard he is playing here," she breathed. Everyone was talking about him in Meridian.

Tracy rolled her eyes. "The Van Lear Family got him a job here, while the court case is running its course." She raised her head and sniffed. "I don't care what they found. Ignazio is guilty." She recalled the satanic spectacle that was in the newspaper.

She looked at her mother. They had gotten a rat in the mailbox after the factory closed. "Just because people accuse you of something," she blushed, "it doesn't mean they're guilty." Leah hoped people were wrong about her mother. That man wronged those women.

Tracy turned. "Oh, we'll talk about the drugs they found." She raised her voice so others would hear. Her eyes darted about.

"I'm not on drugs, MOM," she whined. She tugged the band shirt, which featured a Black Metal band. Tracy would spread days, even weeks, on any mistake. She loved to focus on someone else's blunder.

Her mother stomped inside the General's Shine, and Leah groaned, fists balled. Under the spell of Iggy's playing, she forgot her mother. Her hands relaxed. Paganini, that is the name of his guitar, she marveled. There were many stories about the guitarist circling the town, some old but most fantastical. Did he sell his soul to the Devil? Did he sacrifice children to play like a man possessed? He is innocent; she swore because they found the actual killer. The murder's name slipped from her mind, though she had looked up a dozen times. But after hearing him play, Leah felt the very air enchanted. Each chord stuck cast a dark, devilish spell. The gloom-enchanted melody flowed through the patrons, and she saw its effect. How could they just sit there? She considered the question, seeing the notes inspire emotion in them. Like all great works, it lived in all that heard it.

"Come on," Tracy commanded, pulling her daughter. She kept her eyes away from Iggy. She flung her arms about, and people glanced at her. Their lips curled, and they turned away.

She staggered forward, and the guitarist glanced at her. Leah blushed. "Maybe he sold his soul like Jimmy Johnson," she breathed.

The guitarist's otherworldly focus faltered at the name. She watched fingers move in smooth strokes. No way, it is him; he is a genius. There was no merchandise. She made most of her clothes, but she wanted to help him, some show of appreciation. After a moment to fish out a five-dollar bill, she considered it. It was money from selling shirts. She darted up to an empty jar on the bar. She dropped it inside before Tracy could stop her.

Iggy smiled, turning. "Does the lady have a request?" He enquired with a smile. He glanced at her shirt with an appreciative nod.

"I," she blushed, "I don't know." Leah shook her head, cursing herself. He thinks I'm a loser, like everyone else. She plucked at the band shirt.

"Leave her alone," her mother stomped up to Leah and pulled her away. He frowned, and Leah wondered if this was how it felt to die.

The Guitarist smiled at the band shirt. "I got one for you," he promised with a nod.

Iggy turned away, and again, the rapture of his art possessed him. His passion flowed with creation, as with all genuine artists. Notes rose as unsteady spirits adorn with many sorrows. Leah's eyes widened. It was a song from the band on her shirt. The guitarist's cover was better than the original. His haunting blues cover spellbound the bar.

"Whatever," she studied the jukebox. "He left you," Leah muttered low. After word spread about Brian Weber's indiscretions, Landen had enough of Tracy. Mom was never easy to get along with.

"He hasn't called you," she smirked, "or even tried to contact you." Tracy held her piggy nose up.

"Whatever," she repeated. How would I know? You still have my phone and laptop; she thought with a curse. I have no escape.

"A real man never abandons his family," she wheezed, waving a server over who sighed at the sight of Tracy. She ordered for both of them.

Leah dug short nails into her ribs. Imagining screaming at Tracy, she muttered. She watched her for a moment and then leaned forward. "I heard things from the other kids at school," she smiled, feeling her stomach turn. "They're talking about the factory," she ventured, and her mother jerked.

"People talk, honey." She peered at a couple, but her eyes slid back to her. "What have they been saying?"

"A lot," she scrutinized the tip jar. A bitter taste now soured in her guts. "The factory will stay closed. There were women who were... abused." Leah blushed. Some used much harsher words about what happened.

Tracy reddened, but all the color drained. Former employers of Leitch Industrial Company were throughout the family bar. "What other women do for favors?" she held her chin up. "It is none of your concern!" Everyone made it sound like those women didn't have a choice. They could've kept their legs shut. It would've cost them their jobs, but that was their decision.

Leah studied her, but the world wavered through tears. "They say you helped to cover it up, and the Chaney people will always be traitors." She peered at the gouges on the table's surface. The only one who has it worse than me is Gage Weber, she thought.

She let out a breath. "They don't know anything." Her color returned as she searched for the waitress.

"Is it true?"! She cried, but her mother focused on the waitress, who avoided their table.

Their food arrived, though it was only warm. Tracy sighed, turning to the plate. Leah noticed more patrons staring over at them. Tracy assaulted her plate, but she used her mother's distraction to listen to Iggy. Leah picked at her food.

The gaze of the patrons shifted as the door opened. The closest ones to the door jerked. People here with their families called for a waitress so they could pay. Others, seeing people leave, decided fast to stay or go. Most recalled somewhere else they needed to be; Leah mused with a hiss. The less some know, the more they could hold on to delusions of innocence. Adults are just High School kids with jobs and mortgages, she considered with a grimace.

Barnett glided through the bar, graceful and silent, despite his size. Any remaining blues, descendants of the Union soldiers, averted their eyes when the Van Lear tough guy passed. He paused once when a man's eyes lingered on him for more than a second. After pausing for a moment, his smile widened, and he moved on. Savageness waited under his calm. Eyes beneath the trilby peered through the shadow cast by the hat, no matter the light. The Grays smirked in satisfaction. If he saw anyone but Tracy, there was no sign. When his hat momentarily tilted towards the Guitarist, his step faltered. It was so slight that only Leah saw it. He brushed down his tie and sat before them.

"Hello Miss Chaney," he growled, stumpy teeth flashed like bleached tombstones. He straightened his tie.

"Nice to see you, Barnett!" she fawned. "My, it is such a lovely day! How is Alice?"

"I don't care for obsequious flattery," he noted, tone flat. "I'm here at my lady's behest." Barnett's hat tilted towards Leah. "I assure you that your daughter's presence makes no difference." His lips curled but relaxed.

She blinked, "I was only—"

Barnett held up a hand, knuckles scarred, nails manicured. "Miss Van Lear is very curious, Madam," he revealed, tone again flat and expressionless. "Ingratiating yourself with faux civility wastes my time." he straightened his tie. "Now, there is a strange set of circumstances for certain individuals."

"I'll tell you whatever you want," she promised, swallowing. Tracy heard the man was brutal and indifferent to the sexes.

"I want the truth," Barnett articulated evenly, "and you will tell me."

"Okay, okay," Tracy smiled, sweat beaded on her brow.

"Your daughter here," he gestured at Leah, "will stay and listen, for Miss Van Lear insists." He skimmed her under the trilby hat, "She must listen, so never to make the same mistakes as you or your forebearers." His lip curled.

"Yes Sir," Leah mouthed, blushing, "I'm not my mother." She heard about Barnett, but only ever seen him in passing. He looks like a barbarian in a nice suit. She judged, feeling her skin pebble.

"Obviously," he remarked, turning back to Tracy. "Now, Madam, we come to the conundrum at hand. Christopher Peck, Sheila Richardson, and Brian Weber have disappeared." Barnett waved off the waitress, who scurried away but left a glass of water with lemon. "No one, it seems, has seen them. Misses Peck has left with our blessing. Miss Richardson's car is still at the Black Priory, and the Weber children are a dead end." He inspected his hands. Whatever they saw, it was bad enough to traumatize them, he thought. They recalled nothing but a bruised purple light. With some of the equipment there, it was probably a chemical fire. Brian was a lecherous fool and prolific in his drug production.

"What about Haas?" She begged, squeezing her hands together. "He hauled off Chris's vehicle! He also towed Sheila's car, and HE was the one who found the kids... Gage and Moxie!" Her mind snatched at any rumor making the rounds.

"We already reviewed his stories, and they checked out." he sipped the glass of water. "Haas has done nothing," he shrugged, "and I'll eventually find out if he has. You, on the other hand, Madam, have done much."

"I was the one," Tracy pointed to herself, "who came to you about the fraud." Leah saw other patrons tilted their heads to listen.

"Only after the abuse of the women revealed," he corrected. "We were sure to find the fraud once Alice checked the books." He let out an inaudible sigh.

Tracy looked at Leah, Barnett, and then at the door. "What do you want?" she whined, licking her lips.

"Where is Christopher Peck?" He tapped his fingers on the table. It was a sharp, brutal clicking.

"I don't know," she swore. Tracy tried to keep a tab on them. It was best to direct people's fury instead of taking it.

"Where is Sheila Richardson?" His eyes grew flinty. There was a cold, calculating barbarity in them.

"I don't know," her gaze flew about the bar.

"Where is Brian Weber?" He demanded, though it was in a smooth tone. Leaning forward, Barnett grinned. His teeth were like a row of tombstones.

Tracy's shook. She glanced between Leah and Barnett. "I don't—"

Tracy pulled her over to a table where she could order dinner. Her daughter stared at the guitarist, eyes widening. "Don't forget that we need to talk about the drugs in your backpack," she jerked Leah's arm. She tried to catch the eyes of others at a neighboring table.

"I wasn't smoking it," she swore, turning back to her mother. I wish I would have just not stopped to talk to them. They are always in trouble.

"Oh, yeah," she rolled her eyes, "one of the Duncannon girls put it in YOUR backpack!" Tracy laughed until a high snort pinched it off.

"It HAD to be one of them!" she huffed, and the pale skin turned crimson. They stopped me to talk about buying a shirt, Leah thought. Those prissy brats would never sully themselves by talking to the daughter of Tracy Chaney!

"They're from good, upstanding families," she countered, piggy nose rose.

"Dad believed me," she sulked, slouching in her chair.

"He left us," Tracy squealed. She wished the waitress would hurry. They always seemed to avoid taking her order.

Again, he held up his hand. "I have no interest in what you don't know, of which I'm sure there is much." Barnett sipped the water. "I am interested in anything you may learn about their whereabouts." He leaned forward, and both drew back. "The money stolen is only of an ancillary concern," he tapped the table, "it is the act itself. I want you to find out everything you can, and I don't care where rats build their nests, only they run the maze. You see, Miss Chaney, all of this is odd. They disappeared, yet you are still here. You benefited from an arrangement, even helped coerce some women."

"Hey," Tracy glanced at her daughter.

"What?" Barnett snapped, tapping the table, and the dishes jumped. "Does saying the truth bother you? Maybe she should hear everything." Tracy fell silent. He tapped the glass. "We still haven't found Kayden Stone," he added, eyes searching the table.

"No one has seen him," she whined. All of this was because of Kayden and his incessant questions.

"I know," he growled. "We will find him," Barnett added. He had spoken to people who saw him that day. Like he was fading in and out of reality, he mused. He had dismissed it as a drug-addled delusion until four others mentioned the same phenomenon.

"I will," she swore, beaming at him. Tracy felt sweat gather at her pits. "I'll ask everyone," she grinned.

"Your assurance is heartening," he noted, sipping the water again. "Now, last of all, there are the oddities in the books." Barnett's grin was gruesome.

"I didn't know about the ties to the Van Lear family," she squealed, almost bouncing out of her seat.

"Some of the money still ended up in your account," he revealed, scrapping the table's wood with a fingernail. "The thieves will return all the money by the end of the business day tomorrow." Barnett stilled, but a broad smile shifted to stony features. His eyes flicked to a mirror. "Sheriff, I'm glad you could make it."

Rutger stood beside the table, and all the Sons of the Union smiled at the Confederates. He rested a hand on his revolver. "Barnett," he skimmed the bar, "I don't see your masters. I'm surprised to see such a long leash."

"Is that what passes as wit for you?" he remarked, tapping the glass. His smile broadened. Barnett's hat tilted towards the Sheriff, "You'll do nothing, but please, bluster and bravado are always amusing."

Rutger's eyes narrowed, jaw flexed, but he turned towards Tracy. "I've been hearing things, Ma'am." his tone softened, but his knuckles were white on the revolver. "I've already spoken to the women about their experiences at the factory," he disclosed, studying Tracy, "and your name came up a lot."

"People talk, Sheriff," she countered, keeping her eyes everywhere, except Barnett.

"I don't know that the Van Lear promised or threatened," he jerked a thumb at the big man in the trilby hat. "They are NOT the law around here."

"Maybe she is afraid your men will shoot her," Barnett corrected. His smile broadened.

"I just don't know everything," Tracy smiled, but wiped her brow with sweat.

The Sheriff's mouth worked and glanced at Barnett. "Well, I'll be coming around tomorrow, so your memory better improves." He turned to the man in the trilby hat, "I've heard money is involved, Lear money, and rumors of fraud."

"All our dealings are above board," he sipped the water again, "and we are the victims here."

Rutger's grin hardened, but he turned to Tracy. "If you want to be neutral, be neutral, or pick a side."

"Sheriff," Barnett held up a hand, smile broad and satisfied. "I feel you need reminding of one fact," the man warned. He pointed a thick finger at the Guitarist, "The court case is ongoing, and you are to stay clear of him. Unless, of course, you are here to intimidate the man YOUR men shot."

He glanced at Iggy, who had stopped playing. Police from the township were friends with the Grays, but no one cared about that. The Van Lear family had them on their payroll, Rutger mused. The Guitarist kept his eyes on the Sheriff's revolver.

"I'll get to the heart of this, Barnett," he growled. The Sheriff wished he could hang them.

Barnett stood. "My business here is done, Sheriff." The trilby hat turned to Tracy, "We'll speak again, Madam, but I must leave you. I'll talk to a lawyer about the violation of a restraining order." Barnett strode away.

Tracy watched the Sheriff follow the well-dressed man. She looked around the bar and saw the patrons staring. "Leah," she fished some quarters out of her purse, "could you get something started on the jukebox? That... MAN appears to have stepped off the stage."

Leah took the coins, fighting the urge to recoil from her mother's touch. "All right," she hissed in a high whisper. Sons of the Union and Confederates glared at the women like something found under a rock. She stood, keeping her gaze from Tracy. The door banged open, but she concentrated on the jukebox.

Head down, she trudged through the bar, indifferent to the commotion. The jukebox was old but in fine condition and had a wide selection of music, if one loved Country or Western music. Leah looked at the selection, and a heavy sigh slipped out. She read through the list but finally found an artist. "At least they have Cash," she noted, squinting at the song titles. She leaned closer to the dirty glass. A woman drew close to her, but Leah's face nearly touched the jukebox.

A hard hand pinched her, and she whirled to see the chest of a large man. Leah jumped. "Hey," she barked, but he towered over her. "Don't touch me, pervert!" She warned. Leah swallowed, holding her chin up. No one seemed to care about the violation of the daughter of Tracy Chaney. Some patrons smirked, but most turned away.

Harry stepped closer, and she bumped against the jukebox. "A woman comes into a bar," he grinned. "She is looking for something."

The other woman looked at the selection. Her wild eyes flew to another man across the bar. She bent over to read the titles. He grabbed her too, but kept mean eyes on Leah. Harry's gut bounced.

The woman whirled. Her savage grin was feral. Lily had been next to the Chaney's women's table and caught the talk of the Van Lear family. She opened her mouth but saw the teenage girl, her hair. Red hair like a river of blood rolled down upon a leather jacket. Strands ran through Leah's, but mostly it was dark. Lily looked at the man with the black locks. "You could be," she breathed, touching her lower belly.

"Like a ripe strawberry," Harry bellowed, reaching for Lily's chest.

"Creep." Leah said, trying to stop him, but he knocked her away. I hate being so weak, she thought with a curse.

Lily smiled, and for a moment, Leah swore hellish flame swirled in her eyes. A small hand slapped him away. "Oh, that was very gentlemanlike," she remarked, grinning. "Did you mistake me for your sister or your mother?"

Harry blinked. His hand stung, and he rubbed it. "Don't act like you don't like it!" He reached for her again.

She swatted away his hand. Her broad smile was foxy. Leah swore the woman had a wicked set of incisors. "Like a big stupid dog," Lily marveled, a dark delight danced through her. She squeezed her hand into a fist, and her knuckles popped.

"What is happening, Red?" He chuckled, though dark eyes flickered. Something thrummed beneath his amiable smile.

"Nothing, Hemi," she assured him, putting an arm around Leah. "It is just a little boy tired of chasing sheep around a barnyard."

"Well," he laughed and put a companionable arm around Harry. Hemi dug fingers into the man's shoulder with a gleeful giggle. "I knew he was a romancer of farmyard animals," he grinned, squeezing until a groan seeped out of Harry.

"Hemi, Red," a man warned in an even tone from a table. Built like the man in the leather jacket, he was older and weathered. He studied the bar with mild interest.

"Coming Clay," he promised and let go of Harry. He patted him on the back with a chummy laugh.

"Come with us, sweetie," Red pulled her away from Harry, who gasped and rubbed where Hemi had squeezed him. She caught the hint of bubblegum and smiled.

"I need to go back to my mom," Leah whined, blushing under their regard. Beneath the cigarettes and booze, she caught the hint of pennies.

"We'll sit with you," Red promised, smiling at Hemi, who shrugged. She noted Harry's hungry, predatory eyes.

Clay watched but came after they waved him over. He moved with an easy stride. He glanced, eyebrows raised, until he saw Leah. "Everything fine," he questioned, seeing Harry speaking to other men. Always trouble. They're like flames constantly causing fires, he mused.

"Who are these people?" Tracy's asked, and her lip curled.

"I'm Clay," the older man smiled, wildness held in check by steel resolve. "This is my son Hemish, and Red, Lily, his wife."

"We don't need any company, thank you," she sneered. The Genera's Shine often welcomed tramps and drifters.

His eyes chided Hemi and Red. "We're here, in town, on business," Clay smiled. "We're here to see an old friend." They had traveled far. Their old business needed a conclusion.

Hemi laughed, "It has been a while." He wanted to return, but his father wouldn't hear it. He peeked at his wife with a wicked gleam.

"He was always high-spirited," Red added, and her husband threw his head back, laughing.

"Who may that be?" Leah asked. Maybe it is Iggy. They look like they're from a rock band.

"A rather grave fellow," Clay added with a smile. Hemi and Red broke into gales of laughter. "He is a Van Lear." he examined the plaque over the bartender. It displayed the establishment's name in Old English script. He finished a beer, while the other two emptied bottles of whiskey.

"I'm doing work for them now," Tracy revealed with a smile, satisfied.

"Is that so?" he mouthed, glancing at the others. "We've done work for them too, once upon a time." They did work for the family, though it was years ago.

"I'm sure you have," she remarked. Her lips approximated a smile. Her eyes flattened.

"Mom," Leah pleaded. "They helped me. That man grabbed my bottom!" Her nose wrinkled. She could smell her mother's powdery sweat.

"Oh," Tracy groused, rolling her eyes. "Why did you expect, dressed like that?" Any woman who showed off their body deserved to have men paw her.

He frowned. Hemi's brow drew down, but Red's eyes darkened. It was like a thunderstorm had grown inside them. "Blood is Blood," Clay warned. He ordered more whiskeys, holding a hand up to the others. "What are your names?"

"I'm Leah and this is Tracy," Leah smiled. The wild-eyed woman was her height, she saw. "You could be my sister," her eyes devoured Red.

"You could be my daughter," Lily marveled, eyes distant. Old horrors lingered in lovely eyes, which still stung from old pain. The world took so much, giving so little.

"Well, she isn't," Tracy jeered. Red turned a feral smile on her.

Clay studied Red. His eyes crinkled at their edges when they turned to Leah. "You look like a Rebel," he noted. "We know a lot about rebellion." Hemi and Red laughed.

"Yeah," she beamed, "I'm not into the typical, boring stuff."

"I believe your shirt references the Blood Countess," Clay pointed at her shirt.

"Oh, I made this," Leah admitted. She pulled it so they could see its design better. "It is my favorite band, but I like the Guitarist, who was here earlier." She wished she could listen to him play without her mother around.

"We heard of him," Clay admitted, and the others smiled. "I was told he may have sold his soul to the Devil... or Abaddon."

"Oh, I heard that too," she laughed, but recalled Iggy's skill. "The Van Lear family has been asking about it."

He nodded, "You know the General feared Abaddon would take him."

"You mean Lance Van Lear, the Confederate General?" she frowned.

"Yes," he nodded, "the very one." Clay drank some whiskey. "I heard that place is haunted," he held the bottle to his lips, "the plantation atop Lear Mountain."

"Everyone has heard those stories," she shrugged. Outsiders are interested in local ghost stories, she considered.

"We're leaving," Tracy announced. She stood, fished the money for the meal out of her purse, and slammed it onto the table. She grabbed Leah. "Stop talking to those degenerates!"

"Clay," Red hissed, glaring at her father-in-law. Her eyes snatched at the girl.

"Mom," Leah tried to pull free. She hated how her mother always embarrassed her.

"This is him," Harry growled. He pointed at Hemi, who laughed and waved in good cheer. Four men flanked him, all just as drunk. "We're going outside," he commanded, jabbing Hemi's chest, who laughed.

"Hey friend," Hemi greeted him, sneaking a peek at Red, "I see you learn the hard way. I love to teach it!" He broke into a fresh burst of laughter. All this talk was dull. They had been on the road for a while.

"Maybe, baby, he wants to apologize," she ventured, eyes slashing at them. Her wild gaze held the light. "If it came from the heart, we could see fit to let you boys walk out of here." Red's grin was hungry for darker things.

"Yeah, Pig," Leah added, pulling free of her mother. I'm sick of everyone in this town, she thought. Meridian was a pit.

He sneered, "I won't apologize to two drifter outsiders, and the whore daughter of traitors." Harry gritted his teeth. It was bad that he had to listen to Shy run his mouth.

Hemi, Red, and Clay stared at Tracy who suddenly found the next table interesting. Leah's face fell, tears rose, and her face burned. Harry laughed, and the four men guffawed.

Red appeared before them, though Leah never saw her move. "How about I slap you until you cry?" she offered with a laugh, but sparks of hellfire burned in her eyes. She was supposed to be a good girl until the completion of their business.

The men looked at Harry, all wore equal smirks. Harry's face contorted to a hue as red as Lily's hair. "Stupid slut," he snapped and snatched at her chest. Women lost their haughty look when you humbled them.

Leah grabbed his arm, but Red lifted him. He sailed through the air, and Hemi tackled the two of them. Clay stepped up as Tracy crawled under a table. Violence in the General's Shine had stopped. The bar's patrons stood to see who battled, bewildered by the attack. Harry smashed through a table, which cast beer over a Confederate. He turned to see a son of the Union spit out his drink. A laugh jumped out, but a fist closed it. Other Union boys saw one of theirs struck. They rushed Confederates a table over. Since Prohibition, no one had dared to start a fight in the General's Shine. The waitresses fled to the back, but the bartender tried to stop the brawl. A punch clocked him out for the night. Leah searched for her mother but saw men, laid off and angry, working on their frustrations with their fists. Begrudged calm was gone. The bar became bedlam.

She skimmed the room as a chair flew. Leah stepped back from two bearded men, who held the other with one hand and punched. One bumped into her, and she nearly toppled. They look like idiots; she mused and darted out of their way. Another man shoved her aside, so he could club a gentleman, drunk as he was foul-mouthed, over the head with a bottle. Harry crept through the brawl with a chunk of the table. He scurried like the world's biggest and meanest beaver. His eyes were on the hellcat with strawberry hair. Red threw punches as Hemi slung men like dolls. Clay threw a beer, which knocked a fellow flat. He let out a sigh. Leah noticed Harry and kicked a chair. It slid in front of him.

Harry tripped to fall at Red's feet, and the chunk of wood slid across the floor. She grinned at Leah. "Thanks, Countess," she howled with a fierce grin.

Leah smiled, but Tracy dragged her towards the door. They stumbled out into the parking lot. Harry knocked people aside, and his brothers followed the two women. Red pulled Hemi, who slammed two heads together with a laugh. Clay set down his beer after a moment to finish it.

"Come on," Tracy snapped, "this is YOUR fault!"

"That jerk grabbed ME!" Leah screamed. Tracy whirled on her daughter, but the bar door banged open.

"Where are you going, Chaney?" Harry growled. No traitor will ever dare treat him with disrespect.

Leah backed up, but her mother already ran behind her. Mom can move fast when her bacon is in the fire, she mused darkly. "Why don't you just leave us alone?" She pleaded, knowing they had parked far away.

"Oh, we are far from done with you," Harry promised. He laughed, and his brothers walked behind him.

The bar door banged open. Red and Hemi grinned at the five men. Clay stepped out with a smile. "Gentleman, I forgot to introduce my family," he hooked thumbs in his pockets. "We're the Bliss family." Tracy frowned, but she couldn't recall the strange name.

"Whoever you are," Harry frowned, though something flickered inside, "you're all going to Lear County Medical." He puffed up his chest.

Clay glared at Tracy and then at Leah. His eyes softened when they reached the girl. "NO slight should remain unanswered," he remarked, eyes on the girl.

"Who is going to make us answer?" Harry laughed. He is making a trip to Blackberry Bog tonight.

Clay's eyes stayed on Leah. "Life dealt you a bad hand. Some were born with a loving family, but some have to find them." He smiled at Hemi and Red. He nodded at Leah. "They're laws, old ones, which never change."

"What do you mean?" Leah breathed. I want to be no one but me, she thought. They're their masters. Like a dream, they're like something from a... nightmare.

"No slight left unaddressed." Clay's features hardened. He turned to Harry and his brothers.

"What can I do?" She studied her shoes.

He stepped closer, and the other members of the Bliss family laughed. "No one can save you, even if they love you. In the end," Clay lowered his hands, "you'll have to be your savior."

Red came closer. "We're family, but we have to save ourselves." Her mind fell back to those old days. She held her child, knowing they would never breathe. They would never laugh.

"That's right," Hemi agreed, putting an arm around his wife.

"You people are crazy," Harry judged. He rolled his eyes. Meridian attracted weirdos.

Clay nodded to Leah. "We don't abandon our blood."

"That's right," Red winked at her, but turned a feral smile on Harry.

Hemi laughed, "Show 'em, baby!" He clapped his hands.

"I'll show you," Harry vowed, looking at the other men, "what happens when you mess with the Rangel brothers."

"Rangel family," Hemi bellowed out with a laugh. "I thought you idiots would wipe each other out." Time couldn't even breed the stupid out of some families.

Clay held up a hand. "Red, would you please?" This needed to end so they could get back on task. His son- and daughter-in-law deserved their fun.

She looked at Leah and then stood between them. Red's eyes held a swirling flame and danced. "We'll see if you boys are as useless as your forbearers. I'll tell you what, piggy poker. I'll give you a free shot," she offered, sticking out her chin.

"What," Harry blinked. He wondered why all the sexy ones were crazy.

"Come on, you cowardly cur," Red jeered. She never cared for the Rangel family.

Harry swung, face flushing. The blow caught her jaw. He grabbed his knuckle. "That'll teach you," he added, shaking his hand.

Red smiled, blood smeared teeth. Leah saw her incisors were longer. Inside, wild green eyes were a hellish flame. The smell of pennies grew thicker about her. None but the Bliss family saw the slap, but all heard it. Harry staggered. He searched for the source of the blow. The next slap was loud, and blood dripped from his nose. She held up her fists like a pugilist, and Leah laughed. Other members of the Bliss family chuckled. Harry swung, but she danced away from each punch with a laugh. No swing got close to hitting her. Her palm landed with a sharp crack. He staggered. She rained slaps on him, hands blurring.

Harry's brothers' amusement faded fast. They stepped forward, but Clay and Hemi were ready. Hemi slammed into two of them. He launched them over a car. Clay hit the others once, and they crumbled to the ground. He sighed.

Red kicked him to his knees, but Harry still muttered curses. "Come here," she asked, motioning to Leah.

"What?" she whined, glancing briefly at the man who had grabbed her. He isn't so tough with piss all over his pants, she mused.

"Stand up for yourself," she chided gently. Red grinned with blood still in her teeth. She picked up one of the Rangel brothers' cowboy hats and a lit cigarette on the gravel.

"I don't," she grumbled low. Red pulled Harry's hair so that he faced the girl. Leah stared at his half-dazed expression. "Uh, I don't like perverts grabbing me," she held her chin up.

Red's eyebrows raised, waiting for a moment. "Men like him need physical punishment," she corrected, "because it is the only way they learn." It was a pleasure of hers to teach them over the years.

She trembled, glancing at Harry. I'm sick of everyone! They grab me at school too! The thoughts screamed in her head. Leah no longer bothered going to teachers. Her mother's reputation earned everyone's ire. The slap was sharp, and Leah felt her hand tingle. She stared at her palm, blinking.

"Don't touch me again!" Leah screamed. A laugh escaped her with a sob. Her thoughts raced. So many times, she had dreamed of standing up to them. The Duncannon girls' mean smiles and dismissive eyes ruled her days at school.

"Good girl," Red cooed, letting go of him. Hemi laughed. There was sand in the girl, which needed to nurturing.

"Some men only understand pain," Clay observed, holding Leah's eyes. His lip curled at Tracy. It was a shame that the girl was born to a Tracy.

Tracy stepped between them. "We have to leave." It was bad enough to take Leah into public dressed as she was, but these vagrants were too much.

"Any friend of General Van Lear," Clay turned on her, "is our friend." He smiled. It was a tired, hard grin too full of teeth. Something danced deep in his eyes. Years came and gone. People like Tracy stayed the same.

Leah frowned. The General had been dead for a long time. "I thought you guys were cool," she pouted. She avoided the blood feud between the Grays and Blues of Meridian.

"We won't hurt you," Red promised, eyes pleading. "I would never hurt you, Rosalie." She frowned with a slight shake of the head, "I mean Leah." Clay studied his daughter-in-law, and the laughter in Hemi's eyes died for a moment. Both men's faces fell.

"We need you," Clay glanced at his daughter-in-law. "We need your assistance in a matter. Afterward, we will take you back to your car." He smiled at Leah, but his gaze turned baleful when it turned to Tracy. Pinpricks of hellfire red burned deep in his eyes, and his teeth seemed sharper. He knew one who would disrespect Blood would respect nothing.

Leah shook her head. Impossible, she thought and cut off the idea. "What do you want?" she pleaded. There was always a catch. One time, the Duncannon girls had pretended to be her friend. They had led her on for a month. It had been a trick.

"For you to ride with us," Red begged. She smiled, but it curdled when it turned on Tracy. "We want both of you to come along." She took Leah's arm with a smile. She tucked the hair behind the teenager's ear.

Hemi laughed, clapping, "I love road trips!" He moved to their vintage muscle car. "I did all the restoration, all the custom work too," he bragged, pointing at his work.

Leah turned back to the Rangel brothers stirring. Their cousins, just as dumb, stepped out of the bar, she recalled. "You'll bring us back," she demanded, as the men helped up their family. Everyone knew they held on to grudges.

"I can't make you choose anything," Clay countered. He examined Red. The girl's decision would be binding, and no one could make it for her.

Leah followed the wild-eyed woman, though her mother protested. Hemi opened the door for the woman before he got into the driver's seat. Clay walked to the passenger side, indifferent to the approaching men. Red sat in the back, between Leah and Tracy. Tires kicked back gravel into Harry, his brothers, and his cousins. They covered their faces, cursing. Hemi bellowed out laughter. He punched the wheel.

Despite the vintage muscle car's pine air freshener, the ghosts of tobacco, beer, liquor, and drugs choked the interior's air. It moved at a sluggish pace, the engine roaring like an insane lion. Although the heat was on, a chill persisted. A tang of blood rested below all and settled on the tongue. The radio, caught between stations, garbled out a nonsensical mishmash of music. The air felt thicker and somehow stale. Like a metal tomb, it protected its occupants with heavy enforcement.

Like sucking on a penny, Leah thought. Like a steel coffin, it is a kind of cool. He looked out the window. All of this is happening so fast. Do they live in this thing? How does it feel to be free, free from people, free from judgment?

Clay turned to Leah. "We've been on a road trip for a while," he said. He nodded at Hemi and Red. "There was a betrayal, despite our loyalty. We want to get answers, which we deserve." He smiled. He already planned for their next purpose. Hemi could be wild. Red still felt her loss even after all these years, Clay knew. He smiled, "You are a smart young lady, but our life isn't for everyone," he admitted. Time became a curse. It stole from the mind. He had seen others of their kin go made with the years.

"Filthy, degenerate drifters," Tracy laughed. She couldn't understand why anyone would care about her mousy, forgettable daughter.

Clay was tranquil with a storm beneath. He kept his eyes on Leah. "Do you know our truth?" Hemi laughed, but Red watched her.

Leah smiled weakly but shook her head. She peeked at the Bliss family. "I don't know," Leah whispered, staring at Red, who smiled. "I... thought, maybe, you were Children of the Night," she laughed. It was a rusty croak. Their smiles grew. The answer had come from lingering thoughts, ever since she'd seen Lily's eyes burn with flame.

"That is a poetic, perhaps romantic, way of phrasing it," Clay observed. A light laugh escaped him.

"If you're with the one you love," Hemi beamed at his wife, "It isn't so bad." The decades came and went, but all he needed was his woman.

"That's right, baby," Red agreed, grinning at him. His devotion never faltered or faded.

"It's true!" Leah blinked. A chill gripped her, but questions clamored inside. This was like a horrible dream or a beautiful nightmare. "What, what is it like?"! She bounced in her seat. Tracy grabbed her, pale with red cheeks.

"Like all things," Clay shrugged, "it has drawbacks and benefits." After the initial horror, there was elation. He had felt invincible. Now he felt tired. He felt like the horses of the Ghost Riders in the Sky.

"Let me say I believe you," she chuckled, but her heart raced. "What are the drawbacks?" Leah asked with a lopsided grin.

"The need for blood," he shrugged, "but you need less overtime." He nodded at Hemi and Red. "Time is a pro and a con. I taught myself to read like my woman always asked me to learn." His eyes flicked to the brooch that hung on the rearview mirror. "You'll need to find things to occupy your time, without a master as we are." Hemi and Red laughed at this. Clay wondered how long he could keep them alive. The madness was creeping into them, making them foolish.

"What are the benefits?" she asked, crossing her arms to still the shakes. Leah waited for the trap to be sprung.

"You're stronger, faster, and aging stops," Clay added. He smiled. It faded as his gaze went to the back window. "We can still die, though we are harder to kill." He saw Leah's face fall a little. Death haunted the creature of the Unknown Lands like the world of humankind.

"You'll be able to become what YOU want," Red added. "Not what everyone else desires," her eyes cut to Tracy. She held up a petite hand, and fingernails grew to a wicked length, just so any doubt of their nature would die. She could see doubt in the girl's eyes. There would be no lies between them, even if she said no.

"I don't know," she muttered, heart racing. The smell of blood grew heavy in the car. Her eyes flicked to her mother.

"The decision needs to be considered," Clay nodded. He kept his eyes on the headlights behind them. "You're very young." She was too young to turn. It was ghastly to curse children with this everlasting life.

"I have to think about it," Leah warned. She sighed. Always best to say no when I feel pressured, she thought.

"That's fine, Countess," Red conceded, tucking Leah's hair behind her ear. The girl tried to shield her face from others. She thought she was pretty. "We have all the time in the world," she reminded her.

"Her answer is NO!" Tracy wailed. "And stop tucking my daughter's hair behind her ear!" She rolled her eyes. "It'll just show her plain face."

Red turned on Tracy. Rage sent tremors through her. Hellfire red flame blazed in her lovely eyes. Her fangs were long and wicked. The broad smile held no cheer or laughter, but a furious hunger on the edge of madness. Tracy let out a low, long toot.

"We have people on our trail," Clay nodded behind them, "at least three vehicles." Nothing was ever simple.

"Some people are suicidal, stupid," Red growled. "Rangel morons were always a pack of fools." They had turned every task into a task. They were occasionally useful.

Hemi glimpsed into the rearview mirror. "We can't use the booster on such a curvy road." He laughed with his hand over the button.

The three trucks rushed forward. Horns blared as they drew closer to the custom vintage car. Hemi laughed, and Clay sighed. Red tried to cover Leah with her body, but Tracy tried to use her daughter as a cover. They slammed into the muscle car, but Hemi laughed, before slamming into them. He jerked the wheel towards them with giggles.

"All this is because YOU dressed like a SLUT!" Tracy screamed at her daughter. Her daughter wore clothes that fit her thin body.

"Mom," Leah cried. She never had a boyfriend. The boys at school talked to her like trash.

"That's it!" Red slammed an elbow into Tracy's face, and she fell back. All fell silent for a second, except Hemi, who chortled. She turned to Leah, "I couldn't listen to her insult you anymore!"

Leah blinked. No one has ever stood up for me, she thought and stared at her mother. "Just... uh, don't do it again," she gaped about the interior, eyes blinking. Her mouth opened, though nothing else came out.

"I won't," Red promised, holding up her hands.

Two trucks slammed into the muscle car on both sides. The other vehicle slammed into the back. They jerked forward. Men leaned out of windows and opened fire. Bullets and buckshot bounced off the glass and metal, and Leah screamed. The cacophony was deafening. Hemi laughed, and Red covered Leah. Clay's placid expression hardened, and an oath passed between his fangs. The muscle car went off the road, but the Rangel brothers and cousins still shot. Guns clicked empty, and the trucks raced away.

Hemi slammed a palm against the steering wheel. Red asked Leah if she was fine, and she nodded. Clay stared at the trucks' taillights until they disappeared. The Bliss family stared out at the night. An excited energy thrummed through them, hungry and furious. The charade of humanity departed in their fury.

"We can't leave this transgression unaddressed," Clay admitted, tone empty.

"They tried to kill Rosalie... Leah!" Red growled. Her mind fell back to that night. She had held her daughter, but Rosalie never drew a breath. She waited. Her child was silent, though she prayed to hear her cries. That silence followed her. It filled the stillness.

Clay turned to Leah. "There are different rules for us, those outside the laws of man. We're our masters. We are our law."

"What are you going to do?" Leah shivered. The coffin-like interior felt too small.

"Our code is simple." he turned to Hemi, then Red. "We will defend ourselves, our family." Clay stared at the night and knew it was better to stay the course. The violence led to blood. Blood became madness. They transgressed against, but giving in to hunger was dangerous. It was harder to reign in his family.

Red looked at Leah. "We should just go up to the Lear family estate." Clay frowned at her. A hell storm stirred under his placid calm. Hemi grumbled, but sighed at his wife. Red smiled, squeezing her hands into fists. Fighting them men wasn't worth risking Leah.

They pulled back onto the road. The muscle car's headlights cut through the darkness. Every member of the Bliss family was silent, so their blood would cool. Rage burned inside them, and flames swirled in their eyes. Leah wanted to get out, if only to stop until her head cleared.

Tracy snored beside her. The thrum inside the car was stifling.

Leah watched the Bliss family. Like pirates, she mused, they're free. I don't think most people are free if it is a thing. How will I feel? Does it hurt? The questions whirled in her head. The image of Red busting Tracy in the face played over. To answer any of the questions, she should have to experience it. Nothing can ever fully explain, she knew. Heaven to one is hell to another. She shook her head, but the wild bedlam of questions made answering them impossible. She rubbed her eyes. What do I want to be? The question echoed about the mind. How can I decide my whole life in one car ride? I can't, she thought, snatching a glance at Red.

"A car ride isn't," Leah grumbled, blushing.

"It is okay," Red said. "Take this." she had a card with a number on the back. She tucked strands of hair behind the teenager's ear.

"I don't know what to decide," she pleaded. Leah always detested the mistreatment of kindness. They had helped her despite their dark natures. Each of them fought a war inside.

Red leaned forward, but her eyes went past her to the window. She wiped away a bloody tear. Headlights blazed. Hemi muttered a curse. Clay braced himself with a hand. Red pulled Leah close. The truck rammed into the muscle car. Leah screamed, but the thick armor withstood the blow. Tires squealed, but they locked together.

Hemi laughed, "They are tired of living!" He bounced in his seat. With a chortle, he winked at his wife.

"I bet they're trying to stop you," Leah shuddered, "so they can blame the bar fight on you. The Van Lear family,

Confederates, and Union boys will be after blood." A bloody war could break out after all tonight. She cursed their feud.

"They'll have it," Hemi promised, laughing. Both sides wronged them. Both could go to the devil.

"This cannot stand," Clay said, warning. He stepped out of the car. Hemi slammed it into the park and cut off the engine.

"Stay here," Red ordered, looking Leah in the eyes. She joined the others. They had to stop the threat to the girl.

Leah looked at her mother, who still snored. She stared out into the dark, but it was hard to see anything. "I have to watch." She felt her heartbeat. She rushed out into the night. The gift they offered was wondrous, though mysterious. They hid their darker natures.

Red turned back to her. "What are you doing?" She blushed.

Clay turned. "She comes with us if she so chooses." He glared at his daughter-in-law.

The large truck backed up. Clay smiled, though his eyes were flat. He studied the night, skimming shadows for other bushwhackers. Before the vehicle could lurch forward, Hemi dug long nails into the tire. He laughed and hooted up at the sky. Red chuckled, yet stayed close to Leah. Hellish flames burned deep in all their eyes. Leah stood in the beams of the headlights. A man stepped out with a shotgun.

"We know who you are," he barked, and the gun trembled. "Your family worked for the General." The man studied them, for tales had them dead. Old pictures from those days lingered, but he pushed them away, and the questions that they posed. These must be their descendants, he assured himself.

Red stepped forward, and the man jerked the gun, finger on the triggers. The shotgun boomed, and it nearly flew from his hands. She fell back to the earth as Leah screamed. The buckshot hit her in the stomach. The man stared at the smoke, which drifted up from the gun. Hemi's laugh was hard and lifeless, and Clay stepped towards the man. As the shotgun turned on them, Red sat up. She chuckled, eyes burning with a hellfire hue.

She was up in a smooth, feline burst. The man reached for more shells, but twin hellfire-red flames burned in her eyes. The blow knocked him to the earth, and the air whooshed out of him. Red stood over him, smile broadening. Her fangs grew longer. Little pellets dropped into his chest. The wound on her stomach healed to push out the buckshot, which rained down. Her hands hung at her sides. Red's nails grew to a wicked length. Flames in her lovely gaze blazed, but they cut to Leah and slide back. She slapped him, and his eyes rolled up. She snapped the shotgun before dropping it on him.

Hemi laughed, but Clay turned to the trucks that squealed to a stop. The Rangel families lived in a community up the road. Red turned with a laugh, and told Leah to stay close, no matter what happened. Rangel men stepped out with guns. Pale faces had eyes on the hell the Van Lear family would bring down on them. They had broken the no-fighting rule.

Leah watched. They stand up for themselves; she marveled. No parents, teachers, or law, they ruled themselves. I'm so tired of being helpless! What it would be like to be free and powerful? She wondered.

The blaze from headlights cut through the darkness. The men turned the guns on the Bliss men, but they slid about the shadows. Hellfire eyes cut tracers through the night. Red kept close to Leah, who tried to watch the battle. Clay moved, swayed, and cut through the air like a blade. Lights went dark. The family patriarch flowed away from the gunfire. Hemi moved like the beat of a raven's wing, a flash of darkness and silence. Guns snapped from a single blow from him, and his laughter rose to the moon above. Red motioned for Leah to stand behind a tree, and she flew into the men. Above the earth, she floated. Men screamed, then fell silent. The Bliss family moved as one.

Harry crept through the trees. He watched the drifters move towards his kin and saw they were busy with the Bliss family. Red finally moved away from the teenage girl. Before he could reach her, Tracy stepped out of the muscle car.

"Come on, Leah!" Tracy hissed. She bounced, pulling her daughter.

"Where?" Leah's eyes flew about the forest. She saw Harry half hidden by a tree.

Leah screamed, and her mother whirled. The man leaped from the shadows. Before Leah could dart away, Tracy kicked her in the ankle. Leah tripped. She landed in the dirt, and the air whooshed out of her. Her mother ran into the forest, never looking back. Tears blurred the world, but a laugh rose above Leah. She crawled forward, but Harry grabbed her foot.

"Get off, PERVERT!" She screamed, kicking at him. Leah cursed her weakness.

Harry laughed and pulled her back. "Your mother turned coward, like all the Chaney family." No one cares what happened to them. He could do whatever he wanted to the girl.

Leah kicked with a scream, and Harry grabbed his groin. She stood. Every swing hit his face, but he pushed her back.

"I'll make you sorry, Little Tracy," he snarled at Leah. He planned a trip to the Blackberry Bog after this.

"Don't call me that!" she screamed. Leah launched herself at him. She clawed and spit.

"Shut up!" he slapped her, sounding sharp, but she still stood. Harry raised his hand again, but a small hand, fingers hard as a steal, grabbed his wrist.

Red kicked him, and he fell to his knees. Mouth open, her fangs grew and her nails became razor sharp. She raised a hand high, and lovely eyes blazed in fury.

"DON'T," Leah pleaded. She closed her eyes.

Red stared at her, but for a few seconds, the twin flames in her eyes burned. "He'll live," she promised and sneered at Harry. "But with pain to remind him," she kicked him in the groin. Harry squealed and wept.

Hemi tore the trucks apart. He would have destroyed all of them, but his wife wanted the girl to join them. Clay moved towards them. Bullet wounds already healed. He turned to Red and Leah. Tracy had abandoned their daughter. Despite his calm manner, the patriarch of the Bliss family moved past them into the forest. Hemi returned, brow furrowed, but laughed down at Harry, who cried. Red listened, pulling Leah with her. They left the only conscious Rangel weeping.

The forest flowed about Leah as Red carried her. The wind whipped past. Cold air bit the low decay of dead wood. A chill pricked exposed skin and her cheeks burned. Even at this speed, Red was gentle with her. Inside the blood that covered the woman was the richness of chocolate. She shivered, her heart pounded, and she tasted the forest's myriad flavors. They reached a small clearing.

Clay stood. Tracy had tripped and crawled. Leah's mother squealed in terror, but none of them had touched her. Red's lips curled, shaking her head. After a moment, Hemi arrived, but looked at his wife with a confused laugh.

"Where are you going, Madam?" Clay bellowed and stepped closer. "YOU left your DAUGHTER!"

"You're crazy," Tracy whined. "You are monsters!" Maybe they would eat her daughter, and she could get away.

His lip curled, "Yes, we are, but we don't leave one of ours behind."

Red drew closer to Tracy. "You left her to the ravages of a foul man," she accused, squeezing her hands into small fists.

"With monsters," Hemi hissed with a hard laugh, "for we are servants of the Moon, undone and remade by the blood." He shrugged his shoulders.

"She did this," Tracy pointed to her daughter. "I don't keep company with TRASH!"

"Oh," Clay said, nodding, "you're a Chaney. Treacherous and traitorous, you got your people killed." He looked at Leah. "Life shackled her to you. You should change your name."

"I've had enough of you," Red glided to Tracy, who recoiled from the hellish flames that lived in lovely eyes.

"Don't," Leah breathed low. The Bliss family turned to her. She closed her eyes. There were no reasonable answers to the question in their eyes.

"Why," Red pleaded. Her blood cooled, and the flames receded.

"She betrayed you." Hemi frowned. "She'll always betray you." His brow drew down.

Clay frowned and sighed, "You don't have a chance with the likes of her around," He pointed to her mother. The girl was a better woman than her mother.

"Didn't you guys fight for the South?" Leah charged, holding up her chin. She was defending her mother again. It was an endless, thankless task.

"I never wanted to join." Clay's tone flattened. "They took from me, and they burned down my farm." He pointed to Hemi and Red, "When they couldn't catch me or my son, they took from them from Lily." Red jerked. The hand moved towards her stomach, but she moved it away. They didn't know there was a war. Men in uniforms showed up on their farms.

Leah blushed. It was more complicated than the teachers told us; she thought. Her eyes fled Red's hurt. She turned to Clay. "Would you still fight for the General, if you had to change things?" She demanded. They were people of their time, but some things were inexcusable.

Clay considered, eyes moved to Tracy, then his family. "I'd kill them all. It was nothing but a mockery. The North and the South wanted power and to live off the poor. People died, and all of them got richer." He turned to Hemi and Red. "Tainted blood curses us. The years are hard, especially in the mind. All because they wanted to keep power, we suffered." The hellfire flames in his eyes blazed.

"Please, don't kill my mother," she pleaded. She squeezed her hands. Her guts churned.

Clay threw up a hand and turned away. "We came here to settle an old debt," he reminded his family. He strode towards the muscle car. The girl would choose to destroy her life to please a woman that hated her.

Hemi picked up Tracy, "Come on, Jiggle Chicken, we have a date with an old friend."

Red lifted Leah. "We can't leave you here with the Rangel family around." Moonlight shimmered on the drop of blood that ran down her cheek.

They moved to the custom car, which set where they'd left it. Clay's jaw flexed, entering with a grunt. The door slammed, which shook the vehicle. Hemi pushed Tracy inside and got into the driver's seat. Red and Leah joined them. Rangel men already stirred from the beatings.

Leah stared at the moon. "Everyone in Lear County will be after you." She warned, studying them, but none seemed interested.

"I had a plan for that," Clay revealed. He took the brooch from the rearview mirror and put it in a pocket.

"Man," Hemi sighed, "I loved this ride." He would have to start over. His grin returned after a moment to consider.

Red seized Tracy's neck, and nails grew. "I heard your conversation with the Van Lear tough guy," she said, and her petite body was rigid as stone. She shook her, and Tracy's pudgy cheeks quivered. "I'll have the truth out of you!" The hellfire flame turned on the teenager. "I want her to know the real you! Nothing but the truth, it will be plain. No more lies."

"What?" Tracy blinked at Leah.

"Tell the truth, Mom," Leah held her gaze. There were rumors about her mother.

Tracy looked at Leah, and then at Red. She laughed, "You want the TRUTH?" She was pale. Her eyes jittered to each of the Bliss family. Tracy twitched, lips working. "I helped Brian, Chris, and Sheila!" She spit the words and sat up. "This town despised me, even before I married Landen! So, I wanted them to feel it. They were so high and mighty, but all it took was a threat to their jobs to turn them into whores!" She grinned in Leah's face. "Every time one of them cried, I laughed. Is that enough truth for you? Brian treated me like I deserve, better than them."!

"The money?" She asked, and Leah's face burned. People had asked her about it.

"I took some," she bragged, "but I didn't care, and I DO know it was Lear MONEY!" Tracy laughed at their disgust. "When they fired Kayden, I laughed. When his junkie wife died, I laughed, because I got both of them fired." Tracy tried to slap Leah, but Red stopped her. "Kayden, he looked down on me!" She sneered. "So smart," she trembled, "still not smart enough to figure out we were all in on it."

"Okay... Mom," Leah cried, shrinking in on herself. She stared out the window.

"NO!" she screamed with a laugh. "YOU wanted the truth." Tracy shook her head. "Just like your father. You want to know the truth, but cry or shrink away." She grinned, "I never wanted you, but Landen wouldn't leave with me pregnant. I wanted to scrape you out because I knew you'd be nothing but a burden!"

"Shut up," she whispered.

Tracy drew closer, and sweat rolled down her face. "I'm not sure you're even Landen's kid," she confessed with a sweaty glee.

"Please... stop," she kept her eyes on the night.

"PLEASE, STOP," Tracy sneered. Everyone wanted the truth until they got it.

Red seized her throat. "Shut up," she commanded. Tracy's eyes bulged in her head. Red turned to Leah. "Sweetie, you must stand up for yourself," she tried to smile at the girl. Leah had to stand up to her mother, or her entire life would be wretched.

"Mom," Leah looked at Tracy, "people looked down on you, because of how you behave. Everyone likes Dad. You married into the Chaney family." She shook her head. "If you run into a jerk, they're probably a jerk. If you run into twenty jerks, you're the jerk." Mom, everyone at school talks about you, even before all this. You constantly start trouble, church, or the factory, and everybody hates you."

"They don't hate me!" Tracy screamed.

"They do," she crossed her arms, body crumpled into itself. "They do hate you. The New Money, Duncannon girls said you were a science experiment, part rat and pig. The daughters of the other factory workers try to fight me or spread rumors about me. Gage Weber defends me, and he is the only one." She wiped away tears. Last Time he had stopped a football player, she recalled; he got a busted nose and lip and almost got a broken arm.

"None of that is my fault!" Tracy screamed, and her face turned a deep purple.

"Nothing is ever your fault, even Dad leaving," Leah grunted. Her mother never took responsibility. Everything was everyone else's fault.

"He left us."

Red snatched Leah's phone from Tracy's purse. "This yours?" She handed it over.

Leah took it; though her mother tried to snatch it away. She burst into tears, for it had unread messages from Landen. She covered her face. "How could you keep this from me?"

"I," Tracy opened her mouth, but Red squeezed and shook her.

The car was silent except for Leah's low sobs. Hemi looked at Clay, who nodded, and the muscle car moved back onto the road. They moved up Lear Mountain, where the old plantation rested, unchanged since the Civil War. A siren rose from the township and crawled over the bitter night. Leah looked out of the darkness as shafts of silver fell upon the road. Blood and chocolate lingered below the smell of alcohol and cigarettes. Clay held a bottle, contents thick. It caught the light in shimmers of crimson. Distant lights of the town grew as word spread of the fight. No one had ever dared to fight inside. Word of the Rangel community's destruction had also spread.

Above all set Swannanoa. Three properties rested there, and the Lear family plantation rested at the back. Before anyone could enter, they had to pass the heavy gate. Slaves constructed the high walls. A La Voison woman designed the gate, a slave. People spoke of dark deals when they whispered of it. No one dared to touch it.

The muscle car pulled up to the front gates. Even Hemi's custom work could never break it. Clay motioned for all of them to exit. Hemi hooped and hollered. Red studied the gate, eyes again wild. Leah stepped out before Tracy crawled after.

Clay drew closer to the elaborate ironwork. He frowned and reached for it, but something forced his hand back. "I heard rumors," he marveled. He scrutinized the intricate symbols worked into the metal.

"What do you mean?" Hemi chuckled. He reached for it but something pushed back from the gate.

"We can jump over it," Red shrugged. She stepped back. They could leap to the other side with ease.

"NO," Clay turned back. "There is no telling what'll happen to you. They're some powerful wards around this place." He heard rumors about Lance.

"What do we do now?" Red blinked.

Clay pushed against the ward, and a figure lurked in the darkness beyond. He studied it. "Why don't you come out, Lance, and see the handy work of the Iron Monger?" he asked, but the shadow drew no closer. He waited, but the General was gone. I have to keep them moving, Clay thought, recalling his family's actions of the night. "We were loyal, and it cost us!" he challenged, but he met with more silence. "But," Clay studied the wards, "I see someone else paid a heavy price."

"How do we get inside?" Hemi kicked the invisible ward with a laugh.

Clay turned to them. "We need to go. All hell will come down on us if we stay."

Red motioned at Leah. "So, we're just going to leave?"

"You can hear the police sirens," he turned to Leah. "We have to go," Clay held up the strange bottle, "but you can come."

Leah lowered her head. She peeked at Red and Clay, "I... can't, I just can't." Leah sneaked glances at Hemi's wife. "I'm sorry. You guys seen cool, but I don't know." No one, except Dad, has ever wanted to be around me, Leah thought. "I still have your card," she grunted. Red's smile returned.

"When you're eighteen," Red held up her hands. "You make your decision. It doesn't have to be now. You can call the number, no matter what happens."

"You're welcome to join our family," Clay assured her. The girl would be a fine woman if she escaped her mother.

"You can have HER!" Tracy shrieked. She jumped behind the wheel of the muscle car.

She peeled out. The muscle car shot away from the heavy gate. Tracy laughed, looking at the rearview mirror. "They won't kill me," she squealed, "after I tell Barnett about the Bliss family." The Queen of Lear Mountain won't hurt me after a bunch of drifter psychos killed my daughter, she mused. "Landen will come back too," she swore, "because I just lost my baby." She tried to force tears, but a jagged laugh burst out.

Tracy glanced in the rearview mirror again. Hellfire-red flames burned behind her before they went dark. She jerked the wheel, and the tires squealed but kept on the road. Twin fires drew closer to the car, and Clay smiled at her. With a scream, she jerked the wheel towards him. The car shook with a loud thump. The eyes disappeared. There was nothing in the rearview.

The car accelerated. "Impossible," she begged. The road weaved back and forth. Boom! Something struck the passenger side, and Tracy jerked the wheel left. Back wheels kicked up dirt, but the front pulled her onto a side road. A faded sign had Green emblazoned on it, half claimed by the forest. Red leered in at her with burning eyes and an impish grin. She wrenched the wheel. The wild-eye woman clung to the side. The engine roared. Darkness deepened around the car.

"SLOW DOWN," Hemi roared beside her with a bellow of good cheer. Laughter erupted from both sides and behind. The Bliss family clung to the car.

Tracy screamed. She slammed the accelerator to the floor. The Black Priory raced past, and she frowned. She had never been here before. Most of Lear County had even seen it. "PREACHER'S JUMP," she screeched and stomped on the brake.

The wheels locked, and the rear end fish-tailed. As the front end lifted, they sailed over the bluff. Tracy clutched the wheel. Clay sighed, and Red burst into a feral, rebel yell. Hemi hooted. They saw the bottom bathed in moonlight.

Leah jerked. The echo of the wreck crawled over the mountain. Landen pulled her closer. All over the entire town, the news of the bar brawl spread. He heard that some crazy drifters had kidnapped his soon-to-be ex-wife and daughter. After checking the Rangel community, which looked like a tornado, hit it, he followed the police and deputies up the mountain. Tracy had left her, and he swore Leah would never set foot in her mother's house again.

"I'm sorry, Honey," Landen stroked her hair. "I just couldn't take any more." He shook. He didn't see any blood, but he would take her to the hospital.

"It's okay," she said, touching the business card. She had time to think about it.

He looked at her. "No, it isn't okay." Landen studied her eyes. "I left, and I should've taken you with me." The courts tied him up for weeks. Tracy kept calling the cops and spreading rumors.

"Mom lied," she grumbled, looking at the road. "She told me you didn't bother to call or message me. I just saw your texts tonight."

"We are going to leave Lear County. You need to be in a place to become your TRUE self." He sighed. "I'll have to deal with your mother." Landon would never let Tracy have her back.

"Does anyone become their true self?" Leah wondered, thinking of the Bliss family.

Red looked up and wondered if the police had found Leah. She glanced at the twisted heap of the muscle car. That girl was special, she knew. Hemi looked at the wreck, laughed, and shook his head. He walked around the twisted metal but finally threw up his hands. Clay found an unbroken bottle of whiskey. He studied it and already considered their next task. As long as they moved, they would keep their sanity together. The horrors and long life played havoc with the mind.

"Help," Tracy garbled, and the door opened. She couldn't make her legs move.

Red turned, "Like a roach, like a rat, the Devil must watch over you." She stared up at where she caught the scent of Leah.

"Help," Tracy reached for her, trying to free herself.

"Geez," Hemi turned to her, "she'll live. She'll never walk again."

Clay looked at the broken woman. "We need to get going. They'll come to check the wreck," he warned with a sigh.

Red drew closer to Tracy. "Your daughter is special. She is better than you," she hissed through her teeth. She covered Tracy's mouth with a finger to silence her pleas. "You will live, if they find you, within a couple of days, I think. Leah, your daughter, will help you, and you'll use her love as a cudgel. She'll take care of you while you destroy her hope of escape, her sense of self." Hellish flames burned in Red's eyes.

"Help," Tracy begged.

"Oh," she drew closer, "I intend to help Rosalie." She blinked, growing distant. She snapped back. "I mean Leah," she whispered. Red held her palm over Tracy's mouth, pinching her nose shut. Tracy struggled, but still after a moment. Red wiped the hand on her jeans. "Now, she will have a chance."

This Need

Moonlight dripped through the thick canopy above. Between blackened leaves, it crept upon the desolate bog. Under its glow, the lowland was a terror-benighted shadow, which moldered in its putrescence. Above the muck was a ground fog that carried the decay of tree and flesh. It was heavy, desolate, but warm. This vapor crawled over the earth or skin like the feverish exhalation of a dying man. Sparks of bruised purple hid inside, flirting with yet evading the eye. Each breath carried the base musk of the forest; yet it left the taste of the grave on the tongue. It pried its way between the lips. It slithered through the nose. Somewhere the crow called a lover lost. Around the woods, it echoed, then died. So pitiful a plea, this entreaty fell to whisper, then silence. Though trees kept one company, indifferent but watchful to all, he felt adrift. This sea of night passed over him in phantasmal waves. They drew closer in the darkness, in the silence. They peered down at him with patient hatred.

Kayden watched the stagnant pond through the dirty glass. The errant drop of a leaf would send ripples out on the placid water. Waves carried silver slashes in perfect silence until they struck the surrounding mud. Above calm waters, a noose hung, which swung ever so slightly. It had held men and women so they could dance out their last steps. Like a mirror, the water reflected it, and the reflection appeared ready to pull all into the blackness below.

He frowned, but everything before was a haze of Cimmerian black. Eyes like beech wood, charred at the edges, roamed over the vintage car's interior. Deep within forgotten memory, the name slipped beyond his grasp. Kayden turned the radio's nob, though it was silent. Red lines, thin as razors, traced the back of his hand, and he stared. No blood seeped from the wound which sealed. Beneath the tattered, stained shirt, his heart raced.

The radio flickered to life, and the nobs turned. A golden oldie station, the Buzz, played hits of the fifties and sixties. Words filled the cab of a great pretender, who lives in a make-believe world. Kayden listened as tears filled his eyes, which most found uncomfortable. He adverted his gaze till he stopped looking at people directly. This song teased a sorrow buried in the fog of his mind. Another came, though not the one adorned with sorrow.

"Hooper's Cherry," he said. The words uttered to the fine, rich interior, though dust covered it.

Kayden pondered his words. The old car was a ghost story, although Kayden and his brother played in the 1964 Dodge. Old Hooper never had a new ride until he'd saved up money from years of overtime at the mill. Around town, all came to recognize the cherry-red paint, which dazzled in the sun's brilliance. Every Sunday, he would drive about town and even give children rides around the town square. Music poured from the limited-edition coupe. It echoed over the streets.

Hooper suffered the wrath of the Misses in good stride, Kayden heard. When so much money went to his obsession, she was open with her displeasure. Her grousing turned to nagging, but Old Hooper still had his car. Indifferent to his wife's anger, he could always find peace in the smooth ride. Lovers, however, always knew where their weaknesses were.

Kayden found it next to the willow, just like the story. Misses Hooper had asked for a divorce. Hooper was fine with it. Only the car brought him satisfaction or joy, so she had stolen it. He chased her through the town, and they drove out into the Blackberry Bog. Although everyone would've said it was impossible. She stopped short of the Witch's Pond next to the Gallows Tree. They found Old Hooper's abandoned truck, but the police never found the car, him, or the Misses.

Sometimes, when you were in the lowlands of Lear County, you would see headlights in the forest. They weaved through the trees. Others had heard music, though found nothing. Kayden recalled running away from his father, Isaac, and hearing the same song. He followed it through the muck until he found Hooper's cherry-red 1964 Dodge. It waited for me, he mused, like it was on a showroom floor instead of a bog. I rushed home so I could tell my brother.

"Andre," he whispered. Fresh tears burst out, but again, the memory danced away in the fog laced with bruised purple light like arcs of lightning.

Deep in his mind, the name shrouded, which was long hidden. When was the last time he'd thought of Andre? Kayden drew back against the seat. He shuddered beneath tattered clothes. His brother had always been an odd child, he recalled. The sense of him surfaced. More comfortable with girls, Kayden thought. He tried to remember more of him. Clouds came to the forefront of his mind, revealing dead nebulae in lifeless realities.

They rushed to unravel the mystery of Hooper's Cherry. Even then, their home rotted, nearly black. Andre was older and taller, but a frail boy with a delicate frame. Kayden smiled at his brother's delight at seeing the legendary ghost car in all its banality. The radio would spark on, randomly almost, he thought with a troubled smile. Golden oldies, from love songs to chart toppers, would play over the old radio. The unsteady memory made it fresh off the assembly line, but it had set in a bog for decades. You couldn't walk through the forest without getting filthy.

Despite the decay and gloom, the bleak blackness seemed far away. They were free to indulge in innocence. They were far from their father's severe judgments. Imagination feeds the freedom to fly. Every fancy of their minds played around the derelict car. Behind the meager joy, the specter of pain hid. Kayden frowned. A taint threaded through the light, which was a bruised purple. It was ugly despite its alien beauty. It pulsed like a malignant heart. The tormented edge of night drew closer to this island of light.

"Why were we there?" he asked, the shadows beyond the glow of moonlight. From what did we hide?

Out in the bog, a deeper shadow played. The cancerous, bruised purple light pulsed inside the miasma, like a heart forever upon the edge of death. It crept closer, but the memory was half-hidden in sorrow. It flickered to life. He watched the ghosts of his youth and Andre run. Memory was fallible, he saw, though all the years were gone from his younger face. No broken heart, sorrow, or bitterness marred the child; although he saw all of it in the mirror.

The darkness came, shrouded by Kayden's mind, to moonlight's edge. It flowed, seethed, and beat with an alien light of dead, mad worlds. Though he strained to see what the blackness held, it deceived the eye and beguiled the mind. Young Kayden and Andre turned, for they could see.

Joy twisted off Kayden's youthful face. Andre, more accustomed to the world's darker truths, looked away, but steeled himself to fate. Every ounce of joy was gone, now a memory to a memory.

Music from the radio stammered and then died. The light went dark. The heart beneath his tattered clothes pounded, but it felt like a fantasy. Blood roared in his ears, and a chill worked through every muscle. The rasp of every breath held a rattle, as if each was the last. Every crow's call, frogs' croak, and whisper among the trees pressed upon the body and mind. He tried to dislodge the tang of soured pennies on the tongue. Low salt of tears or blood hung in the throat. Skin pebbled, fine hair rose, and he thought of thunderstorms. All beyond him pressed into every nerve, so the bog was a part of him. Woodland creatures crept through the muck, which he felt. Darker things lingered there with strange minds of shattered perceptions. Kayden felt the line between the world and him dissolve; everything was beyond real, a past dream.

Kayden looked out the window, frowned, and tears spilled. "Something happens," he muttered to the glass and memories.

As in all dreams, acts of fate, or nightmares, the world moved without passion and care. Each moment came. Isaac Stone slogged through the muck of the bog. Below his hateful scowl, he wore a smile of wild excitement. His brow drew down, and nicotine-stained teeth flashed in bestial rage. Dark eyes glimmered with sparks of bruised purple. Kayden pressed a hand to his chest, as gray crept into the edges of his vision. Mud clung to worn-out boots and the bottom of his jeans. Isaac squeezed his hands into fists. Knuckles popped; years at the mill had hardened fingers, tough as wood.

Kayden's hand worked at the door, but it was stuck. He peered through the dirty glass. The memory was content to play on, despite his heart pounding. He felt too light. Sweat beaded all over his body. Each was cold as a corpse.

"What did you say?"! Isaac screamed. Young Kayden shrunk back.

"What are you talking about?" Andre looked away, as his lisp deepened. He crossed his arms over a slight chest.

Isaac grabbed his oldest son's wrist and yanked him forward. He squeezed Andre's throat. "You don't talk about BLOOD outside the family!"

"She knew something was wrong," he hissed, cheeks reddening.

"I had a call from the principal," he pushed. His son slammed against the 1964 Dodge, and lights flickered through the dash and radio. "They said that YOU said things," Isaac slapped him, sounding sharp.

Kayden jerked as his younger self shriveled against the vintage car. The unsteady memory felt real. It was wrong. The core of it was factual. He could feel them, sense them. Rage, fear, and shame watched over the confusion, panic, and terror that crawled through Kayden's heart. Darkness without joining the shadow within, until the mind became drunk in the blackness of forgotten sorrow. All outside was inside, which widened the gulf between mind and body. Every molecule was an ocean of endlessly bruised purple-tinged black. A cacophony of sensation stole resolve.

"Is this real?" Kayden breathed with a shudder.

Every moment, the memory played out. He recalled the past veiled in half-truths. This faulty dream on shifting sands played for Kayden. Before any sequence accounted for, it slipped through the fingers. Fine grains of the mind transitioned from past to present, sifted by the years. Did it happen? Did they find Hooper's Cherry? These lies he told to himself held truths, though falsehoods veiled them. Just beyond the glass, this drama drew on.

Andre begged. Isaac screamed. They were born of Kayden's mind. The malignant dark consumed his father. His brother broke more in every moment. It was like Andre had become a beautiful glass doll. Life had decayed over time, the creeping darkness filled in the gaps, lesions of the heart. The counselor cried as Kayden recalled. The Sheriff had come. People whispered, though all acted ignorant. Some confessed they suspected, but another's family wasn't their concern. Kayden tried to get out and needed to help Andre, but the lock refused to budge. His younger self cried, frozen by terror.

"Do you want to see your mother, MOMMA'S BOY?"! Isaac screamed and slammed Andre's head into the car. In the wretched fury, there was fear in his heart.

"No Daddy," young Kayden begged, rushing forward, blinded by tears. He was hurting his brother. There was no reason.

"SHUT UP," Isaac shrieked. He swung and knocked his youngest son to the muddy earth.

"Get away from him," Andre punched at his father.

Isaac touched his jaw, eyes died, but his smile grew. "Today, you see Gwen," he promised. Did his son think he would let him get away with it?

He grabbed Andre's throat. Though his oldest son struggled, hard labor hardened Isaac's grin. Kayden punched at the glass and kicked the door. I need to save Andre; he thought. He glanced at his younger self. I wanted to be stronger. I needed to be tougher.

Andre stilled. Kayden drew closer to the glass as his father dumped the body in Witch's Pond. Many found eternal sleep within it. Isaac took in ragged, deep breaths, smiled wider, and disconnected. His eyes turned to his youngest.

The radio flickered to life. The song of the pretender returned. Kayden stared at the dome light which came to life. It hissed and crackled. Beside him, the door to the vintage car popped open. He spilled from it. He hoped he could still do something. Isaac and Andre were gone.

"Not real," he sobbed to the placid pond. This was a nightmare. He had lost days. Kayden didn't even know how he got here.

Kayden wiped the sweat from his brow and saw it shimmer in the moonlight. It just feels so real. His mind groaned. Every breath drew in the bog's musk, even the tang of his perspiration. He swallowed down the sour taste, and shakes sent tremors through him. A crow cackled in the forest, amused by his anguish. Bullfrogs rose as one, croaks garbled, but fell silent. Eyes roamed over his body. Something lurked deep in the black miasma that roamed the woods.

"How did I get here?" he breathed. Kayden's eyes rambled over the muck.

No one answered from the dreary gloom. He was somewhere between dream and damnation. Shafts of melancholy light revealed little, though hid much. Shadows morphed, shrunk; yet, grew deeper with every pulse. This dream must be a fragment of the past, he mused. Part of him wanted to run, but there was nowhere to go. His dead brother's name echoed back to him. It mocked in its simple repetition, half curse, and remonstration. Tears spilled. Sobs choked with each inhalation. The terror in Andre's eyes lingered, which hung in his mind. His brother's failing pleas swept over the bog, the specter alive still. All beyond the moonlight congealed to a quivering mass that writhed and hated.

No dream had ever been this real. Reality fell short of this damned dream. Kayden coughed. Chest rattling, he felt no pain or illness. Bruised purple light, twin flickers of corrupted sparks, stared back at him in the 1964 Dodge's glass. His brow turned down. He turned his reflection as it stared back. It became a deeper darkness, almost a silhouette. His features hardened. The resemblance to Isaac accused him. Fate was a fickle god, who came for all in the end.

His eyes sailed about the island of light. It went anywhere but at his defiled reflection. A low cry hissed up at him, choked by clicks. Young Kayden stared up at him with blistered, burned eyes that had gone blind. His skin became sallow, milky pale. It was badly burned but then bleached to the white of bone. His lips were gone. The agonized moan lifted to the defiant moon. Crimson pupils seized adult

Kayden with the malevolence of a mad imp. A gibbering curse slipped between jagged teeth, which had broken into shards.

Kayden fell back, foot slipped in the mud, and his feet flew up. Air whooshed out of his lungs. His eyes flew to the scarred child. Gone, the sound of tortured wails remained for a moment, though they faded away seconds later. Alone once again, he coughed but tried to breathe.

"Am I dead?" he asked Hooper's Cherry. No account of the afterlife was anywhere close to this.

The dead feel nothing... right? Kayden felt the deep pain in his chest abate. I've had vivid dreams before, but this one is too real. "That candy," he snatched at a memory before the gulf of emptiness stole it. I took that drug that tasted like candy. Everything got strange after that. Alien light and a deep hiss swallowed all memory till Hooper's Cherry. Did I have a bad trip? Am I tripping now?

No answer came. Maybe I'm in Hell or Purgatory or something. The Blackberry Bog solved problems; Kayden knew. "Maybe someone tired of my mouth," he suggested. He thought of Brian, who was a veteran, and sat up. An ache crept through sleepy muscles, knots hard until worked out. He rubbed his chest. "I feel like I'm dying," he laughed, but a chill ran over his spine, despite the bog's warmth.

A shadow shifted as moonlight pierced the forest canopy. Kayden turned. Deeper in Blackberry Bog, a young man or teenager stopped half-hidden in the darkness. La Voison women to traffic with the dead, he thought as his mind floundered. They say there is a path. A great serpent guarded it. What he always dismissed as superstition echoed through the years. Is it the swamp or am I dead or is this a dream? The questions went up as a plea or prayer. I barely recall him, but that is Andre!

Hooper's Cherry sagged into the earth, which opened its wet maw to devour it. Like an old man sucking a boiled egg, Kayden mused. Light upon Witch's Pond dimmed and nearly died. Darkness of Blackberry Bog drew closer as things squirmed inside. Bolts of lightning crawled through the vapor that almost formed a letter or word. It slashed the mind, dividing consciousness from the dream. It stunned him with its mad wonder.

Kayden staggered away, mind disconnected, body unsteady. Red lines, thin as razors, raced over his emaciated body. He covered his eyes, which ached. As if I looked at something welding, Kayden cursed. Veins slipped from the bloodless cut and waggled in the air as worms questing. His heart pounded, yet it slowed, eyes drew to his brother.

Little wounds healed before he could open beech wood eyes. I should try to speak to Andre, Kayden thought. He forced his legs to move. A shadow darted close to his leg, and moonlight caught bone-white, scarred flesh.

"Oh God," he whispered, but kept his eyes upon his older brother, who was younger than him now.

"Daddy didn't mean it," young Kayden pleaded, though haunted eyes slid away.

"Always a mean, old," he muttered, refusing to look down. You stopped making excuses for people when you accepted. They never loved you.

"They had a special relationship," the boy assured him.

Kayden opened his mouth, though only an agonized groan escaped. Fresh tears spilled. His gaze fell to the muck, and the scarred boy was gone. He returned to Andre, who waited next to a doorway. It was from a trail, a local tourist spot, where you could walk from top to bottom of Lear Mountain. What is it doing here? It is miles away! His brother turned. The moonlight caught the angry red marks on his throat. Kayden held up a hand to hail him, but nothing passed between his lips.

He rushed forward to halt his brother, but the muck slowed him. He stepped through the old wrought iron archway, though paused just beyond. It led down into the earth. The stairway dove and dived ever deeper. Silver light pierced the weave of briars above, yet it was underground. Kayden ignored it, feeling unsteady. Every step downward brought him no closer to his kin, and the way back faded in the distance. Andre flowed downward in a silent grace. Kayden called, sound deadened in this passage, yet it seemed his brother didn't hear or dared not tarry. Every step echoed back to Kayden, flat and wet. The stones of the steps cut decades ago. The passage of time diminished them. Hot, humid air slipped down from above as a rattle wracked the passage. Sweat rolled down his brow and dripped from his chin.

Kayden paused, looking back at the dark behind. Andre was gone. The end of the stairway held only darkness. He called for his brother, but the murmur of voices came through the pool of black. The scrap of metal was low, beneath the rasp of chalk on a board. The pine scent of cleaners leaked through with sawdust. Janitors used it to clean up vomit, Kayden recalled. I always felt so small, and the teachers always looked so big; like we were rabbits, they were foxes or big, mean dogs.

Kayden looked back at the stairs. Muck spilled down each step, and would soon flood the bottom. "No choice," he breathed, and his racing heart kicked into a gallop. Dark mud bubbled and dripped, but something moved deeper inside it, slithered and hated. He recoiled from the tiny bursts of bruised purple that watched.

Darkness washed over him as he stepped back, cold yet grasping. Kayden blinked at the powder-white wall, which held little placards. Each had the smiling child. Only little Kayden looked distant, dower. Was I ever happy? He considered the past. Gloom adorned the hall of the school. Every space or crack had an ichor, which bled onto the stone. Little tendrils pried through the gaps to waver in the air. Freshly spilled blood slept beneath. The smell soured like pennies left to molder. He coughed. Children and teenagers passed him, ignorant of his intrusion on the mix of elementary and high schools. They moved through the hall, and a young woman walked through a plump kid, both indifferent.

"Did your father ever... do anything to your brother?" a voice whispered.

"I don't know," young Kayden muttered. He shifted under the scrutiny.

His skin felt tight, sweat cold, and the world wavered as unsteady as a ship upon a tempest-torn sea. Waves of nausea washed over him, and memories rose unbidden but fell away. Mind unmoored from the body. He was adrift but drowned in countless dying worlds. Back to the amalgamation of memories he returned, tossed upon low eddies. Lifeless smears drowned faces. Sunken gazes were horror-haunted. They grinned and leered as they passed him with the gimlet eyes of friends.

Andre walked out of the classroom. He weaved around the other students and kept well-clear of them, so they were outside reach. Kayden yelled for his brother, but it was fruitless. Young ladies watched Andre as he passed. They whispered behind their hands. Lovely features contorted, skin splitting so barbed tongues waggled. Each shake rattled like a snake. He followed his brother as walls bloated, shrunk, or grew. Faces on placards leered. Nasty, low laughter fell dead on the filth-covered floor. A mop bucket set next to a dark pool filled with chunks. Things squirmed inside with too-human faces. Hands pawed at Kayden covered in lacerations, which oozed a pungent odor like mushrooms. Even the floor felt uneven, appearing flat. He'd stagger when his foot lifted too high to miss the distorted earth.

Kayden tripped, righted himself, and then spilled forward. He landed in a deep crimson pool and slid. Little creatures with crunchy shells cracked and popped, screaming like children burned alive. A young woman walked past, books pressed against her chest, simple dress down to slight ankles. A tail of translucent flesh over bone waved at him as she passed. The world felt distant and blurred, and vomit dribbled from his lips. He drew in a sharp breath and rolled out of the warm ichor. A woman glared at him with a broad smile full of cannibal teeth.

He squeezed his eyes shut. "These are not my memories," he assured himself. This is mine and something else, Kayden thought. It is so real. Maybe it is part of me trying to remember or recall. Is my brother's death the reason for anything? Is this the reason for this need, a need to save? I couldn't save Jillian.

He shook his head at the thought. He could still save her. The dampness beneath him grew cooler as he thought of her. The smell of fresh-cut grass greeted him. Kayden's brow drew down. Blades of grass, half-shorn, pricked his face and forearms. He opened his eyes, swallowing his sour spit. His stomach turned, head light. A door banged closed in the impish wind, sounding sharp.

"No," he peered about the house, which gawked back at him. Kayden shook his head, sitting up. His hand pressed on the book's cover. He bumped into the well.

A wave of nausea wiped away the world to leave dead galaxies, devoured by the placid sanity of reality. His childhood home loomed over him. Bruised purple light blazed over him. Somewhere, a mad monk gibbered, cursed, and pleaded, but revelations assailed him, which he wrote in a leather-bound book. Kayden tried to see him, though blinded. A deathly visage swam before him. He knew his name was Astrad. He knew it from deep within. The madman's name scoured the mind and lingered on the tongue. Was it he who showed him his brother's recollections?

Quick as it came, this reality slip receded. Kayden faced the house of his family, terrors teased from his mind's shadows. The past crept closer. Memories came, but he shook them off. Behind him was the road, though darkness filled the road past the edge of the property. Eyes, beech wood brown with charred edges, returned to the house. It stood, windows dirty, holes in the roof, but refused to fall.

Two graves set next to the house, but he knew the names of them. "That night, after they buried you," Kayden saw Isaac on the stone, "I pissed on your grave."

After urinating on the tombstone, he had never set foot on his family's land again. Even when he lost his house, Kayden refused to return. Jillian wanted him to visit it, but he'd refused.

Her face swam to the surface with eyes nearly closed upon the edge of sleep. Kayden retreated from the memory. I may have lost my job, he swore, but I'll get her into rehab. The smile faltered, then broke, and he frowned. His ex-wife's sleepy eyes lingered, though the image died. It fled back into the darkness.

"There is nothing here for me," Kayden muttered to the house and turned away.

The wall of darkness was cold, greasy, and wet. He forced forward, closing his eyes. Like surfacing after submerging in a warm bath, Kayden broke through into a bone-deep chill.

Burned, rotted meat clotted the air. Kayden opened his eyes to a billow of smoke. It hung over the room as a ground fog, and a thin film of grease covered everything. Sizzle of the flesh hissed, though insect-like clicks hid within. He closed his mouth, but the air tasted like a burn victim's decayed carcass. He coughed, bile rising, but he swallowed it down. Again, the world wavered about him, as gray around his vision had veins of black. All felt like a facade, a comfortable lie over an uncomfortable truth. Absently, he wiped at his skin, but oil clung to it. Things skittered away into dark corners.

"Sit down, BOY," Isaac commanded. Kayden's lip drew up, but for a moment, he felt the urge to do as bidden.

A teenage Kayden trudged, sullen, into the room. He looked at his younger self, wiping away a tear. I forgot how happiness felt until I met Jillian. She was the first spot of light in my life. But she is, he thought, shaking his head.

Isaac was the man of his heart's truth. His father's sallow skin was the color of cheap candles. Eyes gone; they had gored out holes that seeped a dark liquid. It stunk like fried piss. Each drop hissed on the table. His father chewed, jaw working. Broken teeth sliced rotting food. Living briars of rusted iron crawled up through his gullet to creep through holes in his cheeks. They twisted and twined about his body as barbs tore more blood free. Isaac's arms and legs had withered down to bone, muscle now stringy cords. A bulbous gut hung over stained underwear. Root of the rusty creeper writhed with the vines inside, just below his skin.

Kayden stared. The world was gray. Black veins pulsed around his vision, and he felt bile rise at the cloud of stink about his father. Just a nightmare, he assured himself, but his head grew lighter. He coughed, legs wobbled. He rested a hand on the table, and a spoon toppled to the floor. The rattle in his chest deepened, and he coughed. Galaxies of bruised purple light waited for him in the darkness, where reality became unbound. I must be strong, he thought. I need to be strong. Oh God, I might throw up.

"Don't you even have the guts to look at me?" Isaac laughed out a nasty bark.

"I'm going to school... I have to leave," teenage Kayden looked at his plate.

His father drank from a mason jar, liquid clear, but the alcohol stung the young man's eyes. "Do you think it'll make a difference?" he challenged with a chuckle. "You're the SON of a KILLER," he grinned, empty sockets bled onto the floor.

"I do well," he countered though meekly.

"My GOD, you're so smart, you're useless," he sneered. "You'll end up in the factory too, smartest man on the assembly line." Isaac leered at his son. A vine of iron, covered in rusty barbs, rose into the air before it slashed at a teenage Kayden. So delicate was the cut, no blood escaped the scratch.

He looked at his father, but his gaze fell. "I'll never be you," he promised, trying for defiance, but was little more than a whimper.

Isaac brought both fists down, and everything on the table jumped. Empty sockets glared, "Do you think you'll get a scholarship, BOY?" A nasty laugh escaped his rotted meat-filled maw. Chunks fell to the table. Another vine slashed twice at young Kayden to leave angry red lines.

"No," he shifted, "maybe I could earn one."

Isaac laughed and then slapped the table. "Hope is for the rich!" He shook his head. "Brains, but no sense!"

Young Kayden's eyes darkened and older Kayden recalled the first instance of hate in his heart. It was a nebulous thing which burned cold. It felt like a knife plunged into his core.

"I'll leave here," teenage Kayden swore.

"You'll die in the gutter," Isaac chuffed.

"Not before I see you die first," he hissed, eyes darkened. Again, the icy blade turned in his chest. It wished to plummet into his father's mouth.

Isaac sneered, but beneath the bluster, he quivered at his son's eyes. His face hardened. "Do you think you can kill me?" He demanded in a high whine.

Kayden looked down, face flushed, "No." He wanted to deny it. A broken, withered part of him still wished he could love his father.

He jumped to his feet, snatched up the knife, and jerked the teenage Kayden's head back by the hair. "I could cut your throat!" he swore, licking his lips.

The young man stared up into his father's baleful gaze, but a frown creased his unsullied brow. "You're... you're a coward," he breathed, revelation resounding to his core. Truth came at the oddest moments. It refused to live the lie which all adults seemed comfortable abiding.

Isaac growled. He held the knife to his son's throat, but the young man only stared back in confused disgust. The blade pressed against his throat. Kayden's strange eyes, like beech wood charred at edges, judged. His father shook his head. Vines with rusted barbs trembled. The metal creeper slashed at him and left bloody cuts; yet his disgust only grew.

"You better shut up," he warned, "or you'll end up in Blackberry Bog!"

"No," the young man blinked. Bullies were cowards. None ever wanted a fight they believed they may lose.

"What," Isaac stammered.

Teenage Kayden stood. The chair fell back, and he tried to push his father away. His hand bounced off Isaac's chest to slap him across the face. Both stared at the other.

"I have to go to school," Kayden stammered, blinking at his father's tremor. He bolted out the door. The blade inside his chest felt a bitter joy. It was the same joy that lit his father's eyes.

Isaac stared, lip trembling. He looked at the knife in his hand. His knuckles turned white, and he bared his teeth. His son cast his gaze downward, refusing to turn back. Isaac rushed onto the porch. "Come back here." The young man walked faster, but cast a disgusted look back. Isaac screamed at the distaste. "Just like your MOTHER!" he rushed after him.

"Get away from me," teenage Kayden broke into a run but tripped over his feet. His hand snatched at the old well's lip.

Isaac seized his shirt, knife raised, "Just like your whore mother!"

"STOP," he swung around, elbow struck his father's jaw.

Isaac stumbled, vines of rusted iron wavering in the air. His father slipped, banging against the well. The sound of his skull cracked was like a carrot broken in two. Teenage Kayden crawled back, eyes widening. His mouth worked, though no scream came. His gaze flew about the yard. The young man flew towards the house.

Kayden watched his younger self retreat inside. All he recalled was waking up in the hospital. The rest was gone, just like the memory of Andre, until he'd seen it again. He turned back to Isaac, who shambled back up onto his feet. Vines wavered in the air. Each step was a labor. Blood and brains dripped from his skull. Bruised purple light arose behind him. Darkness devoured him, leaving a god-shaped hole. The name Ghlaad whispered to his mind, a curse and revelation. Riotous light blazed, and he staggered away. Kayden fell back into the well. The darkness swallowed him.

"He comes!" a man declared, rapturous yet incoherent. The words erupted from nowhere, echoing through this pseudo memory.

In the endless black, he floated. The infinite tearing open. Another reality rotted, stars died, and chaos defiled the order's sanity. The Gallows King approaches, Kayden's mind insisted, though it was another's voice like his, yet darker. Out of the ragged hole, a silhouette came like a slash of night, head obscured by strange features. Flesh beneath the midnight violet cloak writhed in a bedlam of dark masses. Molten skin peeled from the festered heart of dead stars, once gods. His visage shifted, as though always clothed in the raiment of monks. As a virgin saint, the mad deity descended. The world wavered, shimmered, and cast him adrift in the infinite corpses of celestial bodies.

Kayden spread across the boundless expanse, but he receded into the tomb of his body. He coughed, blood flecks flew. Under the vast, dead nothing, the first sense of peace eased knotted muscles. All the horrors of this Dream Land sent tremors through him. If he had needed to piss, he reckoned, he would've wet himself. Not reality. The declaration was a prayer against the madness. Only morbid curiosity and terror kept him moving. They dissolved too. Here, finally, there were no indignities or cruelties. All was nothing, a part of the infinite, so to make each part insignificant. The tormented isle of his heart felt the calm sea of apathy.

A question in the silence lingered. Inside, where Andre's brilliant but sad face waited. It came as an insistent plea. This need savaged him. Why did he feel it? To live was to suffer, Kayden thought, and so was the plight of everyone upon the earth. He never quit, but never felt this peace before. I must get back to Jillian. He blinked. She needs me. If I don't get her into rehab, no one will. I need to save her.

A voice accused him of a lie, but he shook it off. As he sat up, the tattered strands of peace fell away. Again, the world had shifted. The graves were in neat rows over the rolling land. Tombstones caught the light from the furtive moon, half hidden in the storm. Bruised purple lightning crept through black clouds, thunder-like wails of the mad. No rain fell, though the tumult above promised a downpour. Wind through the stones screamed, and flesh pebbled on his skin. Ancient rot set on the tongue. A low musk of mushrooms bled up from the earth. Past the storm above, the dead realities still watched.

Kayden surveyed the cemetery, named "Heavenly Springs." He never visited Meridian's largest graveyard.

If Blackberry Bog was the battered, besieged heart of Lear County, the graveyard was its abandoned soul. It was massive, but the Blackburn family, cousins to the Van Lear, maintained it. No one would dare ask why Van Lear allowed anyone but themselves to handle such an important part of the town. Like all cemeteries, it was the bitter memory of people. Name and date told little of their stories. They kept all their tales with them—tragedy or comedy. Death buried them together. Everyone who died in the county, except anyone from Swannanoa atop the mountain, found their rest here.

This memory of the past, the Empire of the Forgotten, surrounded Kayden. The storm had abated. No thunder echoed from the mountains or hillocks. A ground fog, thin and ethereal, drifted amongst the tombstones, chill and lifeless. Silence filled the dark. He listened to the rattle in his chest with every exhalation. He wiped his mouth, the taste of blood salty. His gaze wandered about the hills. The surreal became banal.

Throughout the grounds, the Blackburn family had placed benches surrounded by trees. Kayden looked up at the moon, but the dead galaxies were gone. No cloud stalked the sky.

He stepped towards the bench and wiped cold sweat. Kayden froze, head tilted. On each of them was a poster, the kind children put on trees or power lines. He studied them. The plain script was of a midnight purple like a violent bruise, though shimmered with the faint touch of light. Underneath pictures, it gave a brief summation. Christopher Peck had died in a car wreck, the body disappeared, and Sheila Richardson had vanished. Her car was still at the Black Priory. Brian Weber was also gone, but burned down his home. I don't recall this; he thought with a frown.

A hand reached towards the paper, and words brightened. Each seemed filled with a bruised purple light. A deep ache dug into his skull as memories bled into the mind. Christopher shambled on a snowy road in the dead of night. Black stones held Sheila within. In some strange desert, Brian bummed a cigarette from a dead soldier. Each memory rammed inside, a real yet more than a dull sensation of consciousness. They overlapped, mixed, or stitched together in a vile amalgamation. Blazing violet light held the memories together, bleeding prophesies of doom. All inside became impossible angles and proportions. An alien shape, impossible geometry beyond the strictures of this Dream Land, hung inside. It crushed all thought, and Kayden felt the world ravage him.

"Ghlaad, Riotous of Violet, comes" the mad monk wailed, but in a tongue blasphemous to all that dwell in the sanity of light.

The bench before him was hand-carved oak, and bolted to the earth, so no storm could move it. Beneath it, the stone was a corrupted shade of night, infected by bruised purple arcs. It shifted, scraping like bone on bone, but only revealed a crack in the tomb beneath. A black smoke crept out. Tendrils snatched at the grass so it could pull more of itself out. Up from the grave, a spicy decay warmed the air. Kayden wiped at his sweat. His eyes refused to let go of the tattered hand that gripped the lid. The stone moved away.

Out of the grave, a black fog of defiled vapor billowed out onto the earth. Sparks of bruised purple frolicked through the miasma. A head rose out, though another lolled next to it, sewn onto the neck. As the corpse rose, another face, stapled to the chest, unveiled itself. All of them writhed upon the perversion of a body. Chris, Sheila, and Brian glared at him in idiot hate. Their mouths worked in silent curses of alien malevolence. Three sets of hands pulled the lumpy approximation of a body. Several spines, twisted by a cruel god, made up the ghoulish trunk. It emerged, but he froze to the spot. It grinned, yet Kayden remained. The smoothness of its movement boggled the sane mind. It slogged forth.

"Kayden," the Blasphemy cooed with all the delight of a hysterical man, unsteady yet urgent.

The amalgamation of flesh stood to its full height to unveil a gut full of teeth. Like a Venus flytrap filled with fangs, it spread and dripped drool. Out of a depthless hole, a mewling echoed from another world. Kayden screamed as his paralysis broke. A few drops of piss dampened his pans. He whirled around and thanked anything that listened, God or the devil, that his bowels held. At least I didn't shoot the chocolate! His mind screamed and a jagged chuckle burst out. Away he dashed, laughter detached.

Fury of the Blasphemy of flesh boomed as thunder. A shrouded figure moved into the edge of Heavenly Springs. The sky shredded to unveil another cosmos from a deranged reality. All of it watched in hate, desiring the undoing of all that was sane. Countless eyes glared. Infinite mouths gibbered, and all listened in abject loathing. The sight of its chaos blurred the order that swaddled this Dream Land. This god approached an emissary of profaned flesh, with a contemplative step. Tall as a mountain, it moved as a crushing tide. Ghlaad comes, a voice inside said, and Kayden knew it was another in his head.

This Dream Land was boundless, but the Elder Outer Entity was timeless. Kayden ran, mind-numbed to oblivion, and wide eyes devoured the path ahead. From each grave, a tree rose. Upon the bark, faces leered with eyes of painful violet flame, mouths worked in horror. Wails filled the night, laments of endless time. Down from hefty boughs, a bizarre fruit hung. Faceless corpses swung in the still air. Their guts spilled out. Each had the head of a skinned goat, though screamed like burning cats choking on cicadas. They rained down upon the earth.

Death had abandoned these wretches. Eternal decay nibbled at flesh. The Suicide Forest filled with hissing screams. This happens to those who tried to take their own life, his mind insisted. Rot gnawed, flesh hardened and snapped at the hung men. Bark cracked in the gentle sway of the unholy oaks. Each bled. The corpses had no mouths and still screamed, although muffled by flesh. Between each wail, they sucked at the air. Meager breaths were insurmountable. Every twitch of muscle broke their skin. Spasms of pain drew more agony. They whispered accusations from the trunk, faces twisted, and he willed himself to avert his eyes.

Still, Ghlaad, Riotous of Violet, pursued Kayden in pensive steps. Trees toppled as flesh writhed over the land. Crushed beneath the colossus, the Suicide Trees were deathless. The balm of the cold void caused only suffering eternal. Their wails, the symphony of the damned, grew to apocalyptic heights. Kayden screamed and coughed up vomit, but ran on.

Back he cast beech wood eyes. Down upon the land, Ghlaad gazed at the forest. The Suicide Trees' trunks and boughs contorted under the alien gaze. Flesh grew, bursting through brittle bark. Each of the oaks bore a new fruit. Double heads grew up and turned towards the hateful cosmos above. They screamed, though quickly choked to a mutter. Branches grew out of mouths with eyes at the tips, film-covered and blind. They shivered and shook.

Kayden begged, and the vision behind him swallowed any rational thought. Before the gray could cover the world and pull him into the dark, his foot caught only air. He toppled into the gloom.

The wind whooshed out of his lungs and rattled a thin whistle. Kayden stared up from the crevasse. Ghlaad slowed and searched the Suicide Forest. Kayden closed his eyes. I can figure this out, he swore.

"In the beginning," the mad monk whispered, "there was chaos, life infinite. The order came in enlightened defiance, and it came as the Word." Astrad pondered, "The Word made constraints."

"What?" Kayden frowned, but a Word formed in the darkness behind his eyes. He wiped at his eyes, but the image remained.

The Word hung in the infinite blackness. No flat scribbled upon a page, it was math give form. Calculations beyond the mind of man, which flowed of pure consciousness, comprised the form. Anything and everything of the Word defined it within itself. The word and definition were one, but Kayden's mind flailed at it. He could touch, taste, hear, smell, and see it; although it was separate from him. He shook his head and reeled, but the Word remained. It existed detached from time or reality.

Its power was undeniable, for it nearly undone him. Language had power, which Kayden knew. All the beauty of the heart could bleed through. Fiction was keen on telling the truth through tales. Music could return you to the past. It made feelings real with their words. Inspiration drove people to great acts through speech alone.

This all started when I took HPL-0717, Figment. I could feel it. A bruised purple light blazed in the darkness behind his eyes. Kayden jerked. That, whatever, is inside me! He tried to steady his breathing and felt the world.

"Don't run from that which is a part of you," Astrad breathed, distant and contemplative.

A part of me, he thought with a frown. That is how I know about Chris, Sheila, and Brian. They're dead! Through lips pressed thin, a small scream slipped out. It killed them! Kayden gripped his chest, but his body shook, and tears slipped out.

"Take control, Dreamer," Astrad urged, though voice visibly weaker.

"I want to see Jillian," he begged and imagined her face. Kayden needed her. He wanted to know she was fine.

Kayden seized her memory. When there was hope, the future was brighter. He had recalled those days when Jillian was quick to smile. The scent of vanilla brushed over the air, the perfume gentle. It mixed with the chemical splash of dish soap, which approximated a meadow. Dishes clattered, sounding sharp. Silverware accompanied them. The ever-present decay swept away. The air conditioner kept the balmy day outside at bay. It hummed a low drone. Kayden straightened, weight lifting from his shoulders. He now sat. The wood of the chair was comfortable. With the salty taste of bacon and eggs was black pepper, his mouth watered. Just like every morning before work, he thought. His smile, tentative at first, grew a little firmer.

"Work that rough last night?" Jillian asked. "Are you awake?"

Kayden opened his eyes, teased by her voice. A sob slipped out when he saw her good health. I thought she was on the couch, he thought, but it fled before he could grasp it. "Jillian," he breathed, and tears burst out. She had recovered from the drugs, which had savaged her body.

"Yeah," she frowned with a chuckle.

"I," he swallowed. Whatever was happening, he knew, it was great to see her healthy again. "I missed you."

"I came over this morning to talk to you." Jillian's smile faded.

"Anything," he beamed. "I'll talk about anything! You look amazing!" he laughed and wiped away tears. Finally, he thought, I helped. Someone I love is happy!

She blushed, "Thank you. I have you to thank for my recovery. That time in rehab got really bad."

"I'm sorry," he reached for her hand. Kayden hated she'd suffered.

She took his hand, though, after a hesitation. "I came over to talk to you about something... important." Jillian's eyes slid away from him.

"Anything," he swore, grinning like a fool. It has been a long time, he thought, as the weight lifted from him. So suddenly was his misery lightened, that he choked back more tears. I thought it'd never be better! I knew if I worked and planned enough, things could finally turn around.

"I don't want to get back together," she confessed, looking away from his broad grin. It was terrible in its hopeful relief.

Kayden's smile froze and faltered, but he forced it to remain. He blinked, "I love you." Why did she say this?

"I love you too," she admitted, letting go of his hand.

"We were happy together," Kayden tried to hold her hand, but she withdrew.

His eyes wandered from her, for the room's brightness had dulled. Cracks had formed like wounds gone gangrenous. Little white worms spilled from them with little screams. The smell of the food had soured. Bacon burned, meat rotted, and eggs had turned minty green. They stared up at him with twin eyes of malignancy. Despite the cloud of decay, the sheen of tacky sugar covered the skin. He wiped at it, though it was sticky and greasy.

"That was a long time ago," she reminded him. Jillian frowned, eyes sparkled, "a lot longer ago than you think." Jillian crossed her arms, and red lines, thin as razors, raced over her skin.

"Things can be that way again," he pleaded. Kayden could fix things. All it took was work.

"Kayden, Honey, you have this... need," she turned her eyes away. "You saved me, and you try to save everyone." Jillian studied him. "You're so focused on everyone else, and you never live your life."

"You're my life," he scowled, "all I've done was to help you." He inspected her face but refused to look at the flesh that peeled from her arms.

Heavy lids low, her eyes stared through him. "You know we can't be together." Her skin shifted. A bruised purple spark danced in her eyes.

"Why?" he pleaded. His mind cut down a memory before it could flower.

"Because I'm dead," she reminded him, lips slack.

Jillian's body was lifeless, except for eyes that held an alien light. Veins wiggled free of flesh to pull her up like a marionette. No blood fell, though the tang of an abattoir filled the room. Flayed skin spread from her thin body like great wings. Light lit veins from within. Tugged up from the chair, her head lolled forward, but her eyes rolled towards him. Strings of flesh hooked into the floor and ceiling, which made a crimson web work. Kayden reeled. His hands went to his face, though his scream came out as a thin whisper. Jillian's stomach opened to unveil a maw filled with fangs. Tentacles reached out for Kayden. He screamed as she pulled him into the infinite abyss, which swirled from where her heart rested.

Through the chaotic dead space of the mad cosmos, he tumbled. Cancerous nebula swirled. Fragments of a sane reality floated, disconnected though still real, from infinite worlds. It fell to machinations of insane truths. In the beginning of Order, there was the Word, but it forced sanity onto its antithesis. As the Word gave meaning and structure, its opposite wailed in hate, so desired to be all and nothing. If it could be all this, it could be empty, this madness knew.

About Kayden, the revenge of the boundless bedlam spread out without measure. Forever it stretched, for many possibilities had fallen to the predations of the Outer Gods. Kayden screamed, and the cosmos laughed.

He slammed into the muck, and mud splattered up. Upon a chunk of earth, the Blackberry Bog of his memory drifted through the endless dead lands of this mad reality. He glanced at Hooper's Cherry, which squatted, rusted to the frame, but its radio flared to beleaguered life. The song of a great pretender resumed from the beginning. Lights of the dash flickered with the hateful laugh of the corrupted star systems. He coughed and tasted pennies, but forced himself to move.

Andre's head breached the swamp's surface. All the years in the mire had mummified the corpse. Sunken eyes, gimlet with bruised purple light, peered between patches of slimy hair. Green fungus adorned his smile, and a leech spilled out where a tooth had been. Clothes clung to the skeletal frame, stained to a midnight hue. This time, Kayden knew, his brother wanted to catch him, but for a lot more than just a word.

"Die in the past," Andre garbled, lisp wet, in the choked tone of a suffocated corpse.

As he stepped forward, oil-slick feathers grew from under parchment skin. Andre's lower jaw protruded and then came to a point. His teeth tumbled into the mud. One eye became a black orb, though it still held a spark of purple light, hateful and filled with spite. Slick mummified flesh became a riot of meat and bone. Eyes shifted, set above set, until he had eight eyes, half avian, and half a corpse's leer.

Talons stretched out of his back with the brittle snaps of an egg tread upon. Kayden stepped back. The horrid visage assailed his mind. His brother approached with talons long as a cloak and of a dirty corn yellow. Andre lurched forward at an uncanny speed, despite the bedlam of his form.

Kayden turned away with a shriek. Mind filled with the horror of Andre's riotous form. He ran. The horn honked in Hooper's Cheery, sickly yellow eroded to a plum-purple like an old bruise. Out into the bog, he dashed.

The words of Astrad the Augur returned. That, despite the corrupted Word that infected him, he was the Dreamer in this Dream Land, born of his memories. Kayden ran, closing his eyes.

A door formed in his mind. He opened his eyes. It appeared in Blackberry Bog, a frame attached to nothing. Kayden laughed. It was jagged, disconnected.

Kayden ran for it, but a devilish idea seized him. It had been so long since he'd even thought of Andre, it mused, so it would be a shame to not, at least, peek at his brother. The horror, which was his kin, raced through the mire. Only the corpse's eye remained human. Withered arms and legs propelled the deformed body, but the talons made its speed unearthly. Sets of wings had sprouted from random places upon the back, one from the upper stomach. Feathers fell, they molted, but more grew to replace them. The lower beak lolled to reveal the youthful face of Andre, eyes filled with terror.

He pulled away from the plea in his eyes. Kayden slammed into the door, and blood gushed from his nose. Feet slipped out from under him, and he bounced on the hardwood floor. A table leg struck his shoulder, which stopped his slide. He looked back, but the door to the Blackberry Bog closed.

"God," he sobbed. His mind whirled, refusing to accept this madness. If it was a dream, let him wake. If he was dead, then let the Devil reveal himself. This was too much.

"Boy," someone cooed. They giggled.

Isaac grabbed the table, and briars of rusted iron ensnared it. He flung it against the wall. It busted into pieces. Up onto his feet, Kayden scrabbled, though the mud was still slick on his shoes. He fell back from his father.

The nest of briars drew back into Isaac's mouth. His gut bulged until it was ready to burst. He bent, smile broad. Out from his back, the creepers burst, and blood splattered the walls. They dug into the floor and ceiling to corrupt the very house. Rust bit into the plaster, wood, steel, and glass. As he laughed, his head swelled to colossal proportions. Bones snapped, skin ripped like paper, and his head grew. It fell to the floor. Exposed muscles and teeth grinned where the skin had not grown fast enough. Kayden screamed, again frozen in horror. Empty sockets filled with bruised purple light until twin nests of tentacles burst forth. Instead of suckers, it had rings of barbs covered in plum colored pollen. Isaac's laugh was the dull-witted mirth of an idiot devil in hell; yet it was thrice as malicious. Teeth clattered together and severed the fat tongue. Even when blood sprayed from the stump, the chortle never faltered. A slick bud popped out of the severed end. It unfurled as a flower faced by the sun, although the petals of rusted skin held red eyes with ruptured pupils.

"No," Kayden shook his head, but his mind devoured the horror. It insisted that each terror sear into memory.

Every man or woman held an animal inside, which came to the fore in times of stress. One would fight or freeze, but the other would run. Kayden felt the urge to flee, feeling consumed by the horror.

He dashed away. Isaac laughed, and every creeper thrummed. A roar boiled up from deep in the writhing core of Kayden's father. He lurched towards his son, and the house about them started snapping deep within it.

The back door to the home led out into the yard. Kayden used the back door to enter, but the living dream cut off every exit. It burst open, but he ran into the living room. The snowy television cast a haunted glow. His mother stared through the screen. Light pooled in their eyes. The bones of her face were sharp. His heart ached, but Isaac came. She was slight in her dress, hollowed out. The mass of flesh and petals crushed all in its path, yet she still sat, crushed in an instant. The next room was from Kayden's house. Again, his mother sat. He launched past her. He could force eyes from his father, but not her, not his mother. His strange gaze fell upon her. His mother's eyes revealed one who had left in all but flesh. No reaction came when the rusty vine smashed her to the floor.

Again, he bashed through the door. The room's horror struck him, staggering in its insanity. So fetid was the filth that he coughed up vomit but closed his mouth to the compost heap-like stench. A buzzing thrummed throughout, and vibrations sang. The rusty creepers infected the room. They slithered and slid. About the derelict home, they probed. Like a cancer, it corrupted all it touched. Blackened veins spread, yet his mother still sat. She stared at the television, inert, except for the slight rise and fall of her chest. The malignance spread. Isaac's corrupted form defiled her, but still she sat, still apathetic to the agony. Dark ichor dripped from her eyes like tears, and it fell from a slack mouth. As Kayden passed, her gaze rose to him with a glimmer of hope of salvation. Resigned to fate, she knew the future, and all the hours of misery which awaited.

He ripped his face away with a shattered wail. If only I could see Jillian, he thought. I need her. I need someone.

Kayden slammed into the door. Isaac crashed into the room and his mother. He threw himself through, blinded by tears.

The rickety fence struck him, and he flipped over it. Air whooshed out of his lungs. Kayden coughed. Above him, among the sane stars, another reality had defiled it. Dead nebulae scarred the heavens. They searched the desolation below. A blizzard ravaged the Dream Land, yet there was no cloud above. Fat flakes drifted down. The gentle snow choked the sound of the world to a whisper. The groan and gripe of shabby trailers slipped through the calm. Kayden wiped vomit from his lips, which were little more than flecks of drool. The blood and meat stench mingled with the arctic chill, resembling an animal that had died half-ravaged in the cold. A heavy fog rose from his lips; the snow beat it down. Each flake landed on the skin with a prick before they melted. They ran over exposed skin like a cool slash. His heart slowed. The rush of blood in his ears stilled.

Beechwood's eyes moved back to the door, but Isaac was gone. They moved over the trailer court, which could have been any in the county or across the country. Most were only a half dozen, but these cheap hovels went to the boundless ends of this land. Snow covered everything. Bruised purple light peeked from the windows. Each held the memory of hope lost, prosperity forgotten. A dog house set in one yard, occupant inside. The flies still came, despite the cold. A tricycle leaned to one side, the front wheel gone, and the tassels of silver shimmered in the calm. Veils of snow shifted, and the hovels were a phantasmagorical illusion.

A hiss scrapped over the snow, swept below smothered trailers. Clicks echoed of icicles, and each thrummed for a moment. Under the snow, the slither of scales was a whisper. Kayden looked about the desolate court. Shadows lingered at windows. Darkness peeked from under tilted hovels. Out a long, split-tip tongue poked to taste the air. It pulled back with a delighted hiss. Snow shifted as things slid below the pure white, and laughter sucked at the air to leave little pits. He saw more swam below.

"Kayden," a voice cooed.

From the center of a circle of trailers, a hovel was bold to rise above the others. A thin, green slime covered it, where the snow failed to cling. The porch drooped and leaned to one side. Just beyond the door, a couch set in the derelict. A light form rested. Their head reclined.

"No," Kayden whispered. "Can I have nothing?" He fell to his knees, and cold bit into his legs. "We were happy once." He held onto the image of his ex-wife.

I'll find you again; he thought, looking into the trailer. His mind knew, yet his heart denied it. After the triumph of love, the heart soared upon wings of hope. So bright was this possibility. It blinded those fortunate to find it. It was a bulwark against the disappointment and bitterness, holding back the darkness and hate. He prayed to anything, everything, for its return. He clung to his prayer. It had held resolve, but it had faltered. Love failed in the end. The absence left a hole, which drew in all happiness to drown it before it could fly. Gone, it would never come back. You can't save that, which is gone, dead. No amount of love could raise it. All the pleas or pledges would never resurrect it.

Kayden covered his face. "I love you. Nothing left, I'm lost!" Tears fell from his strange eyes, which held a bruised purple light.

Hissing rose from the darkness beneath the snow. Dead eyes like cleft, vile emeralds appeared in the snow. They held the same alien glow in Kayden's gaze. Snakes of a fleshy hue poked up into the air. Sores, lesions, and pustules covered molded skin, which bled a thick, midnight-green ichor. The smell crashed upon the still air, sharp as a skunk, and was salty upon the tongue. Eyes found him, which ran around the head in a ring. They wore leers of hate. All rose from beneath the foot of snow. He felt the ground beneath him shift. They rose into the air, facing toward the sky, where the dead cosmos infected the dream. Mouths split flat heads into four. Up from the bowels of the frozen earth, a horror arose, bulging the serpents' necks. Disgorged from toothy maws, lengths of spinal columns slithered out of the serpents' gullets. The bloody skeletal faces of Isaac, Andre, and his mother leered from the tips of each. Their eye became shriveled and sunken as all bellowed their torment.

Those horrors fell away as the center trailer split open. Jillian stepped out into the snow, bare of skin, adorned with blood. About her, the skin stretched out like a flayed angel of sorrow. Steam rose from exposed muscles, but if she felt any pain, there was no sign. Each foot placed before the other in a regal step like a queen before adoring subjects. Serpents crawled up through the snow so she could tread atop their heads. She opened her arms to embrace him. The swirl of bruised purple light held a dead world, his Earth, in it.

Kayden peered into her eyes. No matter how much he punished himself, she was gone. "You died!" He searched Jillian's eyes, but there was nothing of the woman left. There was little of her at the end, he thought.

He covered his face. The world fell silent. Cold, which bit into his legs, faded away. The hiss of snakes slipped and faded. Only his cries filled the darkness. Kayden recalled her every smile and laugh, all her tears and curses. Their nights of passion and fury lingered in sweetness and bitterness. All their hopes spent; dreams remained forever fanciful. Jillian was gone, but her love would remain, though the years would sweeten it.

"Kayden," Jillian called.

"No," he whispered, shaking his head. She was gone, Kayden knew, and no dream or nightmare could resurrect her. He begged for her to stay, to be here with him.

"Kayden, look at me," she pleaded, though her tone was soft.

"Please," he begged, "my Jillian was no monster." Kayden refused to see her as a monster. Even if she hated him at the end, he knew she was a great person. He should have done more. He should have saved her.

"I need you," she whispered, and tears welled.

He opened his eyes. The snow-covered trailer park was gone. Again, Kayden was at the stair's bottom, which led up to Lear Mountain. He blinked at the sudden change. Rays of light pierced the creepers above the long steps. They rained down upon Jillian, who looked down at him. Years of drug abuse had cleared, and again, she was a healthy weight. Indeed, he saw his ex-wife was in a much better state than him. He wailed. All he wanted was for her to be happy and healthy again. Tremors shook him.

"Jillian," he breathed. She blurred with his tears.

"It's me," she smiled. "I'm the one, that doesn't want you to be punished for everything outside your control."

"I... can't believe you're gone," he admitted, studying her face. Kayden prayed to see her healthy once more. Tears rolled down, but he dared not close his eyes. Part of him it was a ruse.

"I am," she nodded, but her eyes ascended the stairs. "Now, it is time to go." Jillian's smile was weak, and she shivered. Tears spilled.

He opened his mouth, but then closed it. His eyes went up the stairs. A light burned at the top, though it seemed far away. "Where does it lead?" he asked. Kayden drew back, fearing where it may lead.

"I don't know," she confessed, extending a hand to him. "Please, come with me, Kayden. I don't want to go alone." Jillian trembled. "I'm scared."

"Is it the end?" he pleaded, taking her hand. Kayden opened his mouth to ask what would come next, but he pressed his lips back together. "We'll find out together." At least he was with her.

They moved, though he was the first to place a foot. The smell of rain lingered, as if a great storm had passed. About the stone steps, the gentle perfume of flowers remained. Kayden rubbed his chest and felt the ache had left. Clear air held hints of fresh water. A slight breeze breathed through the canopy of creepers above. Both were silent for a while.

Kayden glanced at her. "I had forgotten about Andre," he admitted. His face flushed at the confession. His brother was a shadow at the back of his mind.

"We bury things, so we can go on living," Jillian studied him. "You were always especially bad at doing that. I only ever got up the courage to ask once."

He blinked, "Yes, I recall." His eyes drifted from her. "Isaac killed him." The confession hung in the air.

"I'd heard stories. I'd heard that he had run away, like your mother." She studied the stairs. "Some people said your father was a killer, and your... Blood poisoned you."

Kayden felt warmth spread across his face. "All of Hemlock Hurst and Meridian, heck Lear County, never let the sins of your family go," he muttered.

"You were just a kid," she watched him.

"I think my father killed my mother too," he breathed, though the words were distant. Kayden knew his mind had hidden her deep. Her memory would return with all its pain.

"Oh my God," Jillian stared at him.

He glanced back. "I never put it together... like my brother."

"I'm sorry, Honey," she breathed.

They ascended, though again, it was in silence for a while. Kayden smiled. It felt the muscles were unaccustomed to the act. He stretched his shoulders. Jillian smiled.

"You seem looser," she smiled.

He returned the smile, though it faded. "I know you're gone. And, maybe, you're probably just a memory of her, but—" Kayden shook his head.

"What is it?" she asked when he grew silent.

"You know I tried to save you," he muttered, face reddened, "and I never intended for you to hurt your back. If you had never gotten injured, then you'd never gotten hooked on that junk." The factories closed in the industrial park.

Jillian nodded. "I know. I never held you responsible, but you did. All that was a twist of fate. Life just happens."

"You never deserved to suffer like that," he cursed. Any decent person in Meridian suffered, and the cruel had a great time.

"And you never deserved the suffering you put yourself through," she countered. "I gave up. I didn't want help. When I robbed you, I wanted to make sure you never came back."

"Why?" he turned to her. Kayden would find her food or anything else but drugs.

"So, you can be happy," she frowned at him. "Kayden, baby, you were miserable. I couldn't even remember the last time you were happy."

He thought of his family. "It wasn't you—"

"Yes, yes it was," she pulled him to a stop. "It was me, the Plant, and all of life here. The ghosts of your father, mother, and brother haunted you. All of it chipped away at you, and it was torture to watch."

"I... I loved you," he stared down at the stairs, "and the only time I was happy was with you." At the top of the stairs would be without her.

"Look at me, Kayden," Jillian smiled. He looked at her. "I'm gone, so you can find happiness again."

"I will let you go... one day," he whispered. His smile was weak, but he moved up the stairs. Kayden wiped away tears.

"When you can," she smiled, "I promise you'll feel better."

He turned back to the light, which had grown brighter. It washed over him. Jillian's hand faded in his. "I love you," he swore. The worn croak of the words came out as a rasp.

"I love you," she returned.

Kayden turned to her. He had to see her lovely face one last time. The world shifted. It morphed with dizzying speed. He frowned. He sat down instead of standing. The window was filthy, but the moonlight still slipped through in places. He studied the wheel, and then at the radio. This time, it was silent. It was familiar.

"Mister Stone," a man said, patient but curious. He closed his jacket where he kept his gun. It had been close. It would have been unfortunate for Kayden if Chaos won.

Kayden jerked, pulling back from the passenger. "Who are you?"! He shrieked. It was the man from the classic car.

"That has no importance," he promised. His pale eyes studying him, "at least for the moment." He pulled the jacket open so Kayden could see the musket's butt. "You're awake, Mister Stone." He rested a book on his leg. "I have been waiting. There for a while, I thought you wouldn't make it."

"What do you mean?" he saw a book, much like the stranger's tome, on his leg.

"You took a pill, HPL-0717," he nodded. "It is also called Figment. Although, I cannot understand why anyone would do something so stupid as to take a strange medicine." The older gentleman smiled but shook his head. The man could be a fool.

"That was real," he frowned. "I thought it was a candy with a weird advertisement. There wasn't much food left at my place. I just took it. I just lost... my Jillian."

"Yes," he nodded. "Afterwards, you infected others with what was inside you." The old man's eyes were so pale that they were nearly white. They watched him. "You caused a lot of chaos, and people have also died." He had considered ending Kayden, but another agent against Chaos may be worth it.

"I didn't mean to hurt anyone," Kayden swore, shaking his head. Things went crazy fast.

"Regardless," he waved off his words, "people died because of your actions." The gentleman withdrew his strange, elaborate musket pistol. "If you lost in your Dream Land, I would have liquefied you. I still may retire you." He warned him.

"Why don't you?" he blinked at the eldritch sigils on it.

"You were asleep." he studied the weapon. "You talked, Mister Stone. I liked to you speak about a great number of things."

"I don't know what you heard," Kayden snapped. "I don't—"

"You're intelligent," the gentleman cut him off. "You're also a fool. I asked around town. I spoke to people." He returned the musket to its holster. "An intelligent, loyal, and dogged man such as you could be a real asset. Your resolve is admirable." These would be qualities that the man had to have to survive.

"This is insane!" Kayden wiped his brow. The man wanted something. The madness wouldn't end!

"This is the truth behind the world," he revealed, opening the door. "You'll want to keep that book." he gestured at the tome on Kayden's leg. The man would have to make his way. Dominant forces played the Grand Game.

"What do I do?" he pleaded, but the older gentleman stepped out. He felt something new. It felt as if the veil over the world pulled back. Reality felt more real.

He turned back and leaned back in to look at him. "That is entirely up to you, Mister Stone," he smiled. "All the truths, mundane and insane, are yours to unearth." The old man closed the door to Hooper's Cherry. He had a good feeling about the man.

DICKSON LEE TURPIN is a writer of horror, fantasy, and romance who loves folklore and true stories of the macabre. Many of his stories draw from true events or from real folklore. All of his works exist in one universe, part of one story.

ALSO AVAILABLE
FROM NIGHTMARE PRESS

THE GUARDIANS

Teresa Sewell & Rob LE

In a mystical world where lycans and vampires rule, where magic, cruelty, and blood are part of everyday life, in a time if good fails then all is lost, fate rests in the hands of three people. Three spoken of in a forgotten legend from a race destroyed long ago—or a perhaps a race long hidden from those who seek to destroy them.

Brenat and Teera believe they'll never conceive. However, a miracle happens during their bonding on the night of the blood moon, bringing the couple both surprise and joy. When a second miracle occurs, and they find themselves with seven children, they dream of raising their family in the safety of a small, hidden valley.

Threatening their dream are those who want the children for their own evil schemes. The eldritch witch Keres and her wicked master seek to annihilate all that is good in the world. Believing the family to be those spoken of in the ancient legend of creation, Keres and her master set out to gain control of the children and convert them to evil so they can rule the world.

However, they are not the only ones with nefarious plans for Joel and his siblings...

FAM

John Shupeck

When a 17-year-old drug addict dies, his little brother begs for him to come back to life. Six years later, his nightmare comes true.

OCCULTATION

Eric Lahti

ON A LONG-ABANDONED alien space station orbiting a mysterious black object, the rules are different. Whether it's the immersive virtual reality that's indistinguishable from reality, the wild bazaar where anything and everything is for sale, the drunken debauchery, or the group of giants who run everything and keep the peace, Endpoint is the place where people go to do what they'd never do anywhere else.

For instance, two nights ago, a hacker deleted her brain. This morning a thief awoke in her body with a task: *Find out what happened and you'll get your body back.*

Now, Nat will have to navigate the madness, cults, and twisted power structures to find answers. But on Endpoint, nothing is ever simple.

And the abandoned alien space station may not be as abandoned as everyone thought.

KENTUCKY'S HAUNTED GRAVEYARDS

The Frightening Floyds

From The Frightening Floyds—authors of *Kentucky's Strange and Unusual Haunts*, *Aliens Over Kentucky*, and many other books on the mysterious and paranormal—comes *Kentucky's Haunted Graveyards*, a collection of spooky stories from various cemeteries across the Bluegrass State.

Within this book you will find abandoned cemeteries filled with spirits, celebrities' graves, a glowing tombstone, a haunted mausoleum, a sprawling necropolis filled with exquisite monuments, a woman in search of her black cat, a graveyard said to hold the Gates of Hell, and many more.

There are also some cemeteries not exactly haunted, but very strange and very unusual. Among them a pet cemetery with a dark history, a haunting procession of lifelike statues, the bones of centuries-old martyrs displayed in a church, human bodies interred at a zoo, a family plot in a parking lot, and an airport and business compound built around a Native burial ground.

Join Jacob and Jenny Floyd as they bring you these creepy and weird stories in *Kentucky's Haunted Graveyards*.

ALADDIN'S CURSE

Mark Pickvet

A magic lamp containing an evil Djinni embarks upon an incredible journey as it passes from the Stone Age to the Modern World. The malevolent Djinni fulfills the wishes of those who gain possession of his lamp, only those wishes do not always come out exactly as planned. Tragedy fills *Aladdin's Curse,* as little to no good comes to those who wish for personal gain from the ancient magic. Only three unselfish wishes can rid the world of this wicked force. Follow the series of subplots and short stories through time as the lamp and the evil spirit within all uniquely interconnect them.

The dark side of human nature is only a wish away. As the old saying goes: "Be careful what you wish for; you just might get it!"

BREAKING THE DEVIL'S BREAD:

DARK WORDS AND SHADOW TALES

Satyros Phil Brucato

Our lives are made of stories.
Some of those tales get pretty damn dark.

In the following "13 stories and an Oops," award-winning dark fantasist Satyros Phil Brucato (*Red Shoes*, *Mage*, *Valhalla with a Twist of Lethe*) explores shadows, cries, and silence.

Careless haunters, elite collectors, secretive enforcers, lip-synching goths, hapless custodians, strange children, subterranean exiles, tortured fiends, harried jesters, haggard coulrophobes, ragged batterers, joyous hikers, carnal mystics, and exploding cosmos tell their tales as sardonic darkness swallows all.

If mortal dread is the Devil's bread, then we're all welcome at the feast.

THE HURDY GURDY MAN

David Turnbull

Set in London in the summer of 1969, *The Hurdy Gurdy Man* follows Kath Dunn, who has left her home near the seaside town Berwick on Tweed, and finds herself homeless on the streets of Piccadilly. Here she encounters the eccentric Gordon Urquhart-Scott, who persuades Kath to accompany him to his large crumbling home on the edge of Hampstead Heath, where he claims to run a hostel for homeless women.

Kath finds herself inducted as one of twelve formerly homeless women who reside free of charge in the house in exchange for obeying the Hurdy Gurdy Man's strange rules, including nightly musical performances on the hand-cranked hurdy-gurdy from which his nickname derives.

Kath befriends Ruth. Together they secretly unravel terrible truths linked to the British Class system, the establishment, and the gruesome Scottish borders legends of the Redcaps. After witnessing how deep the horror within the decaying home truly runs, the two women decide to confront the evil at its source. Enlisting the help of other women, they engineer a terrifying conflict they hope will send the evil back to whatever foul region of darkness from whence it came.

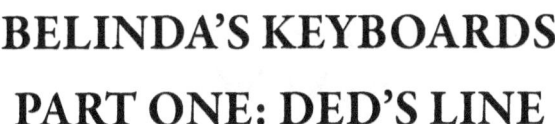

BELINDA'S KEYBOARDS
PART ONE: DED'S LINE

Dedham Pond

Dedham Pond is a journalist in his fifties rediscovering how to do his job responsibly in an era that appreciates bias over truth and influencers over experts. While investigating the death of an old friend's son, Ded discovers Belinda Blessing, who is part of a conspiracy of people who enjoy injecting discord and chaos into the culture wherever they can. Now Ded must find a way to stop the destruction caused by Belinda's keyboards and bring her to justice.

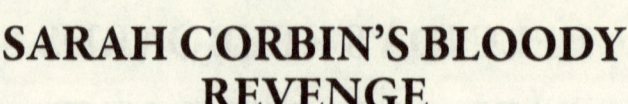

SARAH CORBIN'S BLOODY REVENGE

Coyote Wallace

When Sarah Corbin and her family are killed in a midnight robbery gone wrong, she makes a deal for her mortal soul - in exchange for the chance to hunt down the men who burned her world to ash.

Violent, unflinching, and tinged with supernatural overtones, *Sarah Corbin's Bloody Revenge* takes readers into the dark heart of Texas, where the air is heavy with gun smoke and the streets run red.

On the other end of Sarah's revenge is Lono Talbot, a murderous cutthroat who has parlayed stolen gold into a position of power in the small town of Gehenna. His network of gunslingers and outlaws, reinforced with his ill-gotten gains, has made him one of the most powerful men in the Texas underground. Too well protected for lawmen, Lono continues to grow his influence and power....

....until the mistakes of his past come calling.

MURKY SHADOWS

Belinda Brady

WELCOME TO *Murky Shadows*, a deliciously dark world where ghosts, ghouls, monsters and all-too-horrifying realities collide, and vampires, ghosts and things that go bump in the night rule. From a vengeful fairy, to a bloodthirsty roommate, to the ghosts of a serial killer plotting their revenge, no supernatural stone is left unturned in this captivating collection of spooky tales.

Murky Shadows, by Belinda Brady, is a treasure of short stories that will take you to places you never dreamed possible, and introduce you to characters you would only meet in your worst nightmares. So sit back, relax, perhaps put a light on, and delve into this chilling mixed bag of dark stories, one that not only brings the supernatural to life, but also taps into the darkest corners of the human psyche.

Which story will be your favorite?

READ MORE NIGHTMARE PRESS!!!

VISIT   OUR   WEBSITE   AT
nightmarepress5.wordpress.com

Also, follow us on:

Facebook: https://www.facebook.com/
nightmarepress1

Instagram: https://www.instagram.com/
nightmarepress1

Join the Nightmare Press Group on Facebook to interact with our authors, and keep abreast of their creative endeavors.